FORTRESS

OF

SHADOWS

Book Two
Stonehaven League

CARRIE SUMMERS

Chapter One

From: @Bradley_Williams_CEO
To: @Customer_Support_All
Flags: [Status - Urgent] [Confirm Receipt - Required]
Message:

Management is aware that a small fraction of the player base has complained about an elevated pain experience. There are a few things you should keep in mind when considering this issue. Foremost, please remember that all in-game pain is simulated. No one is being harmed. Furthermore, there have been no instances of a complaining player canceling their account or even reducing their play time. If the issue were as bad as many of the reports claim, these users would not continue to subject themselves to the experience.

However, this does not mean that management is ignoring the claims. We have, in fact, worked with our hardware partner, Entwined, to develop a solution.

Going forward, all customer complaints about the game's pain sensitivity will be handled as detailed below.

1) Open the user's account details. Set the Pain Sensitivity field to "muted".

2) Respond to the customer support ticket with the following (VERBATIM, people. This isn't the time to get creative).

Greetings, [Player Name],

My name is [Your Name], and I will be happy to assist you today. I understand that you are concerned about the pain levels in Relic Online.

Please be aware that the extreme immersion offered by the state-of-the-art Entwined implants may feel overwhelming at first. Although we have verified that the pain response is working as intended, conveying only mild discomfort for the worst in-game injuries, your mind is likely trying to synthesize a pain sensation as pronounced as the other sensory information your implants convey.

Keep this in mind during your next in-game injury, and the phenomenon will likely cease. If this does not occur, please seek quiet locations for your adventuring and questing to give your mind time to become accustomed to the disparity between sensory and pain input.

Thank you for playing Relic Online!

Any breaks from this procedure will result in termination. We cannot lead the user base to believe there is something wrong with the hardware—that is simply not the case. Though we are reducing the pain response for these players, it is only to help them adjust, and the system will slowly bring them back to normal.

-Bradley

Chapter Two

STONEHAVEN'S CARPENTER, PRESTER, shuffled in the sun-dappled grass and touched his brow.

"I can't build that, Your Glorious—sir—ma'am."

Devon planted her fists on her hips and cocked her head. "I know it's not on your list of plans, but you're good at improvising, right? Building a defensive wall isn't so different from building just one wall of a"—she pulled up his list of known plans to make sure she had the wording right—"*One-room Shack, Flat Roof,* is it?"

The man grimaced, his gaze on his feet. "It really is different, I'm sorry to say."

Devon glanced toward the front of the village, already envisioning the construction. "Of course we'll want the wall to be taller than a single story. And it'll need to be long enough to surround the parts of the village that aren't sheltered by the cliff..."

She glanced back at the semicircular ridge of stone that formed the back wall of Stonehaven. A pair of sentries from the village had climbed the ramps leading to the cliff top. Shading their eyes, they scanned the jungle for campfires or other clues to the location of Henrik's army. They'd come to wipe out Devon's followers and settlement, and no doubt planned to take the *Greenscale Pendant* relic for themselves. Though Greel and Devon had dealt with their leader, Henrik, there was no reason to think the army would give up after marching all this way.

Because the far side of the outcrop was so sheer, would-be attackers would need significant *Climbing* skill—15 at least—to approach from that aspect. But the front side of the village lay open to attack.

"You see, I could probably *build* sections of wall, but they'd never hold up in the way you need, Your Gloriousness."

"Why not? What if you and Deld worked together?"

In the aftermath of her completed quest for the *Greenscale Pendant* and the raging kegger that had followed, Devon had been looking through the settlement interface. She hadn't been able to figure out how some of the buildings—in particular, those requiring both stonemasonry and carpentry experience—were supposed to be built. When she finally gave up and asked Deld, the stonemason, he'd chuckled then invited Prester to a group. As if by magic, the missing plans appeared in both craftsmen's lists.

Prester shook his head. "I'm afraid it's just not possible. You see, I craft buildings and furniture and vehicles, but I have no knowledge of warfare. It's possible I could *help* construct this wall you need, but I'd never succeed without expert guidance."

Devon sighed as understanding finally sunk in. "You're saying I need to assign someone to a different profession if I want to build village defenses?"

The carpenter nodded, eyes wide as if this was such a basic fact, he hadn't even considered she might be ignorant of it.

"Can you tell me what the profession is?" She didn't remember seeing any jobs related to defense when she'd assigned trades to the members of the Tribe of Uruquat following the ogre's demise.

"Of course, Your Devon-ness. You need a master of fortifications."

She pinched the bridge of her nose and muttered under her breath. "Guess it would be too easy to let me use the trades I've already got people for, right?"

A game popup appeared in her vision.

Is that question supposed to be rhetorical?

"Well, I can't claim to know Veia's plan," Prester said, shifting on his feet.

Devon sighed and cast him a smile. "Sorry, Prester. I was mostly talking to myself."

"Did you need something else, Your Gloriousness?"

She tapped a finger against her thigh. "If I were to promote you to an advanced citizen, that would allow you to take a second profession, right? Could you become this master of fortifications?"

The man actually flinched at the question. "Unfortunately, though I'm quite skilled in carpentry, you may recall that I have little ability to grow in other areas."

Oh, right. She remembered why she'd chosen him as the settlement's carpenter a split-second before a window shoved into view showing her the list of professions Prester was suited for. Though he was capable of *learning* farming, lumberjacking, and a few others, everything but carpentry had a negative bonus to advancement. But as a carpenter, he gained skill at twice the average rate. A regular savant, this guy...

Devon waved the window away. "Thanks, Prester. You can keep upgrading the huts to cabins for today."

As the man gave a quick little salute and dashed off, Devon shook her head and surveyed the village. The truth was, the human followers she'd inherited from the ogre, Uruquat, were too busy to take on a second profession even if one of them had the aptitude.

But she *had* to get the village secured. Soon. Henrik's army wasn't the only threat. Despite the buzzing insects and choking jungle, more players would show up any day. Without a wall and organized defenses, they'd be just as likely to try to "clear" the village by killing everyone inside as they would be to slow down and listen to trade proposals.

She'd need to talk to Dorden about the abilities of the Stoneshoulder dwarves. Fortunately, she'd have a chance in the next few hours. She and a few of the village NPCs had a foray planned, an expedition that hoped to spot Henrik's army and assess their strength *before* the force from Eltera City struck.

Hacking through the jungle. Squishing around in armor turned slimy with sweat.

Should be the perfect chance for a nice conversation.

***

The party set off late in the morning, heading roughly northwest. Besides Dorden, who clanked along in his various pieces of plate and chainmail, Devon had recruited the dwarf's wife, Heldi, to supplement their fighting force with her crossbow. Stonehaven's scout, Hazel, was already roving ahead, her stealth skill rendering her invisible in the thick foliage. And walking at the front of the group—she wasn't quite ready to turn her back on the man—was Jarleck, the brawler who had been a Stonehaven prisoner until recently. For weeks, he'd been on the edge of death due to necrotic poison, but the village medicine woman, Hezbek, had finally managed a cure.

Before his capture, Jarleck had been one of Henrik's lackeys. If anyone could offer insight into the approaching army, it was him. Unfortunately, the situation made him difficult to trust.

As they crashed into the wall of jungle a few hundred paces from the village perimeter, Devon cast a glance back. The sentries on the cliff top stood straight, eyes shaded as they searched the jungle. Three of Dorden's dwarves guarded the front edge of camp, hands near their bastard swords and warhammers, gazes scanning the surroundings. But it was the skulking figure just inside the village perimeter that gave her the most peace of mind. Greel might not be the most likable guy, but he was loyal. She'd learned *that* the hard way.

"Ye sure this is how we ought to spend such a lovely day, lass?" Dorden asked as he pulled out his warhammer and started flailing at a vine that had snagged in his breastplate.

Devon pulled out the *Crude Machete* she'd borrowed from the village stores and hacked the offending foliage off the dwarf. "I thought you'd be dying for a chance to stretch your legs."

"Are you trying to suggest I'm too short?"

"What?"

"Me legs, lass. Ye suggested I stretch them." Dorden laughed as he held out a stumpy leg and wiggled his hardened-leather boot.

Beside him, Heldi rolled her eyes. "You'll learn quickly to ignore his jokes. They're never funny."

Raising his warhammer, Dorden shook it at her in mock outrage. With a belly laugh, he turned and tromped after Jarleck. For the brawler's part, he trudged with a grim sort of determination. As Devon watched him aim a kick at a fallen branch that crossed their path, she wondered what was going through his head. The man was leading them to reconnoiter the strength and movements of his former allies. She focused on his back, willing an inspection window to spawn in her vision.

Jarleck:
Level 13 Brawler
Health: 271/271

Skills:
Unarmed Combat - Tier 2: 16
Grapple - Tier 2: 12
One-handed Slashing: 9

Jarleck views you with 25 esteem, a rating slightly above **neutral.** *Your reputation with this individual can be adjusted by actions that please or displease him.*

Twenty-five reputation really wasn't great, but considering that her tribe had held him prisoner for weeks, it wasn't bad either. He probably wouldn't turn on them unless she did something to provoke a negative hit to her reputation, sending it below 0. Still, she let him get a few paces ahead before she turned to Dorden. Better to keep village business amongst her loyal allies.

"I know you're an advanced citizen, but you never told me what your second profession is." Of course, she could inspect him to find out, but the inquiry gave her a chance to strike up a conversation.

Dorden snorted. "It's not obvious by my strapping musculature?"

"Uh..." She glanced at his bare forearms. They *were* well-muscled, but then again, so were his wife's. In addition to her primary training as a fighter specializing in ranged attacks, Heldi had recently taken up hunting to help with the village food supply. Neither of those professions seemed like a path to beefcake-ness, yet she was as muscular as the holograms with oiled flesh and six-pack abs that posed in front of the 24-hour gym near Devon's condo.

"I'm just joking with ye, lass. Of course, me impressive physique is no laughing matter, but it's more due to me training with Agavir the Pummeler than anything else."

"Agavir?"

He grinned and patted the large head of his warhammer.

"I see." Devon stepped over a rotting log, her sandaled foot sinking into a tangle of downed vines on the other side. "So what is your second profession?"

"Blacksmithing, o'course. A fine dwarvish trade, I'm proud to say."

A smile tugged at the corner of Devon's mouth. Now *that* was good news. The village was in sore need of new weaponry, simple tools, and repairs to existing implements.

"We figured ye knew," Heldi said. "Dorden's been complaining day and night that ye haven't got to work on building 'im a proper forge."

"Now just a minute," the dwarf patriarch said, cheeks reddening. "I was only voicing me curiosity. I'm sure our wise leader has plenty to occupy her attention before getting down to building me a place to play with me toys."

Ahead, Jarleck grunted as he ripped through a screen of low-growing brush, shredding leaves and twigs with mighty yanks of his bare hands. Devon raised an eyebrow, wondering if she should suggest a machete. Probably not. It would likely just offend his brawler sensibilities.

"Yes and no. We're sorely in need of a smith, to tell the truth. I had Deld working on a forge and only took him off to build the shrine to Veia. He's back on the forge work now..." She chewed her lip and checked on Jarleck's distance. The man still seemed occupied with his raging battle against the jungle. "But you're also right about me having a lot to occupy my attention. We need to fortify Stonehaven. I thought that our carpenter and stonemason could accomplish it, but apparently I was wrong."

"Ah. Ye need a master of fortifications," Dorden said with a knowing nod.

She sighed. Apparently, she'd been the only ignorant one. "Do you think any of your dwarves would be interested?"

The dwarf gave a sorrowful grunt. "Afraid I can't help ye there, lass. Stoneshoulder Clan lived in our ancestral halls for so long, we genuinely forgot the art of building fresh defenses."

Well, crap. Devon's shoulders slumped. It seemed so simple...couldn't they just cut down a bunch of trees, strip the branches, and...what? Replant them in a trench to construct a wall?

Up ahead, Jarleck grabbed a thick vine as if he intended to throttle the life from it. Plant juice seeped from between his fingers as he squeezed and yanked the green rope. Overhead, a branch crackled, then broke with a snap, crashing down inches from the man's head.

"I could do it," he said in his typical growl.

Devon slowed. "Pardon?"

"I don't yet have the formal mark of a fortifications master, but I've got the head for it," he said, still marching forward.

Did her voice really carry that well, or had the man just been listening in? Devon supposed she couldn't blame him. If she'd been kept prisoner and held within a few hitpoints of death for weeks, she'd probably pay close attention to her former jailers too.

She stepped over the branch Jarleck had pulled down while considering the man's offer.

As a village-sized settlement, Stonehaven could support just seven advanced NPCs, and they already had four. As of yet, Jarleck wasn't even an official Stonehaven citizen. To become their master of fortifications, he'd have to join and *then* receive a promotion from basic to advanced NPC.

Not an easy decision, and not one to be made quickly.

"Thanks for the offer," she said. "Let's sit down and talk about it when we return."

As the man's shoulders tensed, she winced.

You have lost esteem with Jarleck: -5 reputation.
Nice going...

Devon cringed. The guy was awfully sensitive for a slab-of-muscle-and-scars type.

Chapter Three

AFTER THE GROUP had been wallowing through the jungle for an hour or so, Hazel burst from the brush inches from Jarleck. The man screamed like a 3rd-grader attacked by a scary clown, then slowly calmed and lowered his fists.

Devon cast a glance at Dorden and Heldi, who shrugged. Was the guy really that big of a wuss?

"Y...Your Devon?" Hazel asked in a shaky voice.

When Devon turned her attention to the small scout, her eyes widened in shock. She'd been too distracted by Jarleck's girly shriek to notice how pale Hazel was. That couldn't be good.

"What's wrong, Hazel?"

"I...It's..." The scout swallowed, looking sick. "I know they were supposed to be our enemies, but I never would've wished something like this on anyone."

Devon ran through the options in her mind. She assumed Hazel was referring to the army. What could have happened? Starvation? Sickness? Attacks by the wildlife?

"The army? What happened to them?" she asked as the dwarves crowded close to listen.

The woman swallowed again, clenching her jaw as if to keep down her lunch. "I think I'd better show you."

***

Devon smelled the blood for a good five minutes before the group escaped the dense foliage into the patch of flattened jungle where Henrik's army had encamped.

The place was a killing field.

Before pitching tents, the army had cleared the understory, piling brush and vines into three large piles. They'd thinned the trees, felling most within the clearing to preserve sight lines. The result was a rough circle of trampled earth around two-hundred feet in diameter with shredded canvas shelters, the remains of the few campfires, a handful of trees...

And bodies.

Around sixty members of Henrik's army lay bloating in the sun, some with severed limbs, most with deep gashes across their torsos. The injuries had a pattern, three parallel lines that made Devon think the victims had been raked with claws.

What the hell?

She scanned the wall of jungle surrounding the cleared area, searching for rustling brush, the flash of teeth, the glint of metal. After a few seconds, she shook her head. These kills were at least a day or two old. There seemed little reason for the killers to remain— especially given the smell of the bodies.

Just to be sure, she leaned toward Hazel. "Any sign of the attackers?"

The scout shook her head. "I circled the area to be sure before fetching you."

"What about their trail? Could you tell which way they went when they left?"

The small woman's brows drew together. "That's the thing. The army came in from the far side." She gestured toward the opposite edge of the cleared area. "But their track is nearly grown over. Three days, four days old maybe."

Devon nodded. The region surrounding Stonehaven and the ruins of the ancient city, Ishildar, was afflicted by a Curse of Fecundity that caused the jungle to swallow everything but the most well-used paths.

"And the attackers?"

Hazel shook her head. "No sign of them. It's like they just disappeared after the battle."

Devon grimaced. Not that it seemed like there'd been much of a battle... Judging from her vantage at the edge of the clearing, it looked like few of the soldiers had even had time to draw their weapons.

"But we're sure they're gone...?"

Hazel nodded. "I didn't check the tents, but I climbed a tree to get a good look at the area. No movement anywhere."

Well, no sense hanging around any longer than they had to. "I guess we should do a quick search," Devon said.

Wrinkling her nose, she tugged her tunic out from under her armor to cover her lower face. As if a heavy footfall would somehow disturb the dead, she edged into the encampment. Clouds of flies rose from the bodies as she advanced.

Why hadn't the game set decay timers on the corpses? Usually, bodies of slain NPCs disintegrated after just a few minutes if the corpse wasn't looted. Was she supposed to learn something here?

Picking up a stick, she nudged a corpse's shoulder. Her nausea eased a bit as the body decomposed into pieces of loot, the decayed flesh turning to dust and vanishing.

She crouched and swept the items from the ground.

You have received: Flint and Steel.
Might be useful if you didn't already know how to conjure fire...

You have received: 5 x Turkey Jerky.
In many countries and city-states, this so-called food item is banned as sacrilegious. In others, it's sold by vendors who also hawk carob chips, veggie burgers, and other fake foods.

With the body removed, the dried blood faded as well. Perhaps it was her imagination, but the stench seemed to weaken.

"Let's get these bodies cleaned up," she said over her shoulder as she strode to the next one. "Gather the loot and we'll examine it after."

Thanks to some quick work by Devon and her companions, the carnage rapidly vanished. Devon sucked in a deep breath of the humid jungle air, now free of the smell of death. A faint hint still clung to the inside of her nostrils and her throat, but that was already fading.

"All right," she said when they'd met up in the rough center of the encampment. "What have we got?"

"A few weapons," Dorden said. "Some armor pieces that Gerrald might be able to repair or repurpose."

"Merhan was carrying a pouch with fifteen gold pieces," Jarleck said, shaking his head. "Dumb fool. If he had that to his name, I don't see why he signed on with Henrik."

"Merhan?" Dorden asked.

The brawler shrugged, his face fixed in a grim frown. "Shared a few campfires with him along the line."

Ahh, crap. Devon should have remembered that the dead soldiers had been Jarleck's friends at one point. She could have at least spared him the need to loot their bodies.

As the big man reached forward, the gold coins shining on his palm, Devon shook her head. "You keep them. You knew these people."

The man grunted and shrugged. "Only because we were all after the chance to earn a spot in Henrik's regime. But thanks."

You have gained esteem with Jarleck: +10 reputation.

"So...theories about the cause?" Devon asked. "What did this?"

It was hard to tell with his enormous beard, but it looked like Dorden pursed his lips. He squinted one eye and looked around the camp. "Never seen anything like it, lass. No tracks. Total massacre. Maybe the beasts came from the sky?"

Devon glanced up, wincing as the tropical sun stabbed her eyeballs. With some of the trees thinned, there was enough room for winged creatures to land, but just barely. Her mind started running toward dragons, but that was usually more of an end-game thing. She wouldn't *totally* put it past Relic Online to send a dragon to smack her around. Still, it didn't seem likely.

She noticed Hazel poking around the outside of one of the tents and called out. "Do you think there's enough space for winged creatures to land and take off here?"

The scout had been lifting the tent flap, and she paused to look up at the patchy canopy. "I'm not—"

An unholy wail cut off the woman's words. Hazel shrieked as a hideous talon tore through the side of the tent, darkness rolling off the wicked claws. The scout backpedaled, caught her heel on a stone, and fell.

The discordant screech sliced the air again, and the tent exploded in a cloud of shredded canvas.

Devon stared at the demon crouching in the remains of the shelter. The thing had red eyes and yellowed teeth dripping with gray juices. Membranous wings in a mottled pattern of gray and blood-red spread from its back, and black fur grew in patches from its wrinkled flesh.

With a snarl, it sprang for Hazel.

Shouting, Devon cast *Freeze* on the beast. Ice encased the demon, paralyzing it. But not for long. Within a second, cracks started to splinter the prison.

Dorden growled as he drew his warhammer.

"For Veia and the Stonehaven League!" he shouted.

Devon caught Heldi's eye as her sturdy husband rushed forward. Heldi shrugged. "He's hopeless when it comes to the battle cry thing."

As Dorden rushed forward and Hazel scrambled clear of the area, more cracks webbed the demon's ice prison. Devon stepped into a pool of sunlight and summoned a *Shadow Puppet*.

She stared at the beast long enough to get a *Combat Assessment.*

Demon Thrall – Level 13
As far as hellish beasts go, this one's kind of a wuss.

Devon sent her sun-cast *Shadow Puppet* arrowing for the beast. Like a lance made of darkness, it speared the monster's chest, bringing another god-awful wail from its throat. She followed with a quick tier 1 *Flamestrike*, drawing a pillar of fire onto the beast.

The demon's health dropped by about a third. It shrieked again and turned its smoldering eyes toward her.

"Oh no ye don't," Dorden yelled. He clobbered the beast with a heavy blow from his warhammer, then gritted his teeth as the demon retaliated, raking claws across his iron breastplate in a horrific nails-on-chalkboard attack.

Heldi had a crossbow bolt loaded and leaned left and right while trying to get a clear shot. "If 'is body wasn't as thick as 'is skull, this would be easier," she muttered.

A few paces away, Jarleck finally shook free of his shock. Bunching his fists, he started forward, but Devon dashed over and laid a hand on his arm.

"Dorden and Heldi are advanced citizens. We can bring them back to life at the Shrine to Veia if the worst happens."

He blinked.

"We can manage without you on this one," she added.

The man's jaw worked while he considered this. After a moment, he nodded.

But it scarcely mattered. As Dorden wound up for another massive, two-handed swipe with Agavir the Pummeler, the demon froze. Its pupils constricted to tiny dots, and then in a flurry of limbs, it ducked and raked claws against the earth faster than a squirrel burying a nut.

Dorden's swing missed, sending the stout dwarf spinning. By the time he recovered, the demon had dug a hole two feet deep. With a last screech, it grabbed the edges of its pit, forced them apart, and opened a rift in the earth. Rays of darkness and purple light shot forth as the beast dove into the rent. A split-second later, the gash closed with a thud.

Devon stared in shock.

"Coward," Dorden snorted.

"What on Veia's earth was that," his wife asked.

Hazel had recovered from her scare. "I think we know where the attackers went..."

Devon blinked, the situation catching up with her. Demons? Here?

Immediately, her thoughts rushed to Stonehaven. Given the demon's exit...did that mean they'd arrived through cracks in the earth too? If so, no perimeter wall in the world would keep them out of the village. The thought turned her spine to ice.

She took a deep breath. "Well, I suppose we don't have to worry about Henrik's army anymore."

The others looked around the ruined camp. Everyone was trying to keep a brave face, but no one was doing a very good job with it.

Veia is offering you a quest: Demon Invasion, part 1
Seeing as a small army was just massacred on your doorstep, seems you might want to figure out what's going on.
Objective: Find out more about the demon attack.
Reward: Knowledge on how to protect Stonehaven

Reward: 10000 experience

Accept? Y/N

"I guess we better search the rest of the tents for surprises," she said.

Hazel's eyes went wide as wagon wheels.

"Sit this one out, Hazel," she added. "Please."

Chapter Four

AS EMERSON STEPPED out of the EM-shielded capsule car and into the canned-air smell of the Las Vegas hyperloop station, message alerts swarmed the edges of his vision. He blinked, stunned by the onslaught—despite having spent weeks with the Entwined hardware piping notifications straight into his brain, he still wasn't used to the experience. Forced to step around his suddenly unmoving form, the other disembarking passengers from Tucson glared and muttered as they passed.

Mumbling an apology, Emerson shuffled forward and stopped to lean a shoulder against a square support pillar. Overhead, an insect-like cleaner bot gave an annoyed chirp.

"You too?" Emerson said as he scooted back out of its path.

The bot chirped again and ran a laser sensor down a vertical strip of the pillar's surface. When the red light passed over a wad of chewing gum pasted into a mortar trough between concrete blocks, the bot spidered down to the offending substance and started plucking at it with tiny pincers.

Emerson grimaced; he'd nearly planted his elbow in the sticky mess.

He ran his awareness over the fleet of icons hovering like radar blips around the edges of his visual field. Most were from E-Squared, flagged with the company logo. Those he herded together to deal with on the two-hour autobus ride to St. George. His mom had forwarded some alarmist chain letter about the government paying biotech companies to incorporate slow-release chemicals into implant coatings. Something about mind control. He took a deep breath but decided not to bother responding and deleted the message instead.

A note from the hospital in Atlanta said that Owen, one of his special recruits, hadn't yet woken from the coma he'd recently fallen into. The doctors still had no theories on the cause of his sudden loss of awareness. Owen's vital signs were strong, and he even had periods of high brain activity—which according to the nurse meant he wasn't actually in a coma, but rather some sort of vegetative or locked-in state. Not that it mattered, as far as Emerson was concerned. Owen had complained about the same issues with Relic Online's pain sensitivity that Devon had. And then he'd become unresponsive to his environment. He moved the report into a cloud folder he'd created to track the issue.

That left just a couple messages, both flagged as unimportant and ghosting at the edge of his vision. Emerson considered leaving them for the autobus ride as well, but as soon as he checked the sender ID, he yanked them forward. After Devon had ignored his increasingly-urgent attempts to contact her yesterday, he'd started to worry she'd suffered Owen's fate and had decided to travel to her home city, St. George, Utah.

Seemed he'd worried unnecessarily. She was clearly still conscious. He stared at the first icon—timestamped twenty minutes ago—and the message opened.

Sorry I haven't responded to messages lately. Had kind of an epic quest line to finish. What's up?

She'd sent another note ten minutes later.

Hey, does this have to do with the message your customer support people just sent me? They said the RO pain system is working as intended and it's my brain creating the problem. So they're trying to tell me it's all in my imagination? BS, dude!

What message from CS? Why were the game masters contacting Devon about the issue when she'd reported it directly to him? Emerson glanced again at the herd of work messages. The answer was probably in there somewhere, but it would take rifling through a bunch of useless crap to find. He selected Devon's message and started subvocalizing a response.

"Looking into that now. Hey, so I was trying to contact you because I—"

Emerson broke off. What should he say? That he'd feared she was in a coma because she didn't respond to his text messages immediately? That wouldn't sound crazy at all...especially since he couldn't explain Owen's situation due to medical privacy laws.

He looked around the station, the bars of actinic LED light illuminating weary faces of business travelers grabbing tubes to dozens of cities across the US, the curtain screens and holograms displaying ads for the latest Vegas shows.

His snap decision to rush to Devon's rescue seemed ridiculous. What had he been thinking? That he'd break down the doorway of her low-rent St. George apartment and tear her from the game before she plunged into unconsciousness?

With a flick of his mental cursor, he selected and deleted his message text and started over.

"I'll look into the thing from CS. No, it's not your imagination. Do me a favor, though. Can you keep your play sessions short until we figure out what's going on?"

As he clicked send, he scanned the station for a link to an autobus terminal. Yes, it was stupid to go to St. George with delusions of playing the hero. The chances that one unconscious player meant that others would follow, were pretty thin. But still...

Anyway, he could use a change of scenery. As long as he didn't *tell* Devon he'd come to Utah in case she suddenly fell ill, she wouldn't have any reason to think he was a stalker. And he wasn't. Really. He'd just had a bad feeling and wanted to follow up.

As he started toward the holostrip marking the proper station exit, Devon's response arrived.

Sorry, but I am away for the next few hours playing RO. If you want to keep reading this auto-responder, keep messaging. Otherwise, I'll get back to you when I log out.

Chapter Five

AS DEVON WALKED back into Stonehaven, she waited for the sense of warm comfort gained by arriving home. But all she could feel was creeping dread. She looked around the village, the mix of jungle huts and dwarven canvas shelters slowly being replaced with simple wooden cabins, the crafting workshop where Gerrald toiled away on his leatherworking, the Shrine to Veia where she'd brought Greel back from the dead. It would be so easy to lose it all.

The players would come soon, and Stonehaven had no walls to keep out invaders. But far worse, she could no longer trust the ground beneath her feet. At any time, a demon horde might simply pry the earth open and crawl out.

She stopped beside the small brook that ran through the glade, crouched, and splashed water over her face.

"Get it together, Devon," she muttered. This was a game. It was supposed to be fun and challenging, but not impossible. A company like E-Squared had to know better than to destroy a player-built village without giving its owner some way to defend the settlement. Even if an army of slavering demons were planning to tunnel up into the middle of Stonehaven, there had to be a way for her to prevent it. She just had to figure it out.

And anyway, the horde wouldn't arrive tomorrow. She hoped.

Somewhat reassured, she ran her eyes over the settlement again. After a day spent hacking through the thick jungle, it seemed almost like the overhead canopy had thinned. Dappled shade still pooled beneath the behemoth trees, but it didn't seem as dark. And the grass around the base of trunks had grown thicker and softer.

She ran her hand through the soft blades of grass. It was definitely thicker than when she and the party had left in the morning.

All at once, she realized what was happening. The Curse of Fecundity played a major part in preserving the ruined state of ancient Ishildar. Five relics were needed to restore the ancient city, and Devon had recovered one, the Greenscale Pendant, from the Temple of Sorrow. She wore it all the time now, slowly attuning the item to her spirit. Thinking of the item, she lifted it from her breastbone and examined it.

Item: Greenscale Pendant

One of five ancient relics created to bind the inheritance of the great city of Ishildar, this relic hums with power. Already, you feel a kinship with the city and a sense that, as you attune your awareness to the necklace, some of Ishildar's power will become yours.

5% Attuned

Maybe by the time the pendant was fully attuned, the jungle would have vanished entirely from the area where the pendant had been found. The Khevshir vassaldom, territory once ruled by an ancient vassal society that owed fealty to Ishildar, included Stonehaven. It would be so nice to be spared the oppressive heat and constant hacking through foliage. And it would be much easier to find resources—right now, they basically had to stumble upon things.

It would also make Stonehaven easier for players and hostile NPCs to find. But it would also make it easier to meet friendly individuals. Stonehaven couldn't stay a village forever and upgrading to hamlet required increasing their population to five times the current size. Right now, that seemed almost impossible.

A small glowing ball dropped from the tree canopy overhead and booped her nose.

"Hi, Bob," she said.

The wisp circled in front of her face as if trying to make her dizzy. "How'd it go?"

Devon grimaced. "You don't know anything about demons, do you?"

Bob stilled, hanging in the air like a stop-motion freeze-frame. "Come again?"

"Henrik's army was slaughtered by demons. One got left behind, but when we tried to kill it, it fled by tearing a hole in the ground."

The wisp jiggled as if shivering. "Demons...this is bad."

"That's encouraging. Any other gems to offer?"

"What do you know about the gods?"

"You mean like Veia?"

"And Zaa."

She considered answering that she knew Veia was a cutting-edge artificial intelligence responsible for making the game's NPCs think they were alive. That didn't seem like a nice thing to say.

"I know Veia is responsible for...for creation, I guess."

"And Zaa is her enemy. Demons are manifestations of Zaa's hatred."

"Okay," Devon said, starting to walk toward the worksite where Deld was busy slathering mortar atop a low wall that would eventually be part of the forge. "But what brings demons forth? How can you shield against them?"

"Would it be too hopeful of me to suggest we treat your encounter as an isolated incident?" the wisp asked.

"Is that a rhetorical question?"

"A historical what?"

"Huh?" Devon asked.

"What did you just say?"

"I asked if it was a rhetorical question."

The wisp took up a momentary perch on her shoulder. "Is rhetorical when you find something really funny?"

"That's hysterical...and never mind," Devon said. "I just need to figure out how to keep demons from appearing like gophers in the middle of town."

"Well, you're still planning to search for the other relics, right?"

Devon shrugged. "I'd planned on it as soon as Stonehaven is secure."

"I'm just saying...if you're looking for ways to stop terrifying dark forces, I don't see why ancient relics holding incomprehensible power shouldn't be on your radar. Back before my previous master became...well, you know."

"Before he became a leathery bag of bones with creepy glowing eyes?"

Bob bobbed as if nodding. "Back when he was just a few centuries old, he corresponded with the last survivors of another vassaldom. Bunch of weird frog people, but they were as loyal to Ishildar's legacy as the Khevshir were."

Devon stopped in her tracks. They'd nearly reached the worksite, and Deld stabbed his trowel into the box of wet mortar as if preparing to give her a tour of the construction. She held up a finger asking for patience.

"Do you know where this other vassaldom was?"

Bob shrank inward as if sighing in relief. "Finally. You don't know how long this thing has been sitting on my tongue."

Bob is offering you a quest: Travel south to the Grukluk vassaldom.

According to your loyal and attractive wisp, the second relic of Ishildar should be somewhere within its boundaries.

Objective: Discover the Grukluk region.

Reward: Knowledge is its own reward, isn't it?

Accept? Y/N

Devon hovered her awareness over the prompt and selected yes.

Circling her in a quick whirlwind of satisfaction, Bob let out a little squeal then zinged off.

She sighed and turned her attention to Deld. "Looks like you're making great progress," she said.

The stonemason grinned. "Unless it rains, should be done by tomorrow."

She patted one of the cornerstones. "Care to give me a tour?"

***

As she left the site of the forge, pleased with the progress, she pulled up the settlement interface.

> **Settlement:** Stonehaven
> **Size:** Village
> Tier 1 Buildings - 17/50 (5 upgraded):
> 7 x Standard Hut
> 5 x Canvas Shelter
> 5 x Simple Cabin (upgraded)
> Tier 2 Buildings (2/6) (1 upgraded):
> 1 x Medicine Woman's Cabin (upgraded)
> 1 x Crafting Workshop
> Tier 3 Buildings (1/3)
> 1 x Shrine to Veia

A little spring entered Devon's step. The ragged jungle encampment she'd inherited was becoming a bona fide settlement. After Deld finished the forge, it would be fun to put him and Prester together, maybe to work on another tier 3 building.

She focused on a little tab that activated the population window. On the way back from the army's camp, she'd quizzed Dorden on the professions of his clan members, and the game had added her newly acquired information into the display.

> Population
> 1 x Stonemason
> 1 x Scout
> 5 x Fighter
> 1 x Cook

1 x Quarryman

1 x Hunter

1 x Leatherworker

1 x Carpenter

2 x Lumberjacks

1 x Armorsmith

2 x Miner

Advanced NPCs

1 x Medicine Woman/Sorcerer - Hezbek

1 x Lawyer/Martial Artist - Greel

1 x Fighter/Blacksmith - Dorden

1 x Ranged Fighter/Hunter - Heldi

Not surprisingly, five of the eight dwarves were fighters—or in Heldi's case, a ranged fighter. Apparently, the dwarf woman had chosen to specialize, gaining massive bonuses to her crossbow and short bow skills, but losing proficiency in melee. The others were generalists. Similarly, Dorden had a range of blacksmithing capabilities—he was as competent at crafting warhammers as horseshoes, more or less. Another of their clan members had specialized beyond general blacksmithing to become an armorsmith, though she could make simple repairs to weapons and tools if needed.

Devon searched around the interface options, but there wasn't any way to view information about settlement fortifications, probably because they had none.

She took a deep breath. No sense in putting off the decision about Jarleck.

It seemed dumb to ignore a resource when they were in sore need, but could she really trust Stonehaven's defense to someone who'd been their enemy just a few days ago? Did she have another choice?

Stonehaven really needed a wall and guard towers. Maybe she could get him started on the work and then boot him if the relationship soured. As long as she kept an eye on him—and her reputation score with the man—it would be difficult for him to sabotage the defenses.

As she brushed away the settlement interface, she noticed the man loitering near the crafting workshop and talking through the open window to Gerrald.

Shoulders straight, she marched over.

"So how about it?" she asked. "Think you could build me a wall around the town?"

Jarleck looked at her with a stunned expression. A crooked grin spread across his face.

Reactivating the settlement window, she invited him to join Stonehaven. A look of genuine pride lit his face as he accepted. It made her wonder whether the mercenary had ever belonged to something before.

> **You have gained esteem with Jarleck:** +10 reputation.
> *Good job. You're starting to realize that scar-faced brawlers have feelings too.*

Before she could change her mind, she promoted him to advanced NPC. Inspecting him and checking his list of compatible professions, she saw that he was, in fact, a good choice for the job.

He had a 1.7 bonus to skill gain in fortifications. As she made him a master of fortifications, his face seemed to mellow. A considering look entered his eyes as he glanced toward the entrance to the glade, then shifted his gaze to the semicircular cliff that guarded the rear approach.

Already, he was nodding.

"Think I could borrow one of the lumberjacks? And I'll need someone willing to help me dig. I'd like to start with a nice timber palisade for the front wall—provided you agree, your...Mayor Devon."

"You are welcome to as much labor as you need—just work things out with Prester so that neither of you are slowed waiting for timber. I can probably talk the dwarven miners into excavating for you. We're short of nice-looking rocks to tunnel into anyway."

The man gave a little salute and trotted off with a gait that was far too snappy for his surly appearance.

Inside the workshop, Gerrald looked up from his work on a piece of leather armor. "Don't think you'll regret that, your Gloriousness. He's a good man."

She didn't want to share any doubt, so she nodded in agreement instead. It was getting late in real-world time—yesterday, she'd configured the little clock in her interface to turn red after midnight. It was a little less shocking than having an alarm suddenly start shrieking in the middle of the jungle.

"Everything good with you?" she asked the leatherworker.

"Just fine. But I heard something you might be interested in."

"Oh?"

"The dwarf guard who's been accompanying Bern to the quarry thought he saw footprints on the far side of the outcrop. Not ours."

"What type of footprints? How did he know they weren't ours?"

"There were horses. The dwarves' mules have been paddocked here since we sited the town. The way the tracks crisscrossed the area looked like they were exploring."

"Fresh?"

"Not especially. Couple days."

Devon sighed. If the tracks had been made by players, hopefully they'd already moved through. She had to log off sometimes. Especially since her sleep lately had been weird. She never felt refreshed on waking.

"Thanks, Gerrald. I'll double the sentries until we get it figured out."

She glanced again at Hezbek's new medicine woman cabin and shook her head. She could check in with her friend tomorrow.

Chapter Six

DEVON SLOUCHED IN her chair at the kitchen table and yawned while the coffee maker finished gurgling and spitting out the last drops of liquid energy into the carafe. She rubbed her eyes, trying to get rid of the sandy feeling. Beyond the hanging slats of her blinds, the brilliant desert sun reflected off car windshields and rooftop solar panels and bathed the red-rock landscape. Heat already shimmered off buildings and asphalt.

She propped her head on her hand and yawned again. It had to be almost noon, but she felt like she'd just slept a couple hours instead of …what? Eleven? Maybe she needed to get back on her Red Bull habit.

A last puff of steam burped from the top of the coffee maker, the appliance's usual sign for a completed brew. As Devon shuffled to the cabinet to fetch a mug, movement on the balcony terrace caught her eye. A second later, a sharp knock came at the door.

"Just a second," Devon said as she set down her mug and smoothed her hair so she wouldn't look like a total slob. She peered through the peephole and saw her friend Tamara's face distorted by the fisheye lens.

The deadbolt and doorknob were warm under her hand, midday heat from outdoors seeping through the metal.

"Hey," she said as she opened the door.

Tamara gave her an obvious double take. "Hey, Devon. Are you okay?"

Devon stepped back to let her friend in, then closed the door to keep out the heat. "Fine, why?"

"No offense," the other woman said, "but you look really pale."

"I do play games for a living..."

Tamara shook her head. "It's not your usual geek pallor. More like you just got over the flu or something."

"I just haven't had any coffee yet," Devon said as she pulled the carafe from the machine and filled her mug. "Want some?"

Tamara shook her head as she pulled out a chair. "It's against the rules. The Mormon obedience squad would come for me."

Devon raised an eyebrow. "You guys have that kind of thing?"

"No," Tamara said with a laugh. "But I'm a good girl anyway."

As Devon tugged the handle, the fridge door opened with a squeak. Blue glow from the LED lightbar inside spilled over the kitchen floor and her bare feet. She grabbed the container of half and half and nudged the door shut with her knee.

"Send some of that cool my way," Tamara said, fanning her face. "You *can* afford AC now, right? If I had your salary, my apartment would be like fifty degrees inside."

Devon glanced up at the slowly whirling ceiling fan and shrugged. "I have a little unit for my bedroom. But I'm online most of the time I'm awake, so I don't notice the heat."

As Devon took her seat and poured a dollop of cream into her steaming coffee, Tamara sat back, seemed about to say something, then shook her head. She tapped her fingers on the table and glanced out the window.

"Been so fricking hot lately. October and November are supposed to be the main reason for living here."

"Guess you haven't been riding bikes?"

Tamara shrugged. "I got in a couple short loops in the mornings before work last week. Planning to hit a trail when it cools down this evening. Sucks, though. I really need something longer for endurance training."

Devon blinked away a stray thought about her endurance attribute score in Relic Online, but not quickly enough, it seemed.

Tamara cocked her head. "What did I say? You got this strange *I'm thinking* look for a second there."

"Oh nothing. Work stuff."

"Just tell me. You sit through all my rambling about bleeding brakes and installing drop seats."

Tamara had a point. She did tell Devon plenty of stuff about her job as a mountain bike mechanic—and recently, about life as a sponsored rider.

Devon shrugged. "I was just thinking that I have four attribute points to spend on my character. Endurance is something I should probably invest in. I don't like getting fatigued... but I wanted to research whether it would do anything for my health or mana regen."

"Regen?"

"Regeneration. How fast those things come back after I get hurt or use magic."

Tamara nodded. "Got it. Seems kinda cool. So you decide how your character improves? I wish I could just click a button to increase my riding skills. Like...click, now I can make that stupid climb on Barrel Trail without wheezing like a dying mule."

Devon took a sip of her coffee now that it had cooled enough not to burn off her taste buds. "So I'm guessing it's your day off, but since it's about three thousand degrees out, you came to hang out in my apartment instead of riding fifty miles?"

Tamara smirked. "I came because I thought for sure you would have turned on your AC. Seems like I need a different rich friend."

"Sorry to disappoint."

"You should be." Tamara paused and chewed her lip. "Actually, yes, it is my day off. And it *is* too hot to ride unless I want to experience heat stroke. But I came by because I've been a little worried. You're working a lot."

"Says the woman who leaves her job working on bikes to go ride bikes."

"I know...I'm not one to talk. But first there was that time you zoned out while we were having tacos. Then the time I couldn't wake you up by knocking. And now you've got an auto-responder set up for messages...it just made me think I should check in. And honestly, Devon, you really aren't looking so great. Got the full-on dark-circles-under-the-eyes thing."

Devon set her mug down and ran a hand through her hair. Tangles snagged her fingers. Yeah, maybe she'd been a little too involved with stuff in the game, but the real problem was her sleep.

"I guess that's fair," she said. "But I don't think it's work. I think my sleep is messed up."

"How so?"

"Seems like no matter how long I'm out, I'm still exhausted when I wake up. I guess I must be waking up a bunch and not remembering."

"Can I make a suggestion?" Tamara asked. "And I swear it's not me being selfish and wanting more women to ride with."

"You aren't going trying to get me on one of those wheeled monsters, are you?"

"What about a short spin on a trail with zero rocks? It will help your biorhythms."

"My what?"

"It will make it easier to sleep."

Devon snorted. "Yeah, when I fall off and get a concussion."

"See, but there's these things. We call them helmets..."

Another warm swallow of coffee slid down Devon's throat. The caffeine was finally starting to hit, and her brain felt a little less squishy. "Didn't you just say it was too hot to ride? Something about heat stroke? Seems like a *great* time to teach someone new."

Tamara glanced at Devon's coffee and shook her head. "Speaking of heat stroke, I don't see how you can drink that. There's this other thing that even Mormons have heard about. It's called cold brew."

"Takes too long, and I'm not good at planning ahead."

"Anyway, yes, it's too hot *right now.* But I could pick you up at like 4:30."

Devon winced. She'd planned to log in right after coffee and breakfast.

"I hear your thoughts working," Tamara said. "You'll be in the game then, right? Good thing your friend Tamara knows a loop we can ride that will have you home and back to work by 6. Call it a lunch break."

"Most people go for deli sandwiches on their breaks..."

"Did I mention you might actually sleep like a normal person tonight?"

Devon sighed and rolled her eyes. "Okay, fine. But if I die on this trail, you have to manage Stonehaven for me."

"I have to what?"

"Just don't let me die, okay? I've got a village depending on me."

Tamara smiled and drummed her hands on the table. "Then I'll leave you alone so you can go rule over your peeps or whatever."

Devon rolled her eyes and chugged the rest of her coffee. "Will I need anything?"

"Just shorts and a t-shirt and a death wish."

"Bye, Tamara," Devon said, opening the door.

***

Dusk was seeping through Stonehaven when Devon logged in, shadows flowing into the village from the deeper areas of jungle surrounding the glade. Bats flitted overhead, diving after unseen insects. Beside the setting crescent moon, a trio of evening stars shimmered against the purpling sky.

Devon took a deep breath of the cooling air, enjoying the damp scents of greenery after the stuffiness of her apartment. She rose from her cross-legged seat beside Veia's shrine and stretched, rising onto tiptoes in her sandals.

A large fire was burning in the center of the village, and she spotted Tom, the cook, stirring the contents of a massive cauldron. She smiled to herself. It had been a while since she'd had a meal with her followers. As she started toward the fire, she noticed that the canopy had thinned even more while she'd been offline. More stars were winking to life between the branches and leaves, salting the heavens.

She heard low voices from above and behind. Up on top of the cliff, four sentries now kept watch over the surroundings. They stood in pairs, dark silhouettes against the sky.

Devon nodded in satisfaction, glad to see that Gerrald had conveyed her message about doubling the guard.

Once she neared the fire, she could make out the progress on the palisade as well. Jarleck's construction looked as if it would incorporate living trees where possible. Two segments of trench had been dug, joining trees that stood in a rough line near the village perimeter. One section had been filled with logs cut from the jungle beyond, adding the benefit of increased visibility in the area just outside the wall. Planted vertically in the trench, the logs created a formidable barrier that was made stronger by heavy beams strung crosswise between the living support trees.

As she stepped into the firelight, villagers moved back to make room. The orange glow illuminated faces tired after a day of hard work. "Nice job," she said to Jarleck. "The palisade is looking great."

He smiled, showing a dimple on the cheek that wasn't scarred from the corner of his eye down to his chin. Jarleck had probably been handsome when he was younger. Devon wondered if he'd ever been married, then caught herself and shook her head. It was so easy to forget they were just NPCs.

"Once the wall itself is up, we'll work on a gate," he said. "As for the first set of watchtowers, Prester told me you helped him improvise the plans for raised platforms. I thought we could maybe use the trees and his platforms as a base then add low walls and cover for the archers to hide behind. That is...if I turn out to be as good at improvising as Prester is."

Devon took a seat on a stump just close enough to the fire to feel the heat. "I have a feeling you will be." Or at least, so far it seemed that any follower who tried had been able to acquire the *Improvisation* skill from her.

"What's for dinner, Tom?" she asked.

The scrawny man blushed, his freckles darkening. He shifted behind the cauldron as if to use it as a shield against the sudden attention. "Sloth stew, Your Gloriousness," he said with a shy smile. "With star anise and some wild sweet potatoes Hazel found while foraging."

Devon felt her smile trying to melt away. Not a good night to decide to eat with the tribe. Granted, the usual turtle soup didn't sound that appetizing either.

"How are the food stores?" she asked.

Tom's face turned glum and he glanced down at the stew. "I'm afraid we won't have enough to make it through the day tomorrow."

"Wait, what? Tomorrow?"

"I'm afraid so," the cook said. "Unless…"

> **Tom is offering you a quest:** Please don't let us starve.
> *You went through a lot to gather these people. Maybe you ditched biology class, but living things need sustenance.*
> **Objective:** Obtain enough basic food units to supply the village for 3 days.
> **Reward:** +5% morale as long as the reserves remain above 2 days' worth.
> **Accept?** Y/N

Devon accepted the quest, then yanked open the settlement interface and activated the resources tab. She skimmed down to the food section.

Food consumption: 22 basic food/day
Food available:
7 x Smoked Turtle Meat
2 x Dried Sloth Meat

Well, crap. She hadn't been paying attention to the food supply after promoting Heldi to be their second hunter. Their first hunter, Grey, had been able to provide enough for the thirteen members of the original Tribe of Uruquat. Even hunting part-time, Heldi's additional contribution should have been more than enough.

As if noticing Devon's consternation, Grey cleared his throat. He was stirring the fire with a poker stick.

"Did you want to say something?" Devon asked him.

"Yes, your Gloriousness. The problem isn't that Heldi and I can't provide enough when there are beasts to hunt. Part of the issue, I believe, is that the forest is changing. The trees are thinning near the village, and the animals are moving away."

Devon nodded. She should have thought of that when she noticed the changes in the biome. But if the jungle retreated, leaving some other ecosystem behind, wouldn't different animals migrate in?

"Maybe different creatures have replaced them. Have you tried looking for different types of tracks?"

Grey set down the stick. "Haven't seen anything yet."

"What about that trail I showed you?" Hazel said, nudging the hunter.

"Too dangerous," he said.

"What's too dangerous?" Devon asked. "Is there another problem?"

Grey shook his head. "The tracks don't come anywhere near here. Hazel found them in an area of dense jungle almost at the border of the old city."

Devon raised an eyebrow at the small scout. "You've surveyed all the way to the edge of Ishildar already?" After the celebration following the recovery of the Greenscale Pendant, she'd asked the woman to start expanding their knowledge of the surroundings, particularly to the north and west where the massive ruins of Ishildar lay beneath a choking blanket of jungle.

Hazel grinned, and a message flashed in Devon's vision.

Your map has been updated.

Devon pulled up the map screen and blinked in surprise. Hazel *had* been busy. And her cartography seemed to be getting better. A wide arc of land had been uncovered between Stonehaven and Ishildar. Hazel had added markings indicating outcrops and freshwater springs and a few scattered ruins on the city's outskirts. At what looked like around a half-hour's walk away, the woman had noted *Massive Footprints and Tail Track*.

"Massive footprints?" she asked. "And what's a tail track?"

"It's the line—or in this case, the deep groove—made where an animal drags its tail as it walks," Grey said. "Hazel showed me the tracks this afternoon. I believe they were made by sloths."

"Massive footprints and a deep tail groove doesn't sound like an ordinary sloth..." Devon had cleared most of the corrupted jungle creatures from the area when preparing to enter the Temple of Sorrow, but there might be some strays. "More red-eyed giants?"

Grey shook his head. "I don't think these beasts are a product of the lich's curse."

"Oh?"

"The tracks were too big and heavy—even larger than we saw with the curse. And it was strange...along with the large sets of prints, there were many that looked as if they were made by ordinary-sized sloths. They led into a dark tunnel of brambles."

"Did you go in?"

"Only far enough to glimpse light on the far end...and a claw as big as my arm." Grey grimaced. "As I headed back out, I heard snuffling behind me. Six or seven normal sloths were chasing me down the tunnel."

"They were attacking?"

"Well... I think so. But they were so slow. They never reached me. I could easily have taken them one at a time and come home with enough meat for the whole village, but I didn't think I could fight that many at once. I ran."

This was sounding suspiciously like some sort of...sloth dungeon? What the hell? Devon tried not to laugh.

"And you didn't get a view of the big one? Other than the claw I mean?"

The hunter solemnly shook his head. "I'm afraid not, Your Gloriousness."

Fantasies of massive experience and skill gain were racing through Devon's head. Of course, that was probably too much to hope for—the experience reward probably scaled to match the challenge. Mobs with a top speed of less than one mile-per-hour couldn't possibly be that much of a challenge, even if the boss sloth had claws as big as a man's arm.

Regardless, a good old-fashioned dungeon run sounded like a fine objective. And she even had an excuse.

Stonehaven had to eat.

Unfortunately, it would be dark soon, her followers deserved a night's rest, and she couldn't bail on her plans with Tamara.

She pulled up both her in-game and real-world clocks and did a little math. Perfect. The sun would rise in Relic Online just around the time she returned—if she returned— from her bike ride.

She searched the gathering until she spotted Dorden and Heldi. "You two up for a little adventure tomorrow?"

Dorden raised a mug of dwarven grog. "By the stones," he shouted. "Tomorrow we battle!"

His wife's eyes gleamed as she raised her own mug, but she settled for a silent toast and a nod.

"Good. We'll leave just after sunup."

Chapter Seven

"SERIOUSLY," EMERSON SAID. He was trying to subvocalize but kept slipping into the audible register and drawing awkward glances from his fellow autobus passengers. He glanced toward the rear of the vehicle and spotted an empty pair of seats. "I have to talk to Bradley. It's important."

As he stood and started toward the unoccupied spots, swaying as the bus bounced on soft air shocks, the CEO's secretary sighed. Her voice was projected straight into his mind by the Entwined implants, the lack of a visible communication device or earbuds no doubt adding to the other passengers' discomfort.

"And I'm saying he's not taking calls. Should I give him a message?"

Emerson rubbed the back of his neck to calm his frustration while—hopefully—pointing out the sub-scalp ridges and exposed circuitry near his hairline. It didn't *actually* matter if the other passengers thought he was mentally unstable, but it was always nice to be recognized as sane.

"Tell him that dropping the pain sensitivity for complaining players is just covering up a problem. Given the situation with Owen, I can't just let my recruits believe that—"

"Listen, Emerson," Bradley Williams' voice broke in, the words delivered at twice the volume of his secretary's. "The engineers at

Entwined have been over this problem back and forth and sideways. Your precious players are the problem, not the hardware."

Emerson clenched his jaw as he sat and scooted toward the window, ducking his head below the level of the seatbacks to escape the watching eyes. "You know full well it's not in their imagination."

"I also know that the problem is isolated to less than a hundred users out of the fifty thousand we've been able to bring online. Speaking of, how are your optimizations coming? It sure would be nice if we could start making some real money."

Once again, Emerson was glad to be speaking through voice via his implants rather than on a video call. Pressing his head against the back of the seat in front of him, he kept his words fully subvocal to avoid anger in his tone.

"Even though Penelope and Zaa continue to use half of our processing resources while apparently adding nothing to the game, I *have* been making progress." He paused, waiting for Bradley to acknowledge his comment about the other AI programmer and her processor-hogging creation. When the CEO said nothing, he finally continued. "I have some new tweaks to Veia's higher-level decision tree running on the test cluster."

"I don't speak programmer, but I gather that means you're going to fix the problem?"

Emerson took a deep calming breath like the yoga ladies in the advertisements were always doing. If he could just get someone to *acknowledge* that the problem was mostly Penelope's fault, it would probably be easier to motivate. It wasn't that he didn't care about greasing the squeaky bits in Veia's code. It was about coder honor. As far as he could tell, Zaa's resource usage was getting worse. It used to spike between about 2 AM and dawn in North America, which at least coincided with a trough in user activity. But lately, the load had spread through a wider time window.

"It means I'm working on it and I should have results soon."

"Good. I'd hate to have to bring Penelope on to consult with your project."

What? Emerson felt like his eyeballs were about to pop out of his head. *Penelope* help *him*?

Bradley's chuckle echoed inside Emerson's skull. "Just kidding. Mostly. But seriously, Emerson, about the pain setting. You're too focused on it. Yeah, you got an in-person complaint. But customer support deals with issues that affect thousands. You're a coder. You should know that you sometimes just have to hack in a solution and move on."

Emerson shook his head. He couldn't let it drop without one more try. "But Owen—"

"I know. Owen's in the hospital. We don't know why, but there's no reason to assume it's related to our tech. And regardless, it's an isolated case. You just aren't seeing the big picture."

Emerson's nostrils flared. His skin felt as red as one of those fools in the hot-chili-eating contests. He took another few...what were they called? Belly breaths or something?

"Speaking of customer support issues," Bradley went on, "I have another task for your plate. Veia has been tweaking the game systems. That's fine. It's by design. But we need to start informing the players of changes. Could you put together patch notes say...once a day?"

Emerson shook his head, dumbfounded. "You understand that most of her decisions and data are buried in multiple layers of neural network, right? It's not so simple as looking through a database for coefficients in the to-hit calculation."

"Again, programmer speak. We hired you because you're the best. I'm sure you'll figure it out."

There was no click or outright sign that Bradley had logged out of Emerson's head, but he sensed the CEO's sudden absence all the same.

"I guess we're done here," Bradley's secretary said cheerily.

Emerson disconnected from the conversation.

Chapter Eight

"HUNGRY?" TAMARA ASKED as the autocab drove away, deserting them in a gravel parking lot with just a pair of bikes, helmets, and Tamara's backpack. "I have a bunch of energy bars. We get crates of samples at the shop."

Devon pushed her sunglasses up her nose and looked around. They were probably only three hundred yards away from a major road where cars streamed back and forth, but the sculpted boulders and spindly brush hid the thoroughfare, making the area feel suspiciously like wilderness. If they got attacked by a cougar or something, it might take hours before someone found their bodies.

"Devon? Food?" Tamara said, wiggling a foil-wrapped bar that crinkled in her grip.

Devon shook her head. "This is going to sound weird, but I just ate a big meal in-game. I need a while before my real body is ready for food."

"Maybe that's why you look so thin. You're only eating for pretend."

Devon picked up a helmet and buckled it on. "I don't usually eat in the game. The system automatically deducts my rations. Just figured I should join my followers since they were having a campfire. It's a morale thing."

In truth, it had become about much more than keeping the villagers' spirits up. Devon genuinely enjoyed their company. She missed it when she was offline. But that would be hard to explain.

"Does that actually make a difference? The morale stuff, I mean?"

Devon shrugged. "It's just like real life. A leader needs to be visible, I guess."

Tamara rolled over the bike she'd borrowed for Devon and stood it next to her. "That's cool I guess. So what did you eat?"

Devon shook her head. "You don't want to know."

"Yes I do," Tamara said with a grin. She reached under the seat of the bike and fiddled with something. A second later, parts of the frame geometry shifted, joints squeaking faintly.

"What's that do?"

"It's new tech we're trying out on our demo bikes. The frames have a few adjustment points, and there's a camera in the headset that scans your body dimensions to calculate a fit. Now tell me what you ate."

"Sloth stew."

Tamara was eyeing Devon and the bike as if judging how well the fitting system had worked. She blinked, then laughed. "Wait, really? What did it taste like?"

"Like really stringy beef, I guess. With licorice. It was actually pretty good as long as I didn't think about the ingredients."

Tamara hit another button and adjusted the seat by hand. "Try this," she said as she moved around to the front of the bike. She grabbed the handlebars and hugged the front wheel between her knees to keep the bike stable.

Devon awkwardly threw a leg over and stood on tiptoes to get her butt on the seat. She leaned forward and touched the handlebars. "Seems good...? I don't know how to tell."

Tamara slid her sunglasses onto her forehead and lowered an eyebrow. "You do know how to ride a bike, right?"

"Yeah, on nice flat streets. I'm still not convinced people are meant to ride these things off cliffs."

"You'll be fine," Tamara said. "This trail only has a few small cliffs. Can I let go?"

Devon nodded, and Tamara released her grip. She picked up her own bike, straddled it, and clicked her feet onto the pedals. She pedaled in a short circle, then stopped and somehow balanced in place.

"So what else did you do in the game this afternoon?"

"After my tasty meal? Just maintenance stuff mostly. We're fortifying the town, so I checked out the progress and talked to the sentries. I practiced casting *Wall of Fire* to gain some spell mastery, but I stopped getting notifications pretty quick because I needed to use it on an enemy to gain any more."

"Meanwhile, I sat in my stuffy apartment and listened to my roommate's shitty music. I think I'd rather have created fire and eaten sloth." Tamara unclipped a foot and stood. "Ready?"

Devon tugged at her helmet strip to make sure it was secure. "I guess."

Tamara pointed to a disturbingly narrow dirt track that struck off from the parking lot and snaked between boulders. "Trail starts there. I'll go behind to pick up any severed body parts."

***

Within fifteen minutes, Devon was sweating through her shirt and wondering whether she'd worn a bra that would keep her decent. She was also having the most fun she'd had outside of a VR game in years. The trail followed a mostly flat course through scrub brush and juniper trees, occasionally rolling over a hump of smooth sandstone like the broad back of a white whale.

Tamara followed behind, shouting out encouragement and advice.

When they reached the point that Tamara declared as "halfway", the sun hung just a short distance above some low mountains studded with outcrops of gray stone that reminded Devon of the limestone fists at Stonehaven's quarry. Devon was breathing hard, as much from the exhilaration of the rolling trail as the exercise, and she pulled over to take in the view.

"Not so bad, right?" Tamara asked as she stopped and set down a foot.

"It's fun. I didn't realize this—"

All of a sudden, the scene vanished, replaced by windswept desolation. The air was as hot and dry as mid-summer in the desert, but without the sweet smells of sage and juniper. Hard stone ground stretched into the distance where a sickly yellow haze pooled beneath a serrated ridge of unforgiving rock. Here and there, jagged spikes of volcanic glass stood from the terrain.

Devon opened her mouth to speak, but a strange shriek came from her throat. She blinked, squinted, reached her...claw forward.

She looked down and saw naked flesh, black and stinking. Her bare feet were twisted and tortured and bleeding, the yellow claws at the end of her toes broken after such a long journey.

The call still echoed through her, demanding her to push onward. She *needed* this. Needed what lay on the other side of those mountains.

But it was so far.

"Devon!"

Abruptly, her vision filled with blue. A dome, wide and welcoming and fading at the edges toward the purple haze of dusk. A tracery of clouds veiled the sky to the east.

Tamara's panicked face suddenly hung above her. "Dev?"

Blinking, Devon planted her elbows in the sand and tried to sit. Brush crackled as she moved, twigs poking through her shirt. She flopped back down flat.

"I..." She licked her lips. What had just happened?

"Holy sh—I mean...what the heck?" Tamara said. "You were just standing there, and all of a sudden, you just fell over. You okay, girl?"

"I think I passed out and...had a dream? Does that happen?"

"I don't know. Here, lemme help." Tamara grabbed Devon's wrist and pulled her up to sitting. She grabbed some packet thing out of a pocket on the back of her shirt and tore off the top. "You might be hypoglycemic or something. Eat this."

Gingerly, Devon took the packet. When she squeezed, a bit of paste squished out through a constriction in the packaging. She wrinkled her nose. "What is it? Space station food?"

"Energy gel."

"If you say so..." Nonetheless, Devon sucked the contents out of the packet. It tasted like gritty cake frosting. She blinked, trying to get her bearings. Already, her dream was fading, yet for some reason, she felt like she'd been through this before.

"You think your taskmaster bosses might give you time off to visit a doctor, Devon?" Tamara said, her brows drawn together in concern. "I don't think it's normal to just pass out like that."

Devon's mouth felt like the aftermath of a toddler's birthday party. That energy gel crap seemed to have stuck to every available surface. "Have any water?"

"Yeah, sec." Tamara jumped over to her bike and pulled a water bottle out of her backpack.

Squirting a good amount into her mouth, Devon swished and swallowed. That was better, even if the taste of not-quite-chocolate remained. She took a deep breath.

"That was weird."

"Yeah. No kidding."

"Maybe my body isn't used to exercise."

"I dunno...maybe. But it's still worth getting a checkup, yeah?"

Devon shrugged. "I guess so. I haven't actually been to a doctor since...I don't know. Since my mom kicked me out."

"You didn't tell me about that."

"The doctor visit or my mom?" Devon said with a weak smile.

Tamara rolled her eyes. "Your mom, obviously."

"It was a long time ago."

Tamara glanced over her shoulder, shading her eyes against the sun. "Do you think you can stand? We still have to get back and order a cab before dark."

Devon swallowed and nodded, accepting Tamara's help as she got to her feet. Tamara picked up Devon's bike and manhandled it into a good orientation for Devon to get on.

"Good?" she asked.

Devon grabbed the handlebars and nodded, swinging a leg over.

"Just ride slow, okay? There aren't any drops or anything, but I don't want you to take a header onto your face."

With a deep breath, Devon set a foot on a pedal and pushed off.

The lingering feel of darkness chased her back to the parking lot.

Chapter Nine

"REMEMBER, DORDEN, TRY not to pulverize dinner," Devon said as they approached the entrance to the sloth's tunnel.

With Agavir the Pummeler clutched in a double-handed grip, the dwarf grumbled. "Some lot of fun you are..."

Heldi shared a glance with Devon and rolled her eyes. The dwarf woman held a one-handed crossbow at the ready, and in case they encountered a situation where they needed serious range, she had a longbow and quiver of arrows slung over her back.

Fresh morning sunlight glittered off dewdrops on the jungle foliage, a mere hint of the heat that would come later. The air smelled of damp earth and plants, and the dew painted the fronts of their trousers and boots with streaks of wetness as they advanced through the thickening brush.

Devon had been putting off spending the attribute points she'd gained at level 11, but on the off chance the area was more dangerous than she expected, she decided to go ahead. She pulled up her character sheet.

Character: Devon (click to set a different character name)
Level: 11
Base Class: Sorcerer
Specialization: Unassigned

Unique Class: Deceiver
Health: 260/260
Mana: 413/413
Fatigue: 5%

Attributes:
Constitution: 23
Strength: 11
Agility: 16
Charisma: 33
Intelligence: 29
Focus: 13
Endurance: 12

Special Attributes:
Bravery: 8
Cunning: 6

Unspent attribute points: 4

Many of her attributes had bonuses from her equipment, and those numbers were rolled into the overall score. In addition, a quick meal of Stonehaven Scramble—one of Tom's tastier creations— had given each of them +3 to their *Constitution* and +1 to *Strength*. As a finesse fighter and magic user, she didn't really need any more *Strength* unless she wanted to form a habit of carrying around heavy objects. Since she'd wanted to focus on the synergy between her two classes, Deceiver and Sorcerer, she'd dumped quite a few points into *Charisma* to grow her mana pool and *Intelligence* to increase her spell damage. But now, it seemed like a good time to balance things out.

Besides, with a *Charisma* score of 33, it was hard enough to keep the stares off her.

She focused on the *Endurance* attribute, and a tooltip came up.

Reduces the rate at which characters gain fatigue while providing a small boost to regeneration of hitpoints and mana (both in and out of combat).

Devon put two points into it. The extra regeneration would be great, and with the quest to find this Grukluk vassaldom, she might be making some long treks that would otherwise be limited by her fatigue rating.

She studied the attributes a little more, then decided to put a point into *Agility* to help accuracy and damage when she fought with her dagger, plus another into *Constitution* for the health gain.

When she gave a mental nod to confirm the changes, her max health went from 260 to 267. A few seconds later, her health bar pulsed and filled to the new max.

As she brushed away the interface screen, a rustling came from the bushes ahead. Dorden stopped and raised his hammer. Moments later, a sloth ambled onto the faint game trail they were following. With a growl, Dorden leaped.

Before he could swing, his wife's crossbow bolt skewered the animal just behind its small ear. The sloth took one slow step then slumped, dead.

You have gained 1 experience point.

But only because that was a nice shot.

Devon rolled her eyes. Yeah, yeah. So this might be a little too easy. But the point was to get food, not to conquer the game's most challenging dungeon.

Dorden whirled in mock anger. "Blast ye, woman. You're going to make me look useless in front of our fearless leader."

Heldi just shook her head and retrieved her crossbow bolt, wiping it off before setting it into the weapon again. As she crouched and touched a skinning knife to the corpse, the sloth disintegrated into loot. Devon scooped up the items.

You have received: 3 x Thick Sloth Steaks, 2 x Sloth Furs - Fine

By her calculations, she needed around seventy basic food units to complete the quest and feed the village for three days. That worked out to between 25 and 30 sloths. As long as they were here, though, she wanted to gather as much meat as would fit in her *Jute Bag* and her friends' rucksacks.

With a nod of satisfaction, she gestured the party forward.

You have discovered: Lair of the Sloths.
You receive 2000 experience.

True to the reports from Hazel and Grey, many tracks crisscrossed a trampled area near the tunnel mouth. What Devon didn't expect was the smell. It reminded her of a litter box in need of a thorough scooping. Wrinkling her nose, she edged forward, intent on cautiously scouting the area before plunging down the entrance tunnel.

Dorden, however, didn't seem to get the hint about stealth. As soon as she neared the entrance, he stomped forward with shoulders set. "Now don't ye risk yourself, lass. I'll take the claws and teeth of these fearsome beasts. That's me calling."

"But I just..." Devon trailed off when she saw Heldi shaking her head as if to suggest protests would do no good.

Devon sighed. She had been thinking how nice it was to have a tank taking the hits. Seemed she'd just have to accept the downsides.

Advancing down the tunnel, Devon couldn't help noticing tufts of fur clinging to twigs and thorns in the walls and ceiling. Some of the creatures that used this tunnel barely fit. Seeing as the ceiling hung at least four feet over the top of her head, Grey's description of an arm-sized claw seemed likely.

At least there would be a lot of meat on the carcass...

When they neared the tunnel's exit, green light filtering through the thinning brambles, Dorden slowed. She exhaled, glad he showed at least a little caution.

He turned and grinned. "Ye were probably thinking I was going to rush in there like an idiot, right?"

"It wouldn't be the first time," Heldi muttered.

"Let's see if we can pull any back here," Devon said, conjuring the first of her *Glowing Orbs*. "Or better, see if you can get them to bunch up somewhere."

"Ye gonna use that trick with yer lightning shadows?" Heldi asked.

Devon nodded and stuck her first orb to the wall, then cast a second and placed it on the opposite wall. "Maybe."

As she started to cast a third *Glowing Orb*, a message popped up.

You can't have more than two Glowing Orbs active at once.
Yeah, we know. No one likes to get nerfed. But you aren't just a
one-trick pony, are you?

A one-trick pony...? What the heck was that? Some weird old-fashioned slang that Veia had picked up?

Regardless, reducing her maximum number of orbs *sucked*! It totally gutted the awesomeness of attacking with lightning-based *Shadow Puppets.*

She yanked open her abilities interface to see the damage to her spell line.

Spell: Glowing Orb – Tier 1
Cost: 10 mana
A ball of lightning materializes in your hand. Unfortunately, you can't hurt anyone with it, but the spell could be useful if you forget a torch or something. Requires some concentration to maintain.

Spell: Glowing Orb – Tier 2
Cost: 22 mana
You can attach the Glowing Orb to another object in order to regain use of your hand. Requires more concentration to maintain.

Spell: Glowing Orb – Tier 3
Cost: 22 mana

You may create two separate orbs, and you can attach each to a different object or surface. You must really like this spell.

Spell: Glowing Orb – Tier 4:
Cost: 22 mana
You can now throw your orbs at a surface to make them stick.

Ugh. So unfair. The ability to throw the orb was small consolation, as was the static mana cost above Tier 2. True, maybe the ability to create six *Shadow Puppets* at once had given her some unexpected advantages, but wasn't that part of the bonus of having a unique class? Devon scowled as she pulled just two lightning-based *Shadow Puppets* from the ground.

Congratulations, you have learned a new spell: Shadow Puppet - Tier 2
You can create compelling illusions with your shadow. Properties of the shadow vary based on the type of light used in its creation.
Tier 2 puppets have 150% health of their Tier 1 counterparts.
Cast: Instant
Cost: 30 mana

Consider the upgrade a consolation prize. (You were close to 100% mastery anyway.)

She sighed. Well, Emerson had said her task was to challenge his Veia AI creatively. Seemed she'd succeeded by finding an exploit in her class combo. Not many players single-handedly caused abilities to be altered to be less powerful—in other words, *nerfed*. She smirked, wondering what ordinary sorcerers thought about the change. If any had bothered to level *Glowing Orb* past tier 2 they were probably extremely confused. After all, to them, all the orbs did was create light. It might even be worth one of her rare visits to the game forums to see their reactions.

Anyway, the instant cast on her new *Shadow Puppet* opened up some nice options—previously, she'd had to wait a second or two before her minion took shape. And where there was one way to use the game mechanics to her outsized advantage, there were surely more.

"Ye ready, lass?" Dorden asked.

Devon drew her dagger. "Go for it."

***

The sloths just kept coming like shambling zombies lining up for headshots. After the sixth or seventh one-shot kill by her companions, Devon gave up on the *Shadow Puppets* and started lobbing *Flamestrikes* at the slow-moving army in hopes to get in on a *little* of the action. To keep the tunnel entrance from clogging, the party looted the kills as fast as they fell, and Devon soon had 55 sloth steaks nestled into stacks in her inventory.

"Ready to move forward?" Dorden asked. "Me hammer never tires of skull smashing, but it's getting a mite boring don't ye think?"

Devon smirked. She considered testing Dorden's patience a little further, but the truth was, she was tired of feeling like the tail end of a sausage grinder. She was ready to see what was going on with this gigantic sloth thing.

"Just be careful, okay? I really don't want the embarrassment of being overwhelmed and slain by a sloth horde."

Dorden raised his hammer.

"Steel yourself," Heldi muttered. "Here it comes."

"For the glory of the Stoneshoulders!" Dorden shouted as he ran forward, taking out sloths with massive swipes.

"Didn't we tell him not to pulverize the meat?" Devon asked.

"I've been telling 'im these sorts of things for *years* an' he still doesn't listen." The dwarf woman shook her head. "Shall we? If we hurry, we might slay some without too much mangling."

Devon plucked one of her *Glowing Orbs* from the wall—just in case—and dismissed the other. "Let's do this."

Beyond the tunnel mouth, the lair widened into a trampled open area dotted with a few scrubby bushes and—much to Devon's dismay—a massive pile of dung. Two more dark tunnels exited the clearing on the far side, but they each turned so that Devon couldn't get a view down their lengths.

Dorden was howling with laughter as he ran around the area trailed by a herd of at least ten ridiculously slow creatures.

There was no sign of the massive sloth Grey claimed to have glimpsed. If it weren't for the tracks outside the den, Devon would have started to wonder whether it had been his imagination.

Squinting to aim her spellcasting just right, Devon conjured a *Wall of Fire* between Dorden and his pursuers. The sloths might have been mindless enough to chase after the dwarf despite the impossibility of catching him, but they weren't so dumb as to blunder through the flames. The herd halted in its tracks.

It took a few seconds, but Dorden eventually realized his pursuers had stopped moving. He turned a glare on Devon. "Trying to ruin all the fun, lass?"

Devon rolled her eyes and, testing out the new properties of her tier 4 *Glowing Orb*, tossed it at the wall. The ball stuck like glue, kind of neat, but an abysmal replacement for getting to cast *six at once.* She shook her head as Heldi popped off a quick series of crossbow shots, felling three of the animals. Devon cast another *Wall of Fire*, sculpting it into a semicircle to hem the creatures in, then pulled a lightning-based *Shadow Puppet* from the ground. She sent her minion into the crowd of sloths.

As electricity arced over the group, sizzling their flesh, Devon stifled a quick twinge of guilt. Yeah, they were just NPCs. And yes, they were—in their own hopeless way—trying to chase down and kill Dorden.

But she still felt kind of cruel massacring the creatures so easily—even if she needed the meat.

"That will probably supply enough for Tom's stew pot, don't you think?" Heldi asked. Faint remorse in the woman's eyes suggested she was suffering the same guilty conscience.

"I'm just wondering what happened to this mythical giant..."

As if in answer, a booming roar shook the jungle. The ground vibrated under a set of heavy footfalls. Moving like an advancing glacier, a sloth the size of a school bus began to emerge from one of the far tunnels. Beady eyes glared. Blunt teeth the size of concrete blocks gnashed as the creature made agonizingly slow progress into the clearing. Devon took an unwitting step back and used her *Combat Assessment* skill.

Behemoth Sloth – level 13 (awakened)

Awakened? What did that mean?

"At last we meet, ye foul menace," Dorden yelled as he broke into a run.

Heldi rolled her eyes and took aim with her crossbow as Devon cast a second orb and hurled it at a nearby section of brambles.

Abruptly, the air seemed to waver. Devon's gaze snapped to the sloth.

Silver sparks glinted deep in the beast's eyes.

"Uh...problem," Heldi said.

"Dorden, wait," Devon called. "Looks like there's a special attack inc—"

Too late. A ripple of silver air raced out from the animal in concentric circles. As the first wave passed through her body, Devon felt as if everything stopped. Her breath, her heartbeat, the bird calls in the jungle. All motion and sound ceased.

No...wait.

The bird still sang, but only with infrequent bass notes. Breath still entered her lungs, just...not very often. She dragged open her combat log.

A Behemoth Sloth casts Slow – Tier 2.
You fail to resist the spell.
The passage of time has been reduced to 10% of normal.

Devon groaned, the noise sounding like some screwed-up brontosaurus roar. A sloth casting *Slow*? Seriously?

She glanced at the corner of her screen where little icons displayed the buffs and debuffs affecting her character. A little timer above the icon for *Slow* showed that ten minutes remained.

Devon dismissed the log and turned her attention to the sloth— her head swiveling from looking at Dorden to looking at the beast over the course of five long seconds.

It almost looked like the stupid thing was smiling.

Dorden's bellow sounded like a cheesy slo-mo sound file as he ran, chariots-of-fire style, toward the beast. Heldi's crossbow clicked heavily as it released a bolt to crawl through the air.

Devon's airborne *Glowing Orb* finally snagged on a branch, wobbling in slow motion as it stilled. Devon mud-walked her gaze between Dorden and the sloth. Already, he was too close for her to send in lightning-based *Shadow Puppets* without catching him in the area of effect. Sighing, she started casting a tier 2 *Flamestrike*.

As Devon's cast bar crawled towards completion, the sloth raised a three-toed paw and bared its teeth. Eyes narrowed, it braced and used the set of three enormous claws as a shield. Heldi's in-flight bolt struck one and skittered harmlessly off. Following through, the beast swiped at Dorden, claws skittering over his leg plates with a low-pitched screech.

Devon's *Flamestrike* descended from a ball of fire that appeared overhead, the pillar growing downward to strike the sloth between its shoulder blades. A cloud of smoke puffed from the monster's fur as around 5% of its health dropped away.

The sloth roared and rotated its enormous head toward her.

"Ohhhh noooo yeeee doonnn't," Dorden shouted, swinging his warhammer as if underwater. The blow connected, knocking the sloth's head sideways.

Heldi readied another bolt.

A sudden sharp pinch on her calf brought a low yelp from Devon's lips. She vaulted sideways like a moon man, staying airborne for a full two seconds. When she landed, she rotated in slow motion to find the source of the pain. Two regular-sized sloths had been chewing on her lower leg. Her eyes widened at the sight of the entrance tunnel. A full-on swarm of creatures was coming down it.

And now they moved as fast as Devon's group.

"Craaaaaappp," Devon yelled as another animal latched onto her Achilles tendon. She stabbed, her arm moving agonizingly slow as the beast sank blunt teeth into her heel. Her dagger's blade pierced the animal's back bit by bit until finally, the guard was flush with the sloth's fur. It released her heel, and Devon aimed a kick for the animal's head as she reached for Heldi to get her attention.

Her fingers brushed the dwarf woman's arm as the sloth sailed away in a slow-motion cartwheel.

"Ruuuuuunnnn forrrwaard," Devon said.

Heldi's mouth made a wide O when she looked back and saw the approaching horde. She pumped her arms like a locomotive gathering speed as her slow strides pushed her away from the tunnel. When the woman was clear, Devon summoned a *Wall of Fire* to seal the tunnel exit.

The sloth she'd punted was no longer moving; Devon ponderously spun back to the main fight. Partway through the movement, she realized that her health had dropped ten points. Just a minor wound, but only a couple days ago, even a scratch had been agonizing. Had customer service been telling the truth about her imagining the pain response? She gave a mental shake of her head.

It couldn't be. But for the moment, she wasn't complaining about the lack of crippling agony.

Dorden was mid-swing with another massive blow from his hammer. Just after it connected with the sloth's shoulder, a retaliatory swipe raked claws across Dorden's damaged leg plate, tearing it free and opening a deep gash that knocked off a third of his health.

"Noooo!" Heldi shrieked, loosing another crossbow bolt. With Dorden on the attack, the beast couldn't get its paw up to deflect the blow, and the bolt stuck into its cheek.

The monster was down to 65% health. They'd done some damage, but not enough.

This wasn't looking too great.

Glancing at the *Wall of Fire,* Devon shrugged and summoned another *Shadow Puppet,* this time focusing on the wavering pool of darkness cast by the light from the fire. At first, she thought nothing happened, but then she saw—and felt—her new creation nearby, flickering in and out of existence. She directed it through the curtain of flame and into the tunnel.

Nothing happened, as far as she could tell.

Another blow from the massive sloth sent Dorden staggering. Devon didn't need to see his health bar at 20% to know he was suffering. Blood ran down his leg, soaking his boot, and he'd been forced to switch his grip on his warhammer to just a single hand.

"Baaaaacck offffff!" she yelled.

"Stooneshoulderrrs doon't surrrrenderrrr!" Dorden said, brandishing his hammer.

"Don'tttt beee succhhh an idddiot!" Heldi yelled as her husband staggered from a glancing blow that shaved off another sliver of health.

Finally, the stubborn dwarf started to retreat. Stuffing a hand into her *Jute Bag*, Devon pulled out a *Jungle Health Potion – Mid*. Praying her *Agility* would give her adequate aim, she threw it toward the dwarf fighter.

The click of Heldi's crossbow caught her attention as two bolts left the weapon, splitting to fly in slightly different directions. Devon waited for the long seconds of the flight, and the moment they lodged in the sloth's chest and shoulder, she cast *Freeze* on the beast to give Dorden some more space.

The man somehow managed to catch the health potion. He gripped the cork with his teeth and slowly yanked it free, then tipped the concoction into his mouth. Devon looked back and forth between the dwarf and the sloth. Still not enough distance to get him clear of the AoE on a lightning *Shadow Puppet*. Shaking her head, she cast *Levitate* on him, then summoned one.

Dorden yelped, long and low, as he rose into the air and started flailing in slow motion.

Ignoring him, Devon sent in both her lightning and fire puppets. Electricity crackled over the sloth's body in pulses, knocking the animal's health down to 40%. A few seconds later, the ice prison shattered. She cast another lightning puppet and sent it in, taking off another 10%, then cast *Freeze* as the sloth started advancing toward the helpless, hovering dwarf.

Though she stared, Devon couldn't see her fire-based puppet for a long while until, finally, it flickered near the sloth. But it didn't seem to be doing anything.

Devon shrugged. "Againnnn, Heldiiii?"

The woman already had another pair of bolts in the air. As if guided by magnets, they flew straight for the sloth's eyes, sinking deep.

Devon couldn't help pulling up her combat log as the behemoth squealed and slowly crashed to the ground.

> **Critical hit!** Heldi's shots SMASHED a Behemoth Sloth for 298 and 323 damage. (+25% chance to hit due to group buff conveyed by your Bravery score of 8).
> A Behemoth Sloth has died!
> You receive 5663 experience.

Just as she brushed the window away, time seemed to return to normal.

"Ahh, thank Veia," Heldi said, panting.

"Ye can say that again, me love," Dorden said, looking down on them and then dropping to the ground with a clatter, presumably after having figured out how to dispel the levitation effect. "Now, if you'll excuse me, I have a little revenge to take."

Devon glanced back at the tunnel in time to see the *Wall of Fire* fading. As it sputtered out, Dorden ran forward, hammer raised.

"Remember not to bludgeon them to... Never mind," she called as the sound of intense battle escaped the tunnel.

Devon turned her attention back to the other dwarf. "You all right, Heldi?"

The woman nodded. "Let's not stick around, though. I'm not keen to experience another encounter like that."

"Me neither," Devon said as she crouched and touched her dagger to the massive sloth corpse. A large pile of loot soon cluttered the ground. Devon scooped it into her bag, all except for a giant heap of fur she couldn't seem to lift.

You have received: 25 x Thick Sloth Steak

Out of curiosity, she examined the fur.

Item: An Absolutely Massive Sloth Skin – Fine
You could parachute with this thing.

"You mind carrying this for me?" she asked. "I'm sure Gerrald could make good use of it."

Heldi grimaced. "Kind of fresh, don't you think? The inside's still a little...damp. Make Dorden do it."

"Will he complain?"

The dwarf snorted. "Just call it a war trophy. He'll be fine."

Chapter Ten

AS DEVON POURED the stacks of sloth meat into the wooden chest holding the village food stores, grimacing at the disgusting wet slapping sound when they landed, Tom sauntered up. He tried to look casual but was doing a terrible job hiding his curiosity.

Devon fixed her face in what she hoped was a crestfallen expression.

"Ahh," Tom said. "So Grey was right about the lack of game. How many days do we have?"

"Depends on how long our bodies can last without sustenance, I guess."

Tom nodded, grim-faced. "Well, I'll do my best to stretch what stores we do have."

Abruptly, Devon couldn't do it anymore. The poor man was just too gullible. "I'm kidding, Tom."

He tugged at one of his oversized ears. "Pardon me?"

"I wish we had some variety in our protein offerings, but there's plenty of food to go around." She stepped back from the chest and gestured for him to look.

Tom leaned forward and peered at the—pretty gross, in Devon's opinion—lake of meat chunks inside the wooden box. His grin stretched so wide she worried his lip might split. A popup flashed to life.

Quest Completed: Please don't let us starve.

Congratulations! Your village will live to fight another day. (4.67 days to be precise.)

Reward: +5% morale while at least 2 days of rations remain in reserve.

Tom was still blinking, awestruck, when she started to back away.

"Do you need any help preserving the meat?" She asked.

He shook his head and started muttering about the new smoking technique he wanted to try.

Devon glanced at her real-world clock. It was only around 10 PM in St. George, which meant she had a few more hours in-game before she needed to log out. The sun had started its afternoon descent, but she definitely had time to make a trip to the quarry and check out the hoof prints Gerrald had mentioned.

As she started for the edge of the village, Bob came drifting from the treetops.

"Nice work on the sloths. Sort of," the wisp said as it circled her head. "Except for the part where your defensive fighter almost died, leaving you to fend off a raging beast."

"Yeah, well, I didn't expect a low-intelligence jungle creature to fire off a massive debuff."

The wisp booped her nose. "Duh...what did you think *awakened* meant?"

"It's not like I've been living in this stupid jungle for the last *one thousand years*." She cast the wisp a pointed look. "Perhaps you could tell me. Even better, maybe you could start sharing this sort of information *before* I encounter a problem."

"Well, even though it's not my job to educate the ignorant, I suppose I could explain. Back when Ishildar was at the height of its power, many of the simple-minded animals and even a few semi-sentient plants were granted powers of thought, strength, and often magic. The good magi and scholars of the city believed it was the duty of a civilization to lift up the less fortunate, and they imbued a set of standing stones with the ability to convey this awakening to nearby entities."

"So they created beasts like that sloth on purpose?"

"Uh...hmm...I'm not sure. You know, memories often get—shall we say—confused after a few centuries. But as I recall, the awakening was more...noble. I remember a tribe of gentle jaguars who would bestow the gift of stealth on worthy adventurers. Awakened horses were known to come to the rescue of lost travelers, often even casting fleetness on the travelers' ordinary mounts while providing directions back to Ishildar via a telepathic link."

"In other words, the standing stones didn't typically create boss mobs with annoying spell lists."

The wisp wiggled back and forth, reminding her of a person shaking their head. "I suspect the stones' auras may be malfunctioning slightly."

"Slightly?"

"Hey...it wasn't like you encountered an *army* of monstrous beasts this morning, right? And you got some nice meat out of the deal. Still, the situation might be worth watching. It's been a while since I encountered an awakened creature."

"How long is a while, Bob?" Devon asked as she stepped onto the quarry trail.

"Since... Ishildar fell into ruin?"

"Oh. So only a millennium."

"I'm going to float the theory that your recovery of the Greenscale Pendant resurrected the awakening process—at least in part."

"So I'm going to run into more of these intelligent, spellcasting creatures?"

"It's possible."

"Great."

Even though Henrik's army had been wiped out, the workers and their dwarven guards still varied the path they took to and from the quarry so that no obvious trail led from the outcropping to the village. As Devon chopped at a small tangle of undergrowth, she wondered how long they'd need to keep up the practice. The need to hack their way through jungle slowed the delivery of stone—it would become a drain on construction eventually. Maybe once the palisade and gate were finished, she could allow a path to become trampled.

Of course, if the forest continued to thin, trails might stop getting overgrown altogether. At that point, it would become impossible to hide Stonehaven's activity.

"Another question for you, Bob," she said.

"I live to serve, master. "

"Master, huh?"

"Not really. I mostly hang around because there's not much else to do."

"That and your previous *master* gave you to me as a pet."

"I prefer the term *guide*."

Devon kicked aside a low branch and winced when her toe hit a rock. Maybe she should take Gerrald up on his offer to replace her *Tribal Sandals* with closed-toed boots. "Well, for a guide, you don't do much guiding. In fact, you don't seem to do much of anything besides boop my nose."

"Maybe you need to ask the right questions, young adventurer," the wisp said, booping her nose.

Devon rolled her eyes. "Maybe you're just a washed-up wizard's familiar living in the past."

Bob gave a strange sound that she guessed was supposed to be a scoff. "Familiars are generally animals, often cats or owls. *I* am a manifestation of elemental energy."

"Whatever. Anyway, if the jungle is retreating because the Curse of Fecundity is lifting from the area that was Khevshir vassaldom—"

"Might I mention that's your theory, not mine?" Bob interrupted.

"You can mention it, but I think it's probably accurate."

"If you say so. I've never seen a thousand-year curse lifted. But maybe you have... Anyway, go on."

"*If* the jungle is fading away because of the pendant, will other wildlife replace the animals that are retreating?"

"How should I know?"

Devon sighed. "Weren't you just saying that you're a guide?"

"And after that, I *also* said I had no experience with lifted curses."

"But you remember when the Curse of Fecundity fell. What happened to the animals that used to live in the area, and how soon did the jungle creatures arrive?"

"Veia's breath, you ask weird questions."

A parrot flew between treetops ahead, and Devon pointed at it with her dagger. "Like that parrot. They don't typically live in pine forests, right? So if pine trees sprout and it migrates away, when will a replacement arrive? If you haven't been paying attention, the village will starve if we don't have a reliable food source. And since we aren't farmers..."

Bob gave something that sounded like a sigh. "Okay fine. I get it. You want to know when there will be more innocent creatures to hunt."

"Unless you want to use your powers as a manifestation of elemental energy to *manifest* another food source."

"By my guess, it will be a month or two after the environment changes before the wildlife adjusts."

Well crap. Months? How is she supposed to feed her village without game for months? A *week* would be a challenge. Even if— and this was a big if—she could stomach going back and clearing the rest of the sloth lair, the population there wouldn't just respawn. At least, given what she'd seen of Relic Online, it wouldn't repopulate outside of normal reproduction rates.

Which made her think...maybe it wasn't just the retreating jungle putting a throttle on the food supply. Maybe the hunters had killed too many of the nearby animals. Or maybe it was a combination of the effects.

If so, it wasn't just a matter of waiting around for new wildlife to migrate in. They needed to start thinking about creating a settlement that could sustain itself. Human civilizations had turned to farming to supplement their food supply once they began settling in fixed locations, and she would probably have to do the same.

But that would require seeds and farm animals and villagers with...what? Cultivation and animal husbandry professions?

Devon shook her head. Running Stonehaven was getting complicated.

Ahead, the forest lightened where the trees thinned at the edge of the quarry area. The sound of a hammer striking a chisel told her Bern was hard at work shaping a block. Since she hadn't seen Deld when dropping off the sloth steaks and leaving Dorden to have his wounds dressed by Hezbek, she assumed he was out here collecting stone chips or manufacturing lime for the mortar. At least one, probably two, of the dwarven fighters would be standing guard over the noncombatants while they worked.

She stopped at the edge of the clearing and was surprised to see how much of the rock had been cut away. Where there had been uneven faces of weathered stone marred by cracks and divots, now a sheer white panel of clean limestone was being systematically removed in rectangular blocks of various sizes. The vein of moss agate ran along one edge of the active quarry area, and the dwarven miners were busy pecking at it with small pickaxes. Devon had noticed that the trench for the palisade wasn't quite finished, but since the wall was rising much more slowly than the trench was growing, she supposed she could forgive the dwarves for— apparently—taking a little time off for their favorite pursuit.

Of course, the moss agate vein was probably a poor replacement for an actual mine with deposits of gold and iron. As disappointing as the ability to throw her *Glowing Orbs* was in comparison to being able to summon six.

Devon sighed and shook her head. She was starting to sound bitter.

Not wanting to disturb the workers, she kept to the edge of the clearing as she circled to the far side. When she spotted the tracks, she crouched and inspected them. Not that she could tell much besides that they were horses, but it made her feel as if she were giving the situation her full attention.

You have gained a skill point: +1 Tracking.
Yup, there were horses here. Good job...

"What do you think, Bob? Were there starborn here?"

"Did you say *were* or *are*?" the wisp said. "Because I think you may want to listen a little more carefully."

"Wait, what?"

"Voices, genius...through the trees a little way."

Devon jumped up and drew her dagger. She slipped closer to a tree trunk and cocked an ear. All she could hear, though, was the work going on behind her.

"This isn't a prank or something, is it?"

"Me, joke?" Bob said, booping her nose again. "Not in this case."

Doing her best to move silently, Devon crept into the forest. As she moved into the thicker trees, the foliage behind her filtered the sound of quarry work, and she could finally catch a hint of the voices. At least one woman and one man were speaking. If she focused very hard, she could almost make out words.

As she advanced, she got ready to summon an orb but didn't want to give away her presence yet. The smell of cooking vegetables—sweet potatoes?—reached her nose before the faint hint of smoke from a campfire. Whoever it was, they must be using very dry wood to avoid obvious smoke. A pretty good trick in a perpetually damp jungle.

When she could hear the crackle of the fire, Devon slowed further, taking just one step every few seconds. Somewhere nearby, a horse snorted. Finally, she peered between leaves. Players, definitely—it was obvious by the way they sat, a confidence NPCs seemed to lack. At least there were only two, not the raid party she feared. The woman looked to be some sort of caster, and if she were to guess, the man was a damage-dealing melee character. Their mounts were picketed on the far side of the campfire, snuffling through the foliage for appetizing greenery.

The players were debating between making for the coast to be the first party to get the discovery achievement or remaining in this area a little longer. It seemed like they were following some quest, but that the directions were vague. Devon found herself nodding in sympathy. At least she and the players could agree on that much.

As she listened to the conversation, the intonations started to sound familiar. Of course, games changed the timbre of voices according to characters' sizes, genders, and races. But they couldn't change the *way* people talked, the words they emphasized.

Devon had spent five long years playing Avatharn Online with a tight-knit group of players. She'd often felt she could recognize her friends by just their voices if they met in real life. Even if she discovered, for instance, that Maya wasn't a twenty-something programmer from California, but rather a burly woodsman from Quebec.

And if she wasn't mistaken, the two players sitting in front of her were Hailey, the druid who had betrayed their party in their final adventure together by live-streaming a boss fight despite their pact, and Chen, the teenage boy from somewhere in the Midwest who had tanked thousands of bosses for their group.

Devon could scarcely move. She could hardly think. Sure, she'd originally decided not to try to hook up with her former guildmates, because they'd already said goodbye. But right now she was desperate to run forward and tackle Chen with a giant hug.

She couldn't though. Because she now understood why they were talking about exploring and discovery and all that. It wasn't the XP they were after. There was no doubt Hailey was streaming right now. The moment she got her betraying little eyes on Stonehaven, the whole world would see what Devon was building.

And no doubt, her settlement would come up on lists of places to smash.

Chapter Eleven

DEVON CAST *FADE*, crouching and pressing her shoulder against a tree. Her heart was thudding so hard she worried her former guildmates could hear it. But they were oblivious. Chen reached into the low campfire with a mail-armored glove and brushed a pair of charred sweet potatoes out of the coals.

Swallowing, Devon focused on him. An inspection window popped up.

> Chendil - Level 9
> Base Class: Knight
> Specialization: Unassigned
> Unique Class: Tinkerer
> Health: 305/305
> Animation Points: 6/6
> Fatigue: 3%

His character name confirmed Devon's suspicion. These were definitely her former friends. She glanced down the rest of his character information. Tinkerer? What was that? The animation points must have something to do with his unique class, but she had no idea what. With the fatigue value of just 3%, it seemed likely that he'd just recently logged in. Maybe that explained why he and Hailey were still near the tracks they'd left more than a day ago.

Speaking of...Devon glanced again at the pair of horses. Why didn't she have a mount? She hadn't even thought about it, really.

Maybe she should ask the dwarves whether one of their mule team would accept a saddle and rider. Compared to a warhorse, a mule wasn't much of a steed. But since the dwarves' wagon was parked due to the impracticality of driving it through thick jungle, and the mules were spending their days chomping grass and swishing their tails at the flies...it couldn't hurt to ask.

She turned her attention to Hailey and inspected the woman.

Haelie - Level 13
Base Class: Seeker
Specialization: Unassigned
Unique Class: Unassigned
Health: 257/257
Mana: 290/290
Fatigue: 5%

Devon rolled her eyes. Haelie? Why even bother to set a character name if you are just going to come up with a different spelling for your real-world name?

As for the woman's class, Devon had no idea what a seeker was. That was another thing she would surely know if she spent time on the forums or if she'd experienced the game's standard character creation. It was clearly some sort of caster class—if Hailey's cloth armor and rune-covered staff weren't enough clues, her mana pool was.

Devon knew she was being a bit petty, but she couldn't help feeling vindicated to see that Hailey hadn't been granted a unique class—not yet anyway. Of course, Hailey's decision to stream their final Avatharn battle against the bog serpent queen wasn't a cool thing to do when the group had decided against it, but it wasn't like the woman had sacrificed their loved ones in a dark ritual or anything.

Still, she had to fight the urge to gloat. It wasn't necessary anyway. It must have been driving Hailey nuts to be grouped with Chen and his unique abilities while she had none.

The level difference between Devon's two friends made sense; just like hers, Chen's experience gain would be reduced to account for the extra power that came from his dual-class status. Devon was faintly surprised to see that Chen was still a couple of levels behind her, but if these two were spending their time trying for first rights on the game's discovery achievements, it made sense. While traveling, they weren't fighting, and when they weren't fighting, they weren't gaining experience.

"You sure you don't want to hit those quarry workers?" Hailey asked as she poked at one of the sweet potatoes. She jerked her hand back. "Ow."

Devon stiffened, nearly breaking her *Fade* effect. *Of course,* Hailey would want to massacre Devon's innocent followers. She clenched her jaw. Why hadn't it been Maya or Owen out here with Chen?

Chen grimaced. "They won't even give XP."

"The guards will. And they removed a lot of stone while we were logged out, right? They must have a town nearby."

"Come on Hailey. They're friendly. I don't care so much about a reputation hit way out here, but it just doesn't feel right, you know? It's like slaughtering civilians or something."

Hailey sighed and used a stick to roll her potato over. "I guess you're right. If it's a friendly town, maybe we could sell some stuff. I kinda want to check out those ruins anyway. My subscribers are getting a little sick of watching us hack through the jungle."

Devon shook her head. Seemed it was still about Hailey's precious subscribers. Back in the Avatharn days, it had made sense. Hailey had earned a decent wage from subscriber donations and pledges, meaning she didn't need to work so hard to sell in-game items and services. They'd all been making income off Avatharn in one way or another. But seeing as Emerson had recruited the whole group, Devon assumed the woman was making the same salary she was. The sensory stream would be a tiny bonus on top of that.

Hailey probably did it for the attention more than anything.

Leaning over to the small pile of firewood, Chen picked up a pair of forked sticks and planted them in the ground on either side of the fire. Then he grabbed the ends of another small branch on which they'd impaled a plucked bird carcass. Chen laid the branch horizontally between the supports and did something strange with his hands, then sat back as the spit began to turn all on its own.

Devon's eyes widened in surprise. She inspected him again and saw that his animation points had dropped by one. She was dying to ask what he'd done there—was a tinkerer some sort of creator of machines?—but of course that would reveal everything to Hailey.

Her calves were going numb, and she shifted, wincing at the faint rustling her movement created. The bird looked like some type of grouse or chicken relative, which was good because she didn't think she could stomach watching them eat parrot. As the bird's skin started to brown, Devon's stomach rumbled. The smell made her mouth water.

"Anyway," Chen said, "yeah, I wouldn't mind a short break from travel. My inventory is pretty full, too. Maybe we should head past the quarry after we eat?"

Devon clenched her jaw. Damn. She'd been hoping Chen would disagree with Hailey's suggestion and that she could just watch them ride away. That might be painful in its own way, but it was better than having Stonehaven discovered. But how was she going to stop them from wandering through the jungle until they found the village? Even if they weren't searching very thoroughly, Stonehaven lay almost directly between the quarry and the edge of Ishildar.

She tugged a hunk of hair as if she could force her brain to cough up a plan.

"But I have to log before 2 AM my time," Chen added. "My mom's pissed that I've been staying up too late."

Hailey shook her head. "Why is she pissed? She gets that you're earning a salary, right?"

"Dude, I still gotta go to school. It's not like I can wake up at noon."

Hailey sighed. "Right. I forgot about that."

"You'd think you'd remember after five years."

"Yeah, but I'd figured they'd put you in some kind of online program."

"No way. Mom and Dad are convinced that the gamer thing isn't a long-term career. They say an online certificate won't be enough to get me into a good school. College I mean."

Hearing Chen talk about his parents, Devon couldn't help feeling a pang of envy. Chen might complain about his mom and dad now and again, but even at sixteen or seventeen—she hadn't quite kept track of his birthday—it was obvious that he recognized how much they did for him. While getting kicked out on her sixteenth birthday, Devon had told herself she *wanted* to leave, that things would be better without her mom and the string of no-good boyfriends dragging her life down. But even as she'd walked out the door with just a backpack and a small suitcase, she'd ached to hear her mother say something—anything—to hint that she didn't want her only child to leave.

The silence in Devon's ears had been agonizing.

Not long after, Devon had found a new family. They'd looked out for each other, even if it was in a make-believe world. Now two members of that family were sitting just five feet away.

And the silence hurt almost as much.

As Devon took a deep breath to try to push away her melancholy thoughts, a loud roar tore from the jungle on the opposite side of the fire. The horses squealed and reared, pulling their pickets from the earth.

Devon jumped up, forgetting her *Fade*, but the wild shaking and tilting of brush opposite the fire captured Chen and Hailey's attention. Quickly, Devon recast the spell and watched, heart pounding, as black and purple rays erupted from the earth in front of her friends.

"Oh, shit," Hailey said as a trio of demons ripped free of the earth, shrieking. All darkness and glowing red eyes, they were similar to the thrall Devon's party had encountered.

"What's the con?" Chen said as he raised a longsword. His helm lay beside the fire, and he held the blade to defend his unarmored head.

Hailey snatched her staff. "Demon thralls. Level 14, 10, and 10. Vulnerable to holy damage. Resistant to fire...oh crap, Chen. My rez stone is out of charges. Don't die."

"Wait, what? You didn't charge it? You said you were going to when I logged."

"I forgot, okay?"

"It's not okay if I die. We're bound in fricking Eltera City."

"*You* are," Hailey said. "I hit the bindstone at the edge of the mountains."

Chen groaned. "Awesome. Then we're even more hosed. It will take days to meet up."

As the demons advanced, shrieking and baring mouthfuls of razor-sharp teeth, Hailey started backpedaling to gain distance. She gripped her staff in both hands. Devon couldn't see her face, but she assumed the woman was concentrating on a spell. A curtain of shimmering energy descended on the lead demon, but the beast shivered and seemed to shake off the effects.

"Charm failed."

"Crap," Chen muttered, swinging at the closest demon. "It's hard for me to hit level 14 mobs."

Devon closed her eyes. If her friends died here, it solved her problem of keeping Stonehaven hidden. Could she do it? Could she watch them fall, especially Chen?

"Holy fricking shit," Hailey said. "There's someone here."

"What?" Chen said, grunting. "Is charm up? Try one of the level 10s. These have to be those demon things people were talking about on the forums."

"Chen, it's a player—wait..."

Devon's eyes flew open to see Hailey staring right at her. She checked the corner of her vision to make sure the *Fade* icon was still active—it was. Beyond the stealth bonus from the spell, she was hidden in the darkness of the forest. The other woman couldn't possibly see her.

Except apparently, she could. "Devon?" Hailey asked. "This has *got* to be a coincidence."

Still, Devon didn't move. How in the hell could the woman detect her?

"Listen, chick or dude or whatever. In case you haven't noticed, I'm a seeker. Your stealth thing isn't working."

"I—"

A shout from Chen cut off Devon's words. He'd taken a hard blow on the arm, and blood was running over his chainmail.

"Fricking hell. Are you just going to stand there?" Hailey asked.

A split-second later, a pop-up appeared in Devon's vision.

Haelie is inviting you to a group.
Accept? Y/N

Gritting her teeth, Devon clicked 'yes.'

***

Devon was still in shock. She stood there like an idiot while Hailey turned back to the fight and started muttering. A casting bar appeared above her entry in the group interface. The words *Guide Vitality* were written over the top the bar. When the cast finished, a faint white halo surrounded Chen, and a little buff icon appeared below his name. A second later his health bar pulsed and gained a few points.

So the seeker class was a healer? As a druid in Avatharn, Hailey had been given the choice to specialize in nature-based healing, but she'd gone for offensive casting and buffs instead.

Chen grunted and took a step back to brace for another block. All three demons were on him, clawing at his defenses. Anchoring the group of enemies, the level 14 thrall hovered at the front of the group, the two level 10 beasts flanking. Between flurries of attacks, the weaker demons fluttered backward, legs dangling just a couple inches off the ground, then landed. The stronger monster remained in place, swinging at Chen with massive forelimbs and making it difficult for the knight to stop blocking long enough to strike back.

As Hailey started casting again—this time, the bar said *Charm*—one of the level 10s rose in the air. Its red eyes flared, and when it opened its mouth, a horrible shriek shook the area, interrupting the cast. Devon winced as sores opened on her forearms.

The attack finally shook Devon from her paralysis. She stepped from the jungle and called down a *Flamestrike* on the demon that had just shrieked. The column of fire engulfed the monster for a moment, singeing bits of patchy fur and leaving blackened spots on its already dark-colored flesh.

"I don't know how long you were in the bushes playing creepy stalker," Hailey said, "but if you didn't hear, they're resistant to fire."

Devon clenched a fist around her dagger. She *had* heard that. She'd just forgotten due to the emotional storm raging in her head. She fought back the urge to snap off a retort. She didn't remember Hailey being this much of a jerk. She'd always been nice enough, even a little shy. Maybe the added fame of being a streamer for Relic Online had gotten to her. Or maybe this was how she always talked to people she thought were strangers.

The pain from her demon-inflicted sores flared as the damage over time effect pulsed. Devon grimaced, but like with the sloth attack, the injury felt nothing like the agony she'd experienced before customer support had messaged her. Something had definitely changed.

Chen batted away another swipe from the lead demon's claw. "I think customer support was serious, Hailey. It just doesn't hurt like it did."

Wait, what? Chen had experienced the pain too? Emerson hadn't told her that. Of course...now that she thought about it, customer support probably wouldn't have bothered to send a message if she'd been the only one to complain. But it also couldn't be *that* widespread, or there would have been a fix sooner. Most players just wouldn't put up with feeling real levels of pain.

Anyway, what were the chances that she and Chen had experienced the same problem if it were just a random quirk?

"I know, right?" Hailey said. "It doesn't feel any worse than the injuries in Avatharn. Anyway, can we focus on not dying?"

Devon stiffened. If the chances that both she and Chen had encountered the same problem were small, it seemed vanishingly unlikely that all three of them would have suffered the same issue.

"Think you could actually land a charm? You seem to forget that I'm not a tank spec anymore."

"Oh fine," Hailey said, grimacing as another damage pulse hit the group. Her charm spell connected this time, and one of the level 10 demons stilled. It stood at attention, looking at Hailey expectantly.

A smaller icon with a little portrait of the demon and its health bar appeared near Hailey's name.

Devon pushed away her shock over learning the others had experienced the pain problem and dashed into a small patch of late-afternoon sunshine. She dumped mana into a tier 2 *Shadow Puppet*. Her creation rose from the earth, all hard edges and sharp angles from the unwavering light of the sun. She formed it into a spear and sent it lancing for the other level 10 demon. The shaft of darkness blew a hole in the thing's chest before shattering, knocking off a third of its life.

"Focus fire," she said.

Chen shook his head. "Remember when our Devon used to say that? They even sound kind of the same."

Another damage pulse rocked the group as Hailey sent her charmed demon to attack its brother. She cast *Guide Vitality* again, and this time, the heal over time spell landed on Devon. At the first pulse, the cool tingling traveled through her body to the site of the sores, numbing the pain. She gained a few hitpoints.

Charm and healing...plus there was that extra information Hailey had called out about the demons, resistances as well as their levels. Whatever the woman's class was, Devon found it confusing.

She dragged another sun-cast *Shadow Puppet* from the earth and hurled it at the demon. The thing was down to 10% life, so Devon ran forward and stabbed it with her dagger—in the back of her mind, she still had hopes of someday skilling up her *One-handed Piercing* enough to wield a necrotic-damage-causing ivory fang she'd looted early in the game.

Up close, the demon smelled like brimstone and hot metal. As she pulled her dagger free, her gaze met the creature's eyes for a moment. A strange sense of déjà vu. Or maybe it was just a vague familiarity. She shook off the sensation as a swipe from the charmed demon's claw finished the beast off.

"What the heck is a deceiver anyway?" Chen asked as he parried a blow from the level 14 monster, then aimed a kick at the thing's knees.

"Can we have circle time and introductions later?" Hailey asked.

"Yeah yeah," the knight said.

Devon focused on a spot between the lead demon's shoulder blades. With a jump, she plunged her dagger into the monster's back. The demon's health dropped by about 10%, taking it down near half.

> **You learned a new ability:** Backstab.
> *Backstab attacks do 2 x normal damage to a distracted target.*
> *You probably aren't sneaky enough to do this without a tank holding aggro. Hint hint... It wouldn't be so terrible to have friends around, would it?*

Hint hint? Really? True, it wouldn't be bad to have friends around. But when one of those friends couldn't be trusted to keep her word and might bring destruction down on Stonehaven, it just wasn't an option.

She struck again, putting more force behind the blow than she probably needed to.

Temper, temper...

"Shut up, Veia," Devon muttered. "And didn't I disable messages in combat?"

"Huh?" Chen asked, deflecting another claw strike.

Hailey's demon flapped forward and dug its toes into its former friend, ripping flesh away from ribs. The level 14 beast shrieked as it lost a quarter of its health. With a mighty shout, Chen did something that made his sword gleam brighter, then sliced his enemy's head clean off.

"I guess it's dead," Hailey said as she strode forward. She pulled a small knife from a little sheath on her belt and approached her charmed creature.

"Wait," Devon said as the other woman laid the blade against the demon's throat. "I have a quest—never mind."

The charmed demon fell without resistance, black ichor spurting from its neck.

"I would say that was fun, except it wasn't," Hailey said. "Thanks for the assist, whoever you are."

A strange silence fell over the campfire area, broken only by the crackling flames and the hiss as grease fell from the roasting bird. A final pulse from the heal spell closed the sores on Devon's arms, and she shuddered as she rubbed her unbroken skin.

Chen was looking at her intently. To escape his scrutiny, she crouched and touched her dagger to the first of the demons, activating decomposition. Remaining in her crouch, she gestured at the loot as if to offer it to them. Chen was still staring.

Devon pressed her lips together. What now? She could leave the group and run, but that would be weird enough they might decide to follow. For that matter, they might follow regardless of how she left the situation. Encountering another player all the way out here just wasn't something she imagined Chen would brush off.

The knight cocked his head. "Your voice...the unique class...the fricking name..." Chen said. "How many people actually choose Devon as their character name?"

"Don't be dumb, Chen. What are the chances?" Hailey said.

"Pretty good, seeing as the game has been leading us in this direction for weeks."

Hailey's slipper-clad feet stopped in Devon's view. "Devon?"

Devon sighed. She wasn't going to be able to fake her way out of this. She stood and met the other woman's eyes as she opened a browser window—the first time she'd connected to the web from inside the game—and searched for Hailey's feed. An image of Devon's character popped into view, the first time she'd seen herself outside of a wavy reflection in a water barrel.

Devon's eyes widened. Holy crap...she *was* hot. Like, really, really hot. Guess that's what focusing points into *Charisma* did for you.

"Cut your stream, Hailey," she said.

A disbelieving grin spread across the other woman's face. "No way. It *is* you."

"I said cut it. Right now."

"Okay, okay. Fine."

The window went black, banishing Devon's view of her extreme good looks. Since she wouldn't put it past Hailey to stealthily restart her stream, she resized the window and moved it to the corner of her view. The feed remained dark.

For now, they were alone.

As Devon glanced between her former guildmates' faces, a flood of emotion rose from her gut. She clamped her lips together to keep her chin from trembling and swallowed to collect herself. "I never thought I'd see you guys again."

Chapter Twelve

AFTER DIVIDING THE loot—Devon had no idea what she was going to do with demon skin scraps—Hailey and Chen pressed into the wall of jungle in search of their horses. Devon hurried back the way she'd come to check on everyone at the quarry. Her shock at seeing her old friends followed by a surprise demon attack had made her forget there were innocent villagers nearby. She feared the worst: that perhaps a second attack had massacred her friends from Stonehaven. But when she stumbled into the quarry clearing, the workers were packing up for the night. They seemed oblivious to the battle that had just occurred.

She didn't really feel like talking, so she melted into the shelter of the jungle to watch and wait for Hailey and Chen's return. After a couple of minutes, the quarry workers formed a little procession and started the short march back to Stonehaven. Around half an hour later, her former guildmates shoved back out of the brush, horses in tow. The animals were sweaty, their eyes still white-rimmed. Devon didn't blame the poor animals for their terror after the sudden demon arrival.

The sun had just set, and the darkness under the trees made it hard to see. Devon didn't know whether either of her friends had darkvision, and she didn't ask. Wordlessly, the group stepped into the brighter light of the clearing. Once out of the trees, Hailey looked pointedly at the quarry then made an act of searching the clearing's perimeter for an exit trail. Devon could see her thoughts working...the presence of friendly NPCs combined with at least one player had to mean a nearby settlement.

Devon crossed her arms over her chest. She wasn't going to endanger Stonehaven for the sake of social niceties.

After a minute or two of uncomfortable shuffling, Chen took a breath. "So, who starts?" He put on a cheery smile despite the obvious tension.

"How about you guys tell me why you're out in the middle of the jungle?" Devon said.

"There's no need to be hostile, Dev," Chen said. "We could ask you the same question, right?"

She pointed her gaze at the ground in the center of their small circle. Yeah, maybe that was a little antagonistic. But she still wasn't going to betray Stonehaven.

Hailey planted the end of her staff in a patch of mud between the slabs of hard stone that made up the clearing. "Actually, let's talk about the livestream of the Thevizh fight. That's why you're pissed, right Devon? We might as well get it out of the way because ignoring the situation isn't going to work in the long run."

Devon took a deep breath, widening her stance. "Of course I'm pissed. You promised."

"Okay, so I promised. But only because you bullied me into it."

"What? I did not. We voted."

"Yeah, we voted. But you had the Daggers of the Sun, which were our only hope of actually downing Thevizh. And since you said you didn't want to do the fight if anyone was streaming, we didn't have a choice."

Devon's hands curled into fists. "I said I would rather have it be just about us, not us and a hundred thousand spectators. But I never said I *wouldn't* go if the group voted to allow streaming."

"You didn't have to say anything out loud. It was obvious in your tone."

"My tone? That's your proof? What if I just had a cold or something?"

"Dev," Chen said quietly. "You didn't have a cold. Let's at least keep this to the facts."

"Okay, so maybe I would've argued pretty hard against streaming. But only because it was our last chance to be together. Our way to say goodbye."

"Only because you convinced us we *had* to say goodbye and break off contact after Avatharn's shut down."

"Wait a minute, Hailey," Chen said, running a hand along his mount's neck. The animal was obviously still nervous, its muscles tense. "We all agreed on that. We didn't know there'd be something like Relic Online, and none of us wanted to be stuck living in the past. We had to move on."

Hailey rolled her eyes. "Okay, whatever. The point is, it wasn't fair to say that none of us could stream. That's how I made my living in Avatharn."

"And the ten dollars you made in tips during our last fight were what got you through until the Relic Online thing came up?"

"Actually, I made almost twelve hundred when you got the killing blow. But that's not the point. For me, streaming was part of playing Avatharn, and I wanted a chance to show our last achievement."

"*That's* not the point either. The issue is that you lied and broke a promise."

Hailey's knuckles were white around her staff. "Did it change your experience, Devon? Honestly?"

"Once I heard we were streamed, it did. The fight was private."

"And since you don't visit forums, if Emerson hadn't told you, you still wouldn't know. All you would remember was riding on Thevizh's head while she flailed around."

Devon closed her eyes, trying very hard to control her anger and not yell. Saddle buckles jangled while one of the horses stomped.

"You know what guys?" Chen said. "You're both right in your own ways. I get why Hailey wanted to stream the fight. We had close relationships with each other, but she had a relationship with her subscribers too. People had been experiencing Avatharn through her sensory stream for almost as long as we played together. They chatted and stuff, you know. I hardly ever streamed, but even I was tempted to forget the pact. I'm still in touch with some of my old subscribers.

"But I get why Devon's pissed too. When I first heard what you did Hailey, I tried to track you down. I was gonna like spam you with hate mail or something. Fortunately, I'm a crappy Internet sleuth."

Hailey stared at her feet, lips pressed into a hard line.

"Anyway, do you think we could just let it go?" Chen said. "Avatharn was pretty much another life..."

Devon blinked and watched a small flock of parrots land in the trees across the clearing. "It's not so much about the Thevizh fight. It's about trust."

Hailey took a deep breath and let one hand fall away from her staff. "For what it's worth, I'm sorry. But don't you think five years of grouping together and watching each other's backs is better proof of trustworthiness than a single incident at the very end?"

What could Devon say? When she put it that way, yes. But the issue was, if Hailey went behind her back to livestream the game experience once, she'd probably do it again. And the last thing Stonehaven needed right now was to be put on the map by a popular streamer.

She forced herself to look at Hailey while she spoke. "We play for different reasons. I get that. Just a little while ago, I was thinking that streaming was about attention for you. But I think it's more about connecting with other gamers and fans. I play..." She hesitated. Why did she play? It used to be for the feeling of achievement and adventure more than anything. Now, it was for Stonehaven. "Let's just say I'm working on something out here in the middle of nowhere. I think it could be great, but it will be ruined if a horde of players shows up. My...my friends will be killed."

Hailey looked over Devon's shoulder as if trying to locate these friends. "So is there a starting location out here? I was starting to think you were the only player around."

Devon held the other woman's gaze. "They aren't players."

Hailey seemed to work this over, confusion warring with disbelief on her face. "NPCs you mean?"

Devon nodded. "Most of the time I don't even think about them that way. Whatever the creator AI has done, my friends here are as real as you are. They experience the same emotions we do. They have histories and people they care about, and none of them want to die. But if you start showing the world what's around here, an army of players is going to arrive and slaughter them just because they can."

Neither of Devon's guildmates said anything for a long time. Hailey reached up and scratched the back of her neck while Chen checked the girth strap on his saddle. Finally, the knight ran a hand through his hair.

Devon's eyes widened at the sight of a slightly pointed ear. "Did you go half-elf, Chen?"

Hailey snorted. "You're just noticing that? Couldn't you tell by his prancing around? The elf runs strong in this one."

Chen's face reddened. "I didn't get a choice, okay?"

The tension broken, Devon looked at Hailey again. "Seriously. I'm happy for you if you're enjoying showing Relic Online to your subscribers. But could you guys please move on through before you turn your feed back on? I just need a little more time to"—she curled her toes, hoping she wasn't making a big mistake—"get Stonehaven defensible. It's not a village to be sacked and cleared. It's my home."

Chen whistled. "A village, huh?" He turned his attention to Hailey. "We can do that, right? I forgave you once for breaking your word. But I wouldn't be able to forgive you again if you screwed this up for Devon. It's clearly important to her."

Hailey's eyes went distant for a moment, and Devon jumped in surprise when bright yellow words appeared over the black screen where Hailey's livestream feed had been playing.

Hey guys. Stream is going offline for a few days. Drop your handle in the notifications box if you want a ping when I'm back online.

"Thanks." Devon wrapped her friend in a hug. "Come on. I can't wait to show you Stonehaven."

Chapter Thirteen

UNFORTUNATELY, JUST BEFORE they reached the partially completed timber palisade around Stonehaven, Chen's mother sent him a message that said he had five minutes to get off-line or he'd lose gaming privileges for three days. Rather than start the introductions only to have Chen vanish into thin air, Hailey and Chen decided to log out just outside of town. They set a time to meet the next day, lay down on the ground, and vanished along with their horses.

In the following silence, the chirr of insects swelled. Faint voices that filtered through new wall. Devon leaned her forehead against the bark of a tree. The community she'd formed in Stonehaven felt so comfortable. The villagers looked up to her and respected her, but more than that, they seemed to genuinely like her. She'd learned a lot from Hezbek and Greel, and she'd sometimes imagined what it would be like to meet someone in real life. Would she have a marriage like Dorden and Heldi, fighting side by side, or like Bayle and Tom, warrior and camp cook? Just the thought made her laugh.

Regardless of whether or not Hailey was trustworthy, there was no question that bringing players into the village would change things. The dwarves had every reason to distrust starborn individuals after having their livelihood undercut by hordes of arriving players. Devon didn't really know how the humans would react, but they wouldn't just ignore the new arrivals. Would her advanced NPCs worry about their status? Would Hailey and Chen act strangely—or worse, laugh—upon seeing the closeness Devon had with some of the villagers?

Would tomorrow be the beginning of the end, or could she somehow turn the arrival of her guildmates into an opportunity to make Stonehaven stronger?

Unfortunately, she just wouldn't know until after they logged back in. And since Chen had school tomorrow, it would be an uncomfortable wait.

Lifting her head from the tree trunk, she left the silence behind and slipped around the edge of the palisade into the village. The bonfire was already burning. Creeping to the edge of the firelight, she scanned the faces of her followers. They were laughing and smiling and slurping down stew. After a moment, Devon tiptoed away and headed for the Shrine to Veia where she sat down and logged out.

***

With her friends list UI active in the corner of her vision, Devon walked around Stonehaven to check the progress of the various construction projects. She still had a few hours to wait before Chen came online, and even though Hailey didn't have school to interfere with her gaming, Devon got the sense the other woman would probably wait until around their agreed meeting time to log in.

Even so, Devon kept glancing toward their grayed-out names to verify that the text hadn't turned green to show they were online. She definitely didn't want Hailey wandering around the area unescorted. For good measure, she also had the yellow-text-on-black window from Hailey's stream shrunk down to a tiny square but still present in her vision.

Judging by sight, it seemed the palisade was about half finished. Near the center of the wall, a gap had been left between two trees that stood about fifteen feet apart. No doubt the gate would go there. Devon squinted and tried to imagine what it would look like once the palisade was finished and a wall-walk had been installed on the back side. Eventually, guard towers and archery posts would add to the defenses. If she were an exploring player who happened upon that level of fortifications, she'd at least think hard about rushing in to attack.

Over the last couple days, Prester had upgraded another of the dwarves' canvas tents and one of the jungle huts to the simple wooden cabins he'd created by embellishing the *One-room Shack* plans. Deld had almost finished the forge; from what she could tell, the building just needed a roof and whatever touches he had planned for inside. She noticed a little curl of smoke coming from the chimney. Seemed he was already testing out the furnace.

Since there was no doubt he'd come running to tell her when it was finished, she decided to leave him to his work and turned for Hezbek's cabin. The door was ajar, and when she peered in, she saw Dorden sitting on a stool. The dwarf looked much improved from his condition after yesterday's fight. A bandage was still wrapped around his leg, but it was clean with no trace of blood. Devon almost wondered if he was wearing it to remind everyone of his recent battle.

"Good morning...I mean"—she checked the position of the sun...definitely past noon—"hey guys."

"Well if it isn't our fearless leader," Hezbek said. "I haven't seen you in a while."

Devon smiled as she stepped through the door. The smell of drying herbs brought instant comfort and a sense of home. Devon might not be bound to Hezbek's cot anymore—it had been awkward to reappear there after death—but she suspected a little part of her character's spirit would always be tied here. A small fire was burning in the hearth, and a pot hung over it, the liquid within simmering gently.

"A new potion?" Devon asked, trying not to sound too hopeful. This concoction actually smelled like something she could drink without gagging.

"Wouldn't you like to know?" Hezbek said with a smirk.

"Yes, I would." As Devon inspected the medicine woman, a window popped up. She selected the tab to check out Hezbek's available potion recipes and the queue of elixirs she would be producing.

- Jungle Health Potion – Minor | 3 per day
- Jungle Health Potion – Mid | 1 per day
- Jungle Antidote – Minor | 4 per day
- Jungle Mana Potion – Minor | 1 per day
- Jungle Mana Potion – Mid | 1 per 2 days
- Blend | 2 per day
- Jaguar's Speed | 1 per 2 days
- Monkey's Agility | 1 per 2 days

The queue of potions was actually empty, which meant that Hezbek was making whatever she felt like the village needed. So far,

Devon hadn't had a need to override that. The medicine woman always seemed to have the right items on hand.

Also, the jungle potions tasted like shit. People did everything they could to avoid drinking them, which made it easier to keep them in stock.

Jaguar's Speed and *Monkey's Agility* were new additions to the list of available options. That was pretty awesome. Hezbek had mentioned her improving skills, but Devon hadn't had a chance to check out her progress.

"Tell me you're cooking up one of those jaguar potions," she said.

Hezbek chuckled. "No, but I have one on hand. Want it?"

"I suppose it couldn't hurt to tuck something like that into my inventory. What's the boost?"

"+3 to speed and a 10% reduction in fatigue gain."

Devon raised her eyebrows. "Sounds nice. Then I guess you're making Monkey's Agility, right?"

Again, Hezbek shook her head. She glanced at Dorden as if seeking his permission.

"Oh, why don't ye just go ahead," the dwarf said. "It will be obvious soon enough."

Shaking her head in confusion, Devon looked back and forth between the two. "Okay, now you have to tell me."

"It's not a potion at all," Hezbek said. "It's a concoction I learned from my mother. Helps with nausea."

Devon cocked her head as she looked at Dorden. "The thought of more giant sloths making you sick?"

"She's kind of dense, isn't she?" Hezbek said.

Devon shrugged and blinked. "What? I'm just trying to figure this out."

"It's not for me, lass. It's for Heldi."

"So *she's* feeling kind of sick after the battle yesterday?"

Dorden sighed and rolled his eyes. "Actually, she's feeling a little better now that it's no longer *morning*. You know, because sometimes certain situations can make a woman feel *ill* in the *morning*."

"If you want to get technical about it," Hezbek muttered. "For lots of women, it's a day-long thing. But we still call it morning sickness for some confounded reason."

"Wait..." Devon stared at the dwarf man. "Are you saying that Heldi's...?"

Dorden gave an exaggerated nod as if addressing a halfwit. "Yes, Devon. She's pregnant," he said with careful enunciation.

"Holy crap! You're going to have a tiny dwarf baby."

"Generally that's what happens when a dwarf man and a dwarf lady love one another *very much*," Dorden said.

Devon turned to Hezbek in shock. "There's going to be a little baby dwarf in Stonehaven." She turned back to the father-to-be. "What kind of toys do they like? Tiny warhammers? Itsy-bitsy pickaxes and candle lanterns?"

"Well, they don't play house and dream of making a tidy little life in some lowland farm village. But otherwise, I doubt they're much different than your scrawny human whelps. Though the most stubborn won't go to bed without a bottle or two of watered ale. Gotta build that tolerance early."

Devon shook her head, still trying to come to terms with the revelation. "Well congratulations, again. Does Heldi need anything?"

"Yeah...a mug of Hezbek's nausea cure."

"I mean besides that. Like a special pillow or something. Do we need to build her a proper bed?"

"She's pregnant, not sick. Most dwarf women work in the mines or lead war parties until the day before they give birth."

Devon cringed. "I don't know if I can send her—"

"Fortunately, it's not up to you," Dorden said with narrowed eyes. "If you try to tell my wife to rest or slow down, I have a feeling you'll lose a Stonehaven citizen. And if she goes, I've got no choice but to follow."

Devon raised her hands in a conciliatory gesture. "Okay, okay. I'm just saying if you need anything, please ask."

The dwarf grunted and gestured with his chin toward the simmering pot. "How's it coming?"

Hezbek plucked a midsized crock off the shelf and ladled in a portion. "Just make sure it cools a bit before she drinks it."

As Dorden stood, Devon moved into position to take his stool. "How's your leg?" she asked.

Dorden grinned. "Fine as a fat vein of gold. Hezbek made me drink another of those disgusting potions last night rather than letting it mend in its own way."

"Then why the bandage?"

"Because how else am I going to get sympathy from my pregnant wife?"

Hezbek picked up a broom and started to shoo the man at the door. "Get," she said.

The medicine woman was still shaking her head after Dorden was long gone. "So what's the news, Devon?"

Devon took a deep breath. It would probably be a good idea to warn Hezbek about her guildmates' arrival. But that conversation might take a while. She had questions first.

"Do you know anything about demons?"

Hezbek had been straightening the contents of a shelf. She dropped her hands to her sides and turned. "You didn't just say *demons,* did you?"

"Did you hear about the attack on Henrik's camp?"

The medicine woman nodded. "But I'd hoped it was just Dorden exaggerating."

"I'm afraid not. I had a run-in with three more last night."

Hezbek dropped to a seat on her cot. "Zaa's stinking pit. That's bad news."

"They can come straight out of the ground, right?"

The woman pressed her lips together before nodding. "In some cases, yes. By my understanding, it takes deliberate thinning of the fabric between Zaa's realm and ours for them to move like that. It's usually localized to an area of conquest."

"Conquest?" Devon couldn't help the shrill edge in her voice. "Are you telling me they're coming to take Stonehaven?"

Hezbek looked down. "Or more likely, Ishildar. But the village should be safe, at least."

"Why?"

"Starborn..." the woman muttered. "Sometimes you are like babes in the cradle. I assume you remember constructing the Shrine to Veia...?"

"Uh, yeah?"

"Then there's your answer. Anything within the shrine's influence—that should cover an area far bigger than we need even once we've become a full-fledged town—is protected from demonic incursions."

Devon took a relieved breath. "Then we won't have a demon army tunneling up from underneath us."

"But if the horde runs rampant over the surroundings, we may as well wish it had happened. And I suppose it's possible that a concerted attack could weaken our protections...but again, why? We're not much of a compelling target."

"If it's just a matter of putting up shrines, can we build more in the surrounding area?"

Hezbek scratched her head. "Hmm. I've only ever heard of shrines connected to a settlement large enough to support them. But there's likely another solution. If I were to guess, there's already a full-fledged Veian temple somewhere in the ruined city. Probably just needs to be cleaned up and re-consecrated."

"So I just need to go into Ishildar and deal with the stone giants that can probably still kill me with one hit..."

The woman shrugged. "Hey, you asked."

You have completed a quest: Demon Invasion, part 1
You learned the Shrine to Veia will defend Stonehaven from a subterranean demon attack.
You have received 10000 experience.

Veia is offering you a quest: Demon Invasion, part 2
Defending the village itself is awesome, but you're still pretty screwed if a full-fledged invasion occurs.
Objective: Clean up and restore the Veian Temple within Ishildar

Reward: Stonehaven won't be overrun.
Reward: 100000 experience
Accept? Y/N

It didn't seem like she had much choice. Devon accepted the quest.

"So how has life as a sorcerer been treating you?" Hezbek asked.

Devon sighed. "I assume you noticed the changes to *Glowing Orb*."

"Finally," Hezbek said with a gust of breath. "I've been complaining about how useless that spell was for *years*. I mean, I complained about it when I was a practicing sorceress. Now I only use it when I need to light a lamp and can't find my flint and steel."

"I kinda liked it the way it was."

The woman shrugged. "Takes all types, I guess. Anyway, complete a couple more adventures, and I'll have another spell to teach you—it's a fun one. You'll surpass me in expertise eventually...not sure where you will find training after that. But we have a while yet."

"Speaking of, will I be able to learn to set the point where a soul is bound anytime soon?"

"Not until you are near the limits of what I can teach, I'm afraid."

Devon tapped her heel on the floor and glanced out the door. Hailey and Chen would be online fairly soon, and it couldn't hurt to have their help on some of her quests. But she couldn't exactly ask them to take on stone giants when their bind points were days away.

"Say I had a couple starborn friends visiting...could you bind them near the shrine like you did me?"

"*Do* you have a couple starborn friends visiting?" Hezbek asked, her voice holding a hint of concern.

"I ran into them yesterday. They're good people, and I think we could use their help."

Hezbek turned to her shelf and started rearranging another grouping of crocks and flasks. "Well, I won't argue with your judgment, my friend. But you have a lot of people depending on you here, so please be sure. I can bind them here if you wish."

Devon swallowed as she stood. "I swear I won't let anything mess up Stonehaven."

"I believe you, then."

"I better leave you to your work," Devon said, rubbing her hands down her leather trousers and wishing for pockets big enough for her hands. "I'll see you later, Hezbek."

"Mmm hmm. Bye, child."

Chapter Fourteen

DEVON SLIPPED OUTSIDE the palisade wall and headed for the spot where her friends would reappear. When she reached the area, she sat down and leaned against a tree. Hezbek's words had brought back all her worries about letting her former guildmates—especially Hailey—into Stonehaven. But now that they were here, there wasn't much she could do to alter her choice.

The question was, what next?

She had two main quest lines to pursue, one to journey south and find the lost vassaldom of Grukluk where she'd likely find the next relic of Ishildar. Her other objective lay in almost the opposite direction. Ishildar's ruins sprawled to the northwest of Stonehaven. The Veian temple could be anywhere inside the city, and searching street by jungle-covered street could take forever. If she could even pass the borders without getting smashed by the Stone Guardians.

On the face of it, it seemed as if the demonic threat was the more pressing issue. Stonehaven's food supply was already shaky, and if the demons started attacking the village's hunters and forager, things would only get worse.

And there was still the issue with these "awakened" creatures. Could she look for the standing stone that was messing with the wildlife while searching for the Veian temple? It would be nice to deal with two problems at once.

She leaned her head back on the tree and looked up into the branches. Almost as if on cue, Bob came flitting down from somewhere in the canopy.

"You want to know what I think?" he said.

"About what?"

"About what to do next."

"How do you know that's what I was thinking about?"

The wisp booped her nose. "Because that's the sort of thing humans do when they sit in a quiet spot and stare into the distance. It was the same with my former master."

"Well let's hear it then," Devon said as she plucked a blade of grass and started splitting it lengthwise.

"It might seem like you should just knock out the quest to restore the temple, but I doubt it's a matter of going there with a broom and sweeping out the leaves. My former master had a hard time letting go of Ishildar and its wonders. Intellectually, he knew that it was doomed to ruin as long as no single person held all five relics. But your race doesn't always behave logically. For years, he tried to beat back the jungle with magic and steel to preserve just a small section of the city. He wasn't a stonemason by any means, but he even mixed mortar and tried filling in the chinks where buildings had started to crumble. But of course it was all in vain."

"So you're saying even if I do manage to restore the temple, it will just fall into ruin again."

"Something like that. I think what I'm saying is that I'm not even sure you *can* restore the temple yet. It's not just the Curse of Fecundity and the Stone Guardians, though those are certainly obstacles. It's the deeper truth surrounding Ishildar. Whatever you do to defeat the decay will be temporary at best. More likely, you'll find yourself as my former master did, fighting a battle that simply can't be won. And meanwhile, Stonehaven will wither and die."

Devon dropped the shredded blade of grass and set her hands loosely on her lap. "It seems like Stonehaven will wither and die anyway. If we can't get resources because demons roam the area, what good is it to keep working on the settlement?"

"When you asked what I know about demons, there was one thing I forgot to mention. From what I understand, they are attracted to certain targets."

"Hezbek said the fabric between worlds thins near places of conquest."

"But this is different. It's less the place, and more the people, that call them once they've neared the boundary. Henrik's army was a large group of trained fighters—they might have been our enemies, but they were still warriors of Veia's creation. It's the same with you and your starborn friends. Veia's flame burns bright inside you, and they come like moths. In comparison, noncombatant citizens are dim embers. Sure, the demon horde is a threat. It absolutely must be stopped. But I don't think your villagers will be massacred tomorrow or the next day even if they leave the shrine's influence."

Devon chewed her lip as she looked into the wisp's light. "Do you really believe that?"

Bob made a motion that looked like a shrug. "Mostly."

As Devon sighed, Hailey's name turned green in her friends list. A split-second later, the woman faded into view. She jumped, startled, to see Devon a foot away.

"Ever heard of personal space?" Hailey said.

"It's not like I mapped your spawn point with a GPS or anything."

Hailey gave Devon's shoulder a friendly shove, knocking her off the tree she was using as a backrest.

"Well, I *was* comfortable," Devon said.

Hailey snorted. "Sorry, Princess." The woman scooted back, took a cross-legged seat, and pulled something out of her rucksack. It looked like an oval of soapstone inscribed with a glowing rune. She cradled it in her palm, bowed her head, and closed her eyes. The rune flared brighter.

"Is that your rez stone?" Devon asked.

The woman nodded and opened her eyes, remaining largely motionless. "I have to channel into it for a little while to charge it. Then I can use it to resurrect someone if they die."

"Is it part of your seeker class?"

"It's just a regular item. You can get them from vendors in the city."

Devon smirked. There were probably lots of things she could get from vendors in the city. "Must be nice to have had the chance to go shopping. What I wouldn't give for a real backpack."

"I was wondering about that," Hailey said. "You're still running around with what looks like a ten-slot newbie bag tied to your belt, but some of your gear has way better enchantments than we've seen. So what's your story?"

"I spawned, got smashed by a giant, got rescued by an NPC but put into servitude to a dimwit ogre, killed the ogre and took over his tribe. We've been building our little village since." For now, she left out the quest line with the relics. She could give Hailey more information later—if it seemed relevant and the woman still seemed trustworthy.

"I know what a sorcerer is, but what's this deceiver class?" A faint flash of envy darkened Hailey's face, probably because she didn't have a unique class while both Chen and Devon did.

Devon tried to sound casual in her answer, downplaying her strengths. She and Hailey were already on somewhat shaky ground. "It's kind of an illusionist. I've got a couple roguish traits, but it's mostly magic. How about you? What's a seeker? You seem like some kind of healer-enchanter hybrid."

Hailey smirked. "You're probably the only gamer on the planet who doesn't know RO's starting classes."

"Believe it or not, I did check into the sorcerer before I chose it," Devon said with a shrug.

"No way. That's probably a first. Anyway, seeker is pretty cool. I guess the backstory is I'm a seeker of truth. I can see through surface appearances to get a deeper understanding."

"Ohhh so *that's* how you saw through my Fade ability." Devon had almost forgotten that the woman had spotted her despite the stealth buff.

The rune on Hailey's rez stone dimmed to the faint glow it had held when she'd pulled it from her rucksack. With a nod, she tucked it back into her inventory. "I have a feeling I can see through most of your illusions. I guess that makes me your nemesis."

Devon laughed, but it felt a little forced. "I still don't understand the healing and crowd control. How does that fit in?"

"My heal spells are about looking into the person's core and guiding their internal healing energies to their injuries. That's why they're heal over time rather than instant repairs. I can only boost the natural process. The charm is similar except—supposedly anyway— I look into an enemy's mind and find ways to persuade them to follow me. In a few levels, I get a fear spell that's a similar concept."

"You are like a one-woman support team," Devon said.

"I haven't even started to explain my debuff lines. I have buffs, too, but I haven't leveled into them yet."

"Hey, so I've been thinking about something one of you guys said last night. You said the game had been guiding you in this direction since day one. What do you mean?" Lying awake last night, Devon had been thinking about that, too. Between the *"hint, hint"* comment when she'd learned the *Backstab* ability and her friends' mention of being guided, she wondered if they were supposed to play together. If that were the case, it would take a little pressure off her regarding the decision to bring her friends into Stonehaven.

Hailey shrugged, another flash of what looked like jealousy crossing her face. "It was more Chen's quest than mine. I got more of the standard new-player experience. Started in a little village called Lokenheim with class trainers and collection quests and stuff. Whereas he spawned on a glacier in the middle of nowhere." She paused, smirking. "Wearing just a breechcloth."

Devon laughed. "Poor Chen. He was probably more embarrassed over showing so much tasty half-elf flesh than he was cold."

"I can just imagine him running around in the snow with his hands covering his man nipples. The shame! Anyway, he was wearing a mammoth-hide robe by the time he wandered out of the wilderness. Looked like a weird love child of Legolas and a cavewoman. He said a quest had led him to me, and now it was pointing him south. Some sort of chosen-one thing about recreating a beacon of light to defend against the dark times to come." Hailey shrugged. "Seemed more interesting than clearing out Lokenheim's rat population, so I joined up."

Hailey probably meant that it seemed more interesting for her subscribers than watching a low-level character beat on rodents, but Devon didn't comment on that. She was probably being too harsh anyway.

"So are you on the quest now too?" she asked.

Hailey nodded. "But it got weird once we descended out of the mountains and into your jungle."

"How do you mean?"

A window popped up asking whether Devon wanted to join Hailey's group. When she accepted, a second popup appeared.

Haelie wants to share her quest: Help the Champion of Ishildar.

The forces of darkness grow stronger every day, moving in ways few followers of Veia can fathom. If there is hope, it begins in the ancient centers of light and power.

Objective: Find the Champion of Ishildar.

Reward: 25000 experience

You cannot accept this quest. Hopefully you understand why. Otherwise, the world is pretty much doomed.

Devon pressed her lips together as she brushed away the dialog. If things weren't awkward before, with Hailey's understandable sense of inferiority regarding the unique classes and so forth, how would the woman react to learn that Devon was the champion they'd been traveling for weeks to find?

"Kind of obnoxious, right?" Hailey said. "Like, where do we start?"

Devon picked up another blade of grass and started peeling off strips. "I might be able to help you guys with that, but I should probably wait till Chen gets on in case you get a quest update."

Hailey looked to the side, probably to hide an expression of annoyance at Devon's assumption that her information would be valuable enough to grant a quest update. "Sure, I guess."

"Want to help me with a little puzzle while we wait?" Devon asked, figuring it would be better than sitting in tense silence.

Hailey shrugged. "Why not?"

Standing, Devon chose a strip of damp ground a decent distance from the new palisade—it would suck to burn down the defenses Jarleck had worked so hard to put up—and cast *Wall of Fire*. She stepped close enough to its glow to cast a shadow, then insta-summoned a *Shadow Puppet*. Her creation flickered in and out of sight. If she couldn't also feel it via a strange sensory connection, she might not even be able to spot it.

"I don't know if you would call this spell an illusion because my *Shadow Puppets* have a physical component. Depending on the source of light I use to create them, they have different properties. But I can't figure out what the point of this one is. Does your truth-seeing show you anything?"

Her eyebrows drawn together, Hailey was staring at the place where Devon's *Shadow Puppet* blinked in and out of existence. That seemed to be a good sign.

"I'm not sure, Devon. I can see a figure. It's like a projection of you. But I don't know what it's doing. Maybe we can try with an enemy around."

"Thanks for trying." Devon dismissed her spells. As she started back for her seat at the base of the tree, Chen's name lit up, and he faded into view.

"So how was school?" Devon asked.

He turned a glare on her. "Don't ask."

With a laugh, she gestured toward the end of the palisade. "Come on. Let me show you around town."

Chapter Fifteen

IF HAILEY NOTICED that Devon had hurried them into Stonehaven and avoided the discussion about their champion quest, she didn't show it. Shuffling along one of the many footpaths that had been trampled down over the last weeks, she gawked at Stonehaven's buildings, the cliff defending the rear half of the village, and especially at the NPCs hard at work.

As the group passed the new cabin that Prester had built for Dorden and his wife, Devon felt eyes on her back. She glanced over her shoulder to see the dwarf couple sitting on the front stoop. Dorden turned a fearsome glower on Hailey and Chen and seemed about ready to reach for the warhammer that was leaning against the outer cabin wall.

Here it comes, Devon thought, tensing for the dwarf man's shout. She didn't blame him really. The dwarves had been forced from their ancestral home by the arrival of legions of players. She'd assured him that Stonehaven would be different and that NPCs and starborn would have equal rights. But they hadn't had a chance to test her promise.

Devon stopped walking, ready to hurry over and intervene. But then Heldi laid a hand on her husband's shoulder and said something in his ear. His expression lightened. Some. The dwarf woman gave Devon a look that suggested she had him under control for now. Devon responded with a nod and resumed walking.

"I'm trying to think," Hailey said, "but I don't remember seeing any threads or news about people establishing player cities. You might be the only one, Devon."

"Well technically, it's not a player city," Chen said. "At least not like they were in Avatharn."

That was just like Chen, obsessed with technical details. If there was a spell list he could analyze, breaking down the efficiency of damage versus casting cost versus cooldown times, he'd have a spreadsheet cooked up within minutes. But he was right about the differences between Stonehaven and Avatharn cities. In their previous game, guilds had built settlements and sometimes hired NPC workers, but there hadn't been the resources—or enough landmass—for individual players to control their own cities.

She let her friends talk rather than butting in. The truth was, it was hard to think of the world in terms of game mechanics. It didn't seem like an alternate reality created on some server farm. Stonehaven and its citizens felt *real*. Part of the reason she avoided forums was because conversations like this one tended to shatter the immersion for her. Of course, she wasn't sure anything could make her new home feel less like the real thing.

Hailey turned and walked backward for a few paces to speak to Devon. "If you change your mind...my subscribers would love to see this." She must have noticed a change in Devon's expression because she quickly showed her palms in apology. "You don't have to be pissed. That's why I asked."

"You really want us to work together on this, Veia?" she muttered under her breath.

Are you presuming to have your creator god on speed dial? Veia's pretty busy running a world, you know. But since you asked, it seems the conclusion should be fairly clear given the information you were presented.

As if she'd been watching for Devon's arrival, Hezbek emerged from her cabin. Actually, she probably *had* been watching...Hezbek had a strong sixth sense when it came to anticipating Devon's actions.

The medicine woman sauntered over almost too casually.

"Hi, Hezbek," Devon said with an amused smile. "Can I introduce you to my friends?"

"I'd be honored," the medicine woman said.

As Devon was making the introductions, she spied Hazel, the little scout, poking a stick into the undergrowth at the base of one of the larger trees inside the village perimeter.

"What you guys think about binding here?" Devon asked. "Even if you move on to the coast like you were hoping, it's got to be a better spot than all the way back in Eltera City."

Chen blinked, his eyes partially hidden in the shadow of his helm. "You have a bindstone?"

Devon glanced at Hezbek. "Not exactly. But Hezbek can help you out. Maybe she could give you a tour as well." The sooner her friends got to know one another, the better the chances this would work out.

When Hezbek realized that Devon's guests had just been pawned off on her, her eyes widened in faint alarm. But she quickly mastered her reaction and turned it into a welcoming smile. "Let's go visit the Shrine to Veia first," she said in a voice that was only a little stiff.

Chen looked over his shoulder, confused, as the medicine woman started leading them away. Devon nodded encouragingly. "I was thinking we could head out together in a little while," she explained. "Maybe earn ourselves a little XP. But I have some maintenance to do first."

Her knight friend didn't look entirely convinced, but he nodded and hurried to catch up with Hezbek. Relieved, Devon set a course for the spot where she'd spotted Hazel.

The slight woman was now down on hands and knees, brushing aside the large leaves of some low-growing tropical plant and plucking little objects from the earth.

"What did you find?" Devon asked.

"Mushrooms."

"Edible?"

Hazel grinned. "Thankfully. Tom's an excellent chef, but his ingredients have been limited lately."

"I'm guessing you're tired of sloth stew."

The scout scanned the surroundings for listening ears before responding. "I don't think I could eat another meal of it without some different flavors. But please don't tell him I said that, Your Gloriousness. You know how sensitive he is."

"It's because he's actually quite talented, I think. But there's nothing he can do if we don't bring him something to work with."

"Exactly," Hazel said. "I'm so glad you understand. When we first laid the village, there were pepper leaves and vanilla beans and little wild onions all around. But it's all been stripped and added to the pot. I just didn't see these mushrooms because they were hidden."

"That's what I came to ask you about, actually."

"Oh?" Hazel said, standing and dusting the dirt off her hands. Her eyes widened when she realized how casually she'd just answered. "I mean, yes, Your Gloriousness?"

"You know, I really don't need a title," Devon said gently.

Hazel stood straighter, not quite meeting her eyes. "I know. You've said it before. But it's not easy to kick the habit, especially when you've done so much for us."

"Well, in any case, I wanted to talk to you about the food situation. I realize you know how to forage for vegetables and nuts and things. But what about seeds?"

Hazel considered the question for a minute. "Seeds for eating, you mean? There might be a few, but not enough to make much difference in our supplies."

"I was actually thinking of seeds we might be able to plant."

Understanding dawned on the scout's face. Her eyes lit as she realized where Devon was going with this. Her enthusiasm was infectious, and Devon felt an answering smile on her face.

"I was just thinking to myself what a shame it's been to pass up some of the edible plants that have gone to seed and turned too bitter to eat. Plus there's a whole field of shriveled lychee fruit over by the old trail to Uruquat's camp. And regular potatoes. All you have to do with those is cut them into bits and they sprout new ones. And—"

"So I'm getting the notion that you are on board with this idea," Devon interrupted.

"By Veia's crooked grace I am," Hazel said with a little hop. But then her face sobered. "Of course, you know I don't have the proper profession to do anything with them."

The trace of hope on the woman's face was faint but noticeable. No doubt every citizen of Stonehaven dreamed of being named one of the last two advanced citizens. Devon liked Hazel, and she wanted to make her happy. Not to mention, if she promoted the woman, death wouldn't be permanent like it was for the basic NPCs. But she had to think carefully about her resources before making any more decisions. Hazel's work as a scout was invaluable, and Devon didn't know how much of that could be sacrificed for farming.

"Once we have enough seeds to start thinking about a crop, we'll figure out how to make them grow," Devon said.

Hazel's shoulders slumped, but only a little.

"If there's nothing else, I wouldn't mind heading out in search of some of these seeds you need," she said.

"Just one more question. You haven't seen any sign of demons since our encounter at Henrik's camp, right?"

Hazel shook her head solemnly. "Thank Veia, no. Nothing."

Devon nodded. "Good. I look forward to seeing what your foraging turns up."

With a grin, the scout turned and hurried for the gap in the palisade where the front gate would be hung. The moment she entered the brush, she was invisible.

***

As Devon was searching for Jarleck to get an update on defenses, a cheer went up from the dwarven area of the village. The sound of running feet warned her to get out of the way just moments before a band of very short and stocky people trampled her. Catching her balance, she blinked in confusion and watched them run for the center of the village.

Dumbfounded, she followed in their wake. Only when she glimpsed Deld standing on an unsteady-looking tower of stone blocks with a bundle of thatch in his arms did she understand.

As he laid it over the final hole in the roof of the forge, a chime rang through the village.

Congratulations! Stonehaven now has a Basic Forge.

A sloshing sound was her only warning before a final dwarf—or rather, the large keg of ale he was carrying—collided with her back. Devon staggered forward and off the trail as the dwarf ran past, his view completely blocked by his cargo.

Another cheer went up when thick smoke started to puff from the forge's chimney, and mugs appeared in dwarven hands as if by magic. By the time Devon reached the building, foam soaked half a dozen beards, and ale sloshed as the dwarves toasted. Heldi and the other dwarf woman, the armorsmith whose name was Garda, had only slightly smaller amounts of foam on their faces and dribbles of ale on their tunics.

Devon grimaced at the sight of Heldi joining another toast but decided not to bring up the dangers of drinking while pregnant. Given that their infants were given bottles of ale in their cribs, perhaps it just wasn't a health concern for the sturdy race.

She did, however, slip up next to the woman. "Congratulations," she said, hugging the dwarf woman around the shoulders.

Heldi seemed to glow with pride. "Thank ye kindly. And thank ye for building a place where we can look forward to raising 'im without fear there won't be enough food or a roof over our heads."

Devon wondered if the coming change to their little family explained how Heldi had calmed her husband down so easily when he'd spotted Hailey and Chen.

"You said 'him.' Does that mean you're hoping for a boy?"

Heldi snorted. "Oh, I know it already. No doubt about it."

"Oh? Is that a dwarf thing?"

The dwarf woman shook her head. "I swear he's already trying to dig 'is way out. Kicking and clawing like 'is little life depends on it."

"And a girl wouldn't do that?"

Heldi gave her a look that was faintly conspiratorial. "She'd be too smart for such antics. Better to save her energy for a time when it would make a difference."

Devon laughed. "Well, I'll take your word for it."

The dwarf's face turned serious. "Dorden told me ye asked about what kind of coddling ye could do."

Devon raised a hand to stop her from going too far down that track. "And he quickly corrected me. Don't worry. If you say you're good for hunting and battle, I won't stop you."

Heldi grunted, apparently satisfied with her answer. "I see me husband's already put down two mugs. Better get to work if I don't want to be a laughing stock."

The woman didn't look pregnant as she stomped over to the keg, though it was hard to tell in all that armor. Devon hadn't thought to ask when the baby was due, and she leaned toward Garda, intent on asking. The look on the armorsmith's face quickly changed her mind. Devon didn't *think* a humanoid being could fall in love with an inanimate building, but Garda's starry-eyed expression as she stared at the forge made her wonder. Devon moved off in search of Jarleck instead.

Hammer in hand, the fortifications master was making his way into the village from the front wall. When he spotted her, he nodded a greeting.

"And? How's progress?" she asked.

"Well, now that the palisade is finished, I was taking some measurements for the gate—especially since we'll soon have iron hinges and reinforcements. Unless you think the guard towers should come first...?"

"Wait, the palisade is finished?"

The corner of his mouth pulled back in an amused smile. "A few of us worked late yesterday. Figured we could surprise you."

Devon grinned as she scanned the front of the village. Sure, she'd noticed that most of the upright logs had been set in place, but with the arrival of her guildmates and her patchy knowledge on fortifications, she'd assumed there was more to do.

"Holy crap," she said. "That's awesome."

He shrugged. "After you brought in the extra food reserves yesterday, most of us were feeling a bit more motivated than usual."

Of course. The morale boost from the quest had encouraged them to work a little harder. She'd suspected the effort she put into raising morale did more than make her feel like a good leader, but she hadn't had solid confirmation. That was cool. If she could find other ways to raise the stat, Stonehaven could advance even more quickly.

Well, construction would be faster anyway. She still had no idea how they were going to grow the population to one hundred citizens to reach the hamlet designation.

"A gate sounds perfect. The guard towers can come after. Do you need help getting the iron components?"

Jarleck shook his head. "Already talked to Dorden. Unless you set him on something else already, we should be ready to drop the bar securing our settlement in just a couple days."

"Sounds perfect," she said, clapping him on the shoulder. "The dwarves just tapped a keg. You deserve a nice frothy mug of ale."

Jarleck smiled. "I don't drink. But I enjoy watching other people make idiots of themselves. As long as you don't mind, I think I *will* take a few hours off."

"Please."

You have gained esteem with Jarleck: +5 reputation.

Devon fell in beside the burly man as he trudged toward the party at the forge. Idly, she wondered if he had a reason for avoiding alcohol. Most thug-type NPCs went straight for taverns and wineskins at any opportunity. But Jarleck wasn't exactly as thug-like as he first appeared. She almost laughed when remembering his shriek when Hazel had startled him.

At the edge of the celebration, Jarleck cast her a nod, then threaded through the crowd to take a seat on a flat-topped boulder. Devon searched the crowd until she spotted Deld.

"Congratulations," she said. "It's the finest Basic Forge I've seen."

Deld blushed with pride. "I'm particularly proud of the furnace. Funnels the air from the bellows and the heat from the fire just right."

"I was thinking...care to get with me and Prester and figure out your next project? He's been stuck upgrading huts to cabins for a while, and I bet he could use a break."

"That would be, as you say, awesome," Deld said, looking a little bashful over using her words.

"You're starting to sound like a regular starborn," Devon replied as she caught Prester's eye and gestured him over. While he made his way through the crowd, dodging a couple dwarves who were having some sort of chest-bumping contest, Devon pulled up her settlement interface and tabbed over to the list of tier 2 buildings.

Crafting Workshop:

A utilitarian building usable by many crafting professions.

Bonus to: Weaving, Woodworking, Leatherworking, Tailoring, Stone Carving (small).

Requires: Carpentry (Tier 3), 50 x Wood Plank, 6 x Wood Beam

Forge (basic):

A forge capable of working basic metals.

Required for: Blacksmithing

Requires: Stonemasonry (Tier 2), 60 x Stone Block, 10 x Bucket of Mortar

- Smokehouse:

Preserves raw meat, fruits, and vegetables at many times the rate of a standard campfire. Does not require a specialized worker to operate.

Can process: 40 units of meat, fruit, vegetables, or medicinal herbs per day.

Requires: Stonemasonry (Tier 2), Carpentry (Tier 3), 10 x Stone Block, 2 x Bucket of Mortar, 20 x Wood Plank, 4 x Wood Beam

Barracks
Sleeping quarters for fighters. Increases squad cooperation. Sleeps 6.

Requires: Carpentry (Tier 4), 70 x Wood Plank, 6 x Wood Beam

Kitchen
Every campfire chef's dream.

Bonus to: Recipe discovery (x3), Tier 2+ recipe output (x2)

Requires: Stonemasonry (Tier 2), Carpentry (Tier 3), 10 x Stone Block, 2 x Bucket of Mortar, 60 x Wood Plank, 6 x Wood Beam

The settlement now had three tier 2 buildings, the crafting workshop, the forge, and Hezbek's medicine woman cabin. Eventually, Stonehaven would need most of the options to support a growing population. In fact, they'd probably need two barracks to round out the six tier 2 structures allowed for a *Village*—and required to advance to *Hamlet*. It would be tough to provide shelter for a hundred citizens otherwise. But for right now, she had a good idea what they needed most.

"Can I help you, Your Gloriousness?" Prester asked. He did a poor job hiding the hope on his face.

"Sick of building cabins?" she asked.

"Well...as you know, my lifelong dream was to become a carpenter. I'm grateful for the chance." He kept his eyes on his feet while he spoke.

"But like any skilled craftsman, you get bored doing the same thing over and over. It's okay to admit it. I hate grinding, too."

"Grinding?"

"It's when you—never mind. You two mind grouping up and...say...working on the kitchen building next?"

Prester gave a surreptitious glance over the crowd, no doubt doing the same thing as Hazel and checking that Tom wasn't in earshot. "Is there a chance it will...help vary the dinner options?"

Devon smirked. "I'm working on that regardless. Tom's ingredients have been limited since we stripped the nearby vegetation and wildlife. But once we do have better variety, a kitchen would give Tom and any other cook who settles in Stonehaven a better chance to discover new recipes. Plus, it won't take nearly as many ingredients to produce double the delicacies."

She could almost hear the carpenter's mouth water. He tried to keep a businesslike demeanor as he nodded. "I would be happy to work on the kitchen if it is your desire, Your Gloriousness."

She nodded. "Build me a dream kitchen, men. Stonehaven is counting on you."

Prester glanced down at the half-full mug in his hand.

"After the party, I mean," she said.

Her overseer's work done, Devon stepped back from the celebration, intent on finding Hailey and Chen to see if they were ready to head out. Much to her surprise, she spotted Chen—still wearing his helmet like a total dork—on the far side of the crowd. He appeared to have a mug in his hand, a fact which caused Devon moderate alarm. Last time she'd seen the teenager drink in game, the evening had ended with him vomiting in the throne room of the Iron Kingdom. They hadn't exactly been welcome guests after that.

She hurried through the crowd and all but knocked the mug from the knight's hand.

"Now hey there, lass," Dorden said, turning his very red face her way. "The boy jess needa wee sip er two."

Dorden staggered and was caught by another reeling dwarf and set back on his feet.

Hailey was standing next to Chen, sipping daintily from her own mug. She caught Devon's eye and shrugged. "They said they watered it down."

Devon shook her head. "Even watered down, a keg of this stuff would be enough to level three frat houses. Seriously. I drank about a shot glass's worth and fell in the creek."

Hailey looked at Chen, only now seeming to notice the stupid grin and unfocused eyes. "Shit," she said.

Moments later, Chen collapsed in a heap of hardened leather and chain mail, his helm bouncing off and rolling to the wall of the forge. He started to snore.

"Well, up for a little duo adventuring?" Devon said. "I don't think we'll get much damage per second out of this one anytime soon."

"No, doesn't seem like it." Hailey stood over their fallen companion, looking down at him morosely. She scoffed. "Lightweight."

Chapter Sixteen

"SO HOW DO we work this?" Devon asked as they crept along one of the faint and braided trails toward the quarry. "Neither of us is a tank, obviously."

"Chen isn't either, though his armor definitely soaks up more damage than mine," Hailey said, plucking at her cloth robes. "I can go with light leather eventually, but only after it's been consecrated."

"So what have you guys been doing tactics-wise?"

Hailey batted at a low-hanging branch with her staff. "Damn this jungle's annoying. I feel bad for you being stuck here the whole time. Anyway, against single targets we've mostly been trying to straight out-damage them. I've been dropping a heal on him at the start of combat."

"I've gotten used to the jungle." Devon brushed a strand of spiderweb off her face. "Mostly, anyway. So what have you done against multiple targets?"

"Depends. Chen has a few tricks depending on the situation, but I won't spoil the surprise. I can do some crowd-control, but I have a hard time charming anything near my level. Makes sense I guess since they're kinda easy to coup de grace while charmed."

"Seemed kinda broken that you could walk up and kill that demon with one hit yesterday."

"Well, I was three levels higher than it. But yeah. It's cool when it works. But sometimes I walk up with the knife and they go berserk. I died that way once."

Devon brushed aside a dangling plant tendril and hooked it on a broken tree branch. "Think Chen will be hungover tomorrow?"

Hailey laughed. "I hope not. But I wouldn't be surprised."

"What's the strength of the knight class?"

"Single target damage. He gets some cool buffs for one-on-one fights...something about valor and trial by combat. There's one whirling attack that hits multiple guys, but it's got a long cooldown. That's pretty much been our only area of effect damage."

"Well, on the bright side, I have an awesome AoE. Except it hits friendly people too. Ground currents from the lightning."

"Try not to shock me to death, I guess," Hailey said.

"I'll do my best."

"So, what's the goal today?" Hailey said. "Or are we just out to get some experience?"

Devon took a breath before answering. At this point, she was either going to have to start telling her friends stuff, or she would need to figure out a way to boot them from the area. And since Veia seemed to want them here...

"I'm guessing you noticed the large expanse of ruins north of us."

"The ruins we're currently heading directly away from..."

"Bear with me. I have a reason."

The sound of chiseling from the quarry pressed through the trees, and Devon hurried her steps. Bern and his guards were missing a massive party and they didn't even know it. As she stepped into the open, she shaded her eyes and watched the quarryman work. Bern was dangling from a rope that had somehow been fixed on top of the outcrop, and he was busy drilling a line of holes to mark off another block. Afterward, he would drive wooden wedges into the holes. By slowly dripping water onto the wood, he'd cause expansion in the wedges, and eventually, the block would crack away from the cliff.

At least, that was the general gist.

"Hey, Bern," she called. "Go home."

"Huh?" he yelled back.

The sound of her voice brought figures from the brush. As the guards stepped into view, Devon recognized Bayle and Falwon, the pair of human fighters. Things were starting to make sense now. The dwarves must have known the forge would be finished in the afternoon, so they'd convinced poor Bayle and Falwon to take over guard duty at the quarry. The cheer had gone up just *before* Deld laid the last piece of thatch, suggesting that the dwarves had been staking him out just waiting for the excuse to drink.

"There's a party in Stonehaven. I'm ordering you home for the rest of the afternoon. The guards can work it out amongst themselves who stays sober enough to keep a lookout."

Bern didn't take much convincing. She must've had him at *party*. He did something with his rope to put himself on rappel and slid down the line to flat ground. With a quick salute, he set off at a trot. The guards hurried after.

"Anyway," Devon said as she resumed walking south, "the ruins have a name. Want to guess?"

Hailey gave a little huff. "I'd rather you just tell me."

"Okay fine. The short story is those ruins are Ishildar. And I'm pretty sure the champion you guys are supposed to find is...me."

As soon as she spoke the words, the jungle gave a muted chime.

"Ding?" Devon asked.

"Level 14," Hailey said in a flat voice. The woman's footsteps stopped. "Well, if you are looking for confirmation, I guess that quest update settles it. My new mission is to help you uncover the *Blackbone Effigy*. Whatever that is."

As soon as she spoke, a pop-up appeared in Devon's vision.

> **Quest Updated:** Travel south to the Grukluk vassaldom.
> *It seems that your loyal and attractive wisp was correct. The second relic, the Blackbone Effigy, is almost certainly somewhere within Grukluk.*
> **Objective:** Discover the Grukluk region.
> **Objective:** Figure out where the Blackbone Effigy is hidden and retrieve it.
> **Reward:** The Blackbone Effigy (duh).

"Well, seeing as you're the boss," Hailey said, seeming to hate every word she spoke. "Where to?"

Devon chewed her lip while trying to order her words. "Look, I know this sucks. No one creates a character in hopes they can become someone's sidekick. Seriously. I get it. I'm tempted to tell you guys to just leave."

"And do what? Travel around and hope the game gives us another purpose?" Hailey sighed. "Yeah, it's kind of lame. You are the champion and we're helpers"—she put air quotes around the word—"but I'm trying to tell myself that we aren't even level 20 yet. This is all just newbie stuff. I mean, shit, Chen isn't even level 10."

"The double class thing is a killer on experience gain," Devon said.

"Plus he has school. I tried to tell him to run away and become a homeless professional gamer. He won't listen to me."

Devon laughed. "So you're good with sticking around? I swear we'll share equally in whatever awesome loot and power we get from restoring Ishildar."

Hailey chewed her lip then nodded. "Can we work out something on the streaming? Like, I don't show a map or anything about Stonehaven, but I can turn my feed on for other stuff?"

A voice in the back of Devon's mind told her she'd be an idiot to agree to any spectators. But she also knew that part of her reluctance was stubbornness. She had to compromise somewhere. If she flat out refused, Hailey might go back on her word out of spite anyway.

"If I swear I won't say no for the sake of it, can we take it case-by-case? You've gotta understand I've been out here totally by myself since launch day. I just need a chance to get comfortable with the idea."

Hailey nodded. "I'd spit in my hand and offer to shake, but..."

"But that would be disgusting," Devon finished.

The other woman grinned. "Let's go find some monsters to slay."

***

Hailey cast a *Crippling Self-Doubt* debuff on the harpy eagle as it screeched and soared down from its nest in the canopy. As soon as the spell struck, the bird's wings flapped with less strength, and it didn't compensate fast enough. It hit the ground hard and lost around 5% of its hitpoints.

From this close, Devon could smell the carrion on its breath. Black eyes glared, piercing from a face patchy with ragged feathers.

She hesitated for a second, trying to decide what to cast. If the eagle tried to fly again, her *Shadow Puppets* might not be able to hit it—she'd learned that the hard way on their last battle, a mosquito the size of a Rottweiler that had been "awakened" with a deep-set desire to cast *Blood Sucker*. As she'd watched little tendrils of blood leak from her pores and fly across the jungle into the stupid thing's proboscis, her *Shadow Puppets* had followed it around, stuck to the ground while the bug had hovered just out of reach.

"Hold on a second," she said when Hailey started muttering something.

A cast bar appeared above the seeker's head before vanishing as she interrupted her own cast. "Yeah?"

"Just looking for a little vindication. Probably best if you back up."

Devon quickly summoned a *Glowing Orb* then cast *Levitate* at the same time as she threw her orb toward a nearby tree trunk. The eagle was half-flapping, half-staggering toward them, its *Strength* cut by a third due to Hailey's debuff. But the bird was still three levels higher than Devon and armed with talons as thick as her wrist, so she had no illusions about how she'd fare at melee range. She cast another *Glowing Orb*, slapped it on a branch overhead, then insta-cast a couple tier 2 *Shadow Puppets*.

The eagle kept coming, hatred burning in its sharp eyes.

She hit it with a *Freeze* spell, and its wings stopped moving midflap. When its weight slumped onto its feet, cracks webbed the ice prison, but the shell held.

She sent her *Shadow Puppets* in. The ice exploded as lightning arced over the bird, frying feathers. Its health dropped to around 60%.

"Nice f-ing hit," Hailey said. "Can I fight now?"

"Go ahead," Devon said as she backpedaled through the air and tossed a *Flamestrike* onto the stumbling bird. At least Hailey's debuff made most creatures slower, a big advantage for two players without a whole lot of defense.

Plus, Devon had her *Wall of Fire*, which deterred pursuit, even if it screwed up Hailey's targeting because it apparently made it harder to look into the enemy's soul for "truth".

Hailey cast *Inner Angst*, hitting the eagle for another 50 damage or so—around 5% of its health. The eagle screeched pitifully but kept coming.

Another cry pierced the jungle. Wings beat the air.

"Oh, shit! Add!" Devon yelled when she spotted the bird's mate.

She threw a *Wall of Fire* in front of the damaged eagle, then hammered it with another tier 2 *Flamestrike*. A shadow darkened the understory as the second bird crashed through branches, heading straight for her.

"Trying charm," Hailey yelled as her casting bar filled and flashed. "Er... nope! Resist."

Claws raked Devon's shoulder. She went flying backward on her cushion of air, losing almost a quarter of her health. The bird hadn't expected its opponent to go skidding away, and it cartwheeled sideways. In a stroke of blind luck, it crashed into its mate, knocking the other bird through the *Wall of Fire.* The double damage from the fire finished off the first bird, leaving it smoldering on the ground.

"We got this," Devon called. "Weaknesses?" A nice bonus of fighting with a seeker was the class's innate ability to get a tier 4 *Combat Assessment* at a glance, even when the enemy had partial to full cover.

Her flame wall faded in time for her to see Hailey's debuff hit the remaining eagle. It staggered while trying to adjust to the weakness, and a small dark cloud from the other woman's *Inner Angst* shaved off more health.

"I'm going to pen it in," Devon said, checking her mana bar. It was down to 30%, but her investment in *Endurance* was helping in-combat regeneration already.

She cast a pair of *Walls of Fire,* molding them into a full circle. After witnessing the death of its mate, the harpy eagle was smart enough *not* to blast through the flames. It tried to spread its wings, but the feathers brushed the fire, and the bird quickly sucked the wingtips back.

A wave of coolness passed through her as Hailey's *Guide Vitality* landed and pulsed its first heal over time effect. The ache in Devon's shoulder eased, and she gained a few health points.

She took a breath, scanning the surroundings. A few feet away, a small pool of filtered sunlight brightened the jungle floor. After casting a quick tier 1 *Flamestrike* to keep the eagle on the defensive, she skimmed over the ground to the patch of light. Hailey hit the bird with another *Inner Angst* as Devon pulled a sun-based *Shadow Puppet* from the earth. She sent her minion streaking under the wall of flame and brought a spear of shadow up diagonally through the eagle's chest. The *Shadow Puppet* shattered, and the blow sent the eagle staggering toward the flames. It screeched, and Devon felt a quick pang of guilt. When had she become such a softy? The damn bird would have gladly killed her and Hailey both.

The smell of singed feathers finally reached her nose, and Devon grimaced. But the bird recovered and kept clear of the flame wall.

Hailey attacked with another *Inner Angst,* knocking the eagle down to less than 10% health. "Out of mana," she yelled.

Devon nodded. "Almost there, too."

Her last *Flamestrike* took off more of the bird's health, but it was still standing. Shaking her head, she dismissed one *Wall of Fire* and her *Levitate.* Sprinting forward, she leaped and landed awkwardly on the bird's wing. A final stab of her dagger finally brought its health to zero.

The jungle chimed.

Congratulations! You have reached level 12!

You have gained a skill point: +1 One-handed Piercing.

Finally! It felt like forever since she'd leveled. Splitting her focus between building Stonehaven and advancing her character made it sometimes feel like she wasn't doing either very well. The piercing skill-up was nice too. Those were slower in coming now that she'd reached tier 2 in her progression. But it was still looking like it would be a *long* time before she could do anything with the *Ivory Fangs* and their crazy necrotic damage.

"Congrats," Hailey said as she crouched beside one of the birds and activated decomposition. "Feathers and eagle meat. Have any fletching skill?"

Devon shook her head. "I've been letting the NPCs cover the trade skills mostly. But none of them are fletchers."

Hailey huffed and shook her head. "Must be nice anyway. Like having an army of servants."

"I don't think of it that way. It's more like we're building Stonehaven together."

Hailey stilled for a moment. "Yeah, I get it. Sorry for the way I've been talking about them...I'm probably just jealous."

It wasn't like Hailey to apologize, just like it wasn't like Devon to forgive easily. Maybe they were both trying to start fresh in Relic Online. "Honestly, I really wouldn't blame you for being kind of pissed, Hailey. I know I already said some of this, but I don't understand why you got the standard newbie experience while Chen and I spawned in the wilderness. Why do we have unique classes and you don't? We were all recruited for the same reason, right? Emerson needs us out here doing our thing to teach his AI how to think more creatively."

"Yeah, I know. I don't think it's personal." Hailey shrugged. "For all I know, I'm still single-classing because this champion quest line needs a high-level seeker. There's a lot of stuff we just don't understand."

"Hey, speaking of classes, I've been wanting to ask...what exactly is a tinkerer?"

Hailey laughed. "Chen would literally kill me if I told you. He is such a showoff about it."

"Okay fine. I guess I can be patient." Devon glanced at her real-world clock. She had another few in-game hours before it would turn midnight in St. George, but it was approaching evening in the jungle. "So how much longer do you want to stay out?"

"How's your inventory space, Miss Jute Bag?"

Devon rolled her eyes. "It might not be the fanciest container, but it was a gift."

She pulled up her inventory screen. On the journey south, they'd taken a little extra time to hunt wildlife despite the crappy experience rewards for their level. Of the ten available inventory slots, four held full stacks of 10 x *Snake Meat*, two held a total of 8 x *Boar Flank Steaks,* and one held a partial stack of *Medium Leather.* Her *Everfull Waterskin* and the *Jaguar's Speed* potion filled two more.

Devon grimaced.

Hailey smirked. "That's what I thought. Since I seriously doubt we will reach this Grukluk place in the next hour or so, maybe we should head back."

Devon opened up her map screen. Their southward journey had revealed a strip of jungle roughly parallel to the north-south mountain range that bounded the jungle to the east. They hadn't uncovered any major landmarks, but they had cut a decent path through the forest. If they traveled the same route soon, the jungle wouldn't have filled it back in.

"Sounds good—wait, do you smell that?" Devon sniffed, wrinkling her nose at the stench of body odor and unwashed bodies.

"The burned feathers—oh, ew!" Hailey squinted and peered into the jungle behind Devon.

A shout that sounded suspiciously like a goblin war cry shook the foliage.

165

Chapter Seventeen

AN ARROW STREAKED past Devon's face and stuck in a tree. Oily feathers trembled while the shaft quivered. In the bushes, a goblin grunted, and a thrown hatchet whirled through the air. Devon tried to dodge, but the small axe glanced off her leather doublet near her shoulder blade and tumbled into the undergrowth.

"Ouch." She winced as a few hitpoints fell away from her health bar.

Devon sprinted forward to try to put some trees between her and the advancing goblins as Hailey scooped up the remaining loot from the eagle and backpedaled, her eyes searching the jungle.

"At least ten incoming," the seeker said. "Level 9s and 10s with a level 12 lieutenant type."

"Mana?" Devon asked as she glanced at her own bar. It had filled back up to just 30%.

"Half. Not enough."

"Same," Devon said. "Run."

The women tore forward along the trail they'd cut through the jungle, leaping roots and ducking low-hanging branches. The gleeful shouts of the goblins chased them through the forest. Ahead, the trail curved. Devon searched the undergrowth as she sprinted, her darkvision flickering to life when her gaze penetrated the deepening evening shadows.

A yelp jumped from her throat when five more goblins leaped onto the path ahead, gibbering and squealing and brandishing notched machetes. Filthy hide breechcloths and bras covered the necessary parts—barely—and their greenish-gray skin was smeared with filth.

Devon cut hard to the right, crashing into the brush. She was sure they'd be caught within a few seconds, but then she burst onto a game trail with trampled hoofprints and piles of dung. Cheered by the good luck, she forced energy into her legs. Her fatigue climbed through 70%, and Devon's lungs started to burn. But if they could get enough distance on their pursuers, they might still have a chance. Maybe they could even take out a few if they could get the goblins spread out.

"Oh, crap," Hailey yelled from behind. "Jump!"

Too late. Devon's foot plunged through the jungle floor, sending her stomach leaping into her throat as she tipped face-first into a yawning pit. Palm fronds, crumbles of dried mud, and branches plunged into the darkness beside her. Wicked spikes jutted from the bottom of the hole, old blood darkening the tips. She clenched her eyes shut. This wasn't going to feel good. Knowing it was futile with a casting time of a couple seconds, she started casting *Levitate*.

The spears pierced her, interrupting the spell as they plunged through her body and out the other side. Distantly, she heard Hailey's footfalls as they circled the edge of the trap.

Devon's screen went black.

You have been slain by a Goblin Pit Trap.
Haha! Watch your step, n00b!

***

Devon respawned in a cross-legged position in the meadow grass beside the Shrine to Veia. She flopped back and spread her arms out, staring at the pink clouds that streaked the evening sky. Well, that had sucked. At least the experience of being impaled hadn't hurt like it used to...whatever E-Squared had changed had *definitely* improved the pain situation. If they'd just admitted to fixing the bug rather than blaming her imagination, it wouldn't even be an issue.

"Run into a problem?" a weaselly voice asked, intruding on her thoughts.

She draped her forearm over her eyes. Of all the people who could have witnessed her humiliation after being surprised by a group of *goblins*, why did it have to be Greel? Though...speaking of lawyers, maybe that's why E-Squared hadn't copped to inflicting real pain on its players. There was probably some law against unauthorized torture.

"Hello, Greel."

"Evening, Devon. Anything exciting to share?"

"Well, the good news is that Hailey and I ran into some monsters that might drop something besides body parts."

"Drop?"

"As in loot. The stuff we get from their corpses."

She sat up and glanced down at her armor. Under level 20, the penalty for dying in Relic Online wasn't too bad—just a hefty durability hit to her equipment. As expected, the leather armor Gerrald had made her now sported ragged tears and broken buckles. She'd have to leave it with him for a few hours for repairs. Which made her think she needed to have a backup set of armor. Now that injuries didn't cause agony, she suspected she'd take a few more chances. Even if she didn't make a habit of dying—she hoped, anyway—taking damage also wore down gear. Just not as quickly.

"I met your friend Chen," Greel said. "Or rather, I listened to him snore. Interesting company you keep."

"Speaking of, I didn't see you at the celebration."

Greel rolled his eyes. "When you or the rest of these schmucks do something worth celebrating, I might be bothered. If you can come up with something better than dwarven ale for the libations, that is. I enjoy a fine sherry, but brandy will do in a pinch."

Devon sighed. "As a non-starborn, you don't get attribute points, do you?"

"Pardon?"

"I just thought it couldn't hurt for you to invest a little in *Charisma*."

He gave her an insincere smile. "How clever of you, insulting my charms because you can't match my intellect."

"I'm beginning to wonder why I brought you back from the dead..."

"Perhaps it's the secret attraction you harbor for this slice of man flesh," he said, gesturing toward his slight and faintly hunchbacked form.

"I'm impressed, Greel. You made a joke."

"Anyway, I didn't come over here just for the sparkling conversation," Greel said. "I thought you should know that while I was surveying the surroundings, I encountered another of the demon scourge."

"Crap. You okay?"

He rolled his eyes. "Do I look injured?"

"It's just something you say to show caring," she said with a heavy sigh.

"Well, for your information, I dispatched it easily. But something occurred which I thought might interest you. As part of my studies, I gained basic proficiency in the demonic tongue. As the monster was dying, it cried out."

"Oh?"

"I would expect it to babble something about Zaa, but if I'm not mistaken, it said, 'I've failed, Ezraxis.'"

Devon paused. The name sounded familiar, but she had no idea where she might have heard it. "Huh...That's weird."

"That's why I—"

Greel stopped speaking and blinked when Hailey shimmered into existence beside the shrine. "I doubt I'll ever get used to that," he muttered.

"I take it things didn't go well," Devon said, taking in Hailey's ragged appearance. The woman's robes were torn, and deep gouges marred the runes on her staff.

"Yeah...no. I killed two of the little shits, which was better than I expected. But obviously fifteen to one isn't great odds, even if they are just stupid goblins."

"Wait, goblins?" Greel asked, cheek twitching.

Devon nodded. "We unfortunately encountered a war party."

Greel's next words were a low growl. "Tell me where. I'll kill every one of those foul cretins."

Greel is offering you a quest: Cleanse the area of goblin presence.

It seems that Greel really, really hates goblins. Inviting him along when you go back would probably make up for murdering him before. You are going back, right? (Hint: goblins often move into the ruins left by other, more civilized races. Even frog people are more civilized than the little green pukes.)

Objective: Clear out the goblins.

Objective: Greel must accompany you and survive.

Reward: 30000 experience

Accept? Y/N

As Devon accepted the quest, Hailey cast her a look that seemed to ask what Greel's deal was.

Devon shrugged. She wasn't even sure she wanted to know.

***

Devon was still laughing about the thing with Chen when she logged out. The dwarves had carried his unconscious body to a tree, lifted him to a branch at head height, and tied him to the trunk sitting upright. They'd replaced his helm with a little cloth bonnet, the dwarven version of a dunce cap according to Dorden. Someone had made purplish red paint from crushed berries and had painted dwarven runes reading 'Kiss me' on Chen's cheeks.

Hopefully, she'd be around when he logged in or woke up or whatever. If anything could teach teenagers the dangers of too much alcohol, it would be an invitation to a virtual-reality party with a bunch of rowdy dwarves.

Aside from the comedy factor, though, the prank showed that the dwarves had accepted her friends—Chen at least. Which was good, because if her guildmates were going to help her restore Ishildar, they would probably be spending a lot of time in Stonehaven.

She yawned and rubbed her face as she sat up, the sofa cushions wheezing with her motion. It was late enough that her apartment had cooled down. The ceiling fan still lazily stirred the air, but otherwise she didn't feel like she even needed to open a window. Closing the blinds, she flipped the light switch and opened the fridge.

Devon sighed. She really needed to get to the store. Maybe tomorrow before she logged in...Chen probably wouldn't even be online until late afternoon when school ended.

With a shrug, she grabbed a carton of milk and a can of beer. Sliding a mostly empty box of cereal from the cabinet, she poured the remainder—including the sugar dust— into a bowl and added milk. Technically, it was after midnight, which made breakfast an okay choice for a meal.

She could just hear Tamara scolding her as she cracked open the beer.

Speaking of, as she sat down, she opened her messages to see if Tamara had sent anything. A little heart emoji popped up next to her friend's name. When Devon focused on it, a line of text unfurled.

You make that doctor's appointment yet? -Mom

Devon flagged it to respond later.

Another little alert showed a text from Emerson.

Anything on the pain?

Devon took a few big swigs of her beer before answering.

"You know," she dictated into the messaging app that came with her Entwined hardware, "you could've told me my friends were having the same issue."

A little icon lit up to tell her Emerson had received the message and was responding. She cringed—she hadn't actually wanted to get into a conversation. She'd figured he was asleep by now.

The message took a long time in coming, a sure sign that he'd been thinking carefully about his response.

To be fair, you didn't ask.

"That's a copout and you know it," she said.

So who did you hear from? Chen?

"Him and Hailey. They randomly turned up in my obscure corner of the world. Did you tell Veia to bring us together?"

No...but that's actually really strange. For what it's worth, I don't directly control anything Veia does. It's more like I give her a toolkit and the overall goal of building a world people want to play and she figures out the details.

Devon slurped a spoonful of cereal then sat back in her chair. "Well, apparently she decided I should reconnect with old friends. How sweet. Anyway, yeah...I think the pain thing is fixed. I also know it wasn't my imagination."

Again Emerson's message took a while to arrive. *I'm not happy with the way the fix was communicated. Or with the lack of diligence in the investigation of the issue. I can't really say more.*

"Lawyers?"

I'll let you draw your own conclusions.

"So has it been hot in Arizona too?" Devon asked as she took another swig of her beer.

Again he took a long time answering. Maybe he was doing something else at the same time...

Record highs in Phoenix.

Okay, but didn't he live in Tucson? Devon shrugged. The guy was crap at small talk. Before she could come up with something else to say, another message arrived.

Hey, Devon?

"Yeah?"

You're limiting your play sessions, right? You still need normal amounts of sleep and all that.

Devon smirked. Between Emerson and Tamara, she had a full set of parents. If only they'd been around when she was an actual child.

"I'm good. My sleep's been kind of weird, but I tried mountain biking. My friend said it would help with biorhythms or something." She decided not to mention the whole passing-out incident. It had probably just been caused by the heat and exercise after weeks as a couch potato.

Well if it's any consolation, my sleep's been rough lately too. Get some rest, okay?

"Yeah, you too. Night."

She closed down the messaging app and finished her cereal. Another image of Chen in his pretty bonnet flashed into her thoughts, and she laughed before finishing her beer.

Chapter Eighteen

EMERSON STARED AT Devon's inactive icon for a few minutes after she logged off the messaging app. Finally, he highlighted the text he'd been considering sending. He was already riding the line complaining about E-Squared's handling of the pain issue. A good lawyer could probably get him for breaking his NDA over what he'd already said. But they wouldn't because no one else could maintain Veia's systems. Not even their precious Penelope. Even if she had the skill, which was doubtful, Emerson had recently decided he needed better job security. He'd stopped documenting his changes to Veia's codebase and configuration. The only comments he left behind referenced Bradley's lack of interest in programmer-speak. Penelope—or any other engineer E-Squared could hire—would have to be inside Emerson's head to understand anything about the code at this point.

Petty, yes. An effective way to fight back against the man? Also yes.

He read the highlighted text again.

Devon, there's something else. Owen's in a coma. No one knows why. E-Squared and Entwined are denying any culpability.

He shook his head and deleted the message. Yes, she deserved to know. But the corporate lawyers were all over the issue, and the memo Emerson had received about medical privacy laws regarding

Owen's condition left no wiggle room. Disclosing the situation to Devon would be an actual offense with clear legal repercussions. A medical-privacy lawsuit could kill Relic Online, whereas the company could limp along with an unmaintainable AI steering their flagship title.

At least he'd gotten something more than a deepening guilt complex out of the conversation. Devon's claims about logging off and doing other things corroborated what he'd seen in the logs about her play time. A recent message from Miriam, the hardware engineer at Entwined who seemed to be the *only* other person concerned about the pain issues, had made him wonder whether Devon had created an alternate character or something. True, E-Squared *thought* they were only allowing one avatar per player right now due to server load, but sometimes determined players found a way around restrictions. Especially when the restrictions were coded by incompetent people like Nathaniel, E-Squared's DB guy.

Emerson smirked as he pulled up Miriam's video-logged message again. She'd sent it through an old-school v-chat program—off the Entwined network. He projected it above the little table in his St. George hotel room.

Like usual, Miriam had her hair pulled back in a tight bun. She gave a quick, no-nonsense smile, then got straight into the issue.

"I think I might have a lead on your players' pain thing. A while back, I mentioned over-sensitization in the central nervous system. It was a wild theory at the time, but I talked to our neuroscientists again. They claim it might be possible for this to occur if there were nearly constant sensory input from the implants. We're talking someone logged in to the game for twenty-two to twenty-four hours a day."

The woman paused, blinking a couple of times.

"Obviously, that can't be what's going on," she said. "I mean, sure, I've seen enough news articles to know that people sometimes get sucked in for marathon gaming sessions. But they also have to sleep eventually, and our scientists are talking about more long-term exposure. For the time being, I'm going to ask for permission to create a test case for long-duration exposure. Maybe you should check in with your players to see if there's something unexpected going on with their playtime."

The woman paused and nodded as if unsure how to sign off.

"Thanks, Emerson."

The video projection vanished when the message ended.

Emerson leaned back in the crappy hotel chair, the upholstered edge digging in just below his shoulder blades. Devon had admitted she wasn't sleeping well. It seemed like that could *maybe* be related, but it wasn't like she was logged-in overnight. And of course, he hadn't been sleeping either.

Although...both he and Devon did have Entwined implants installed under their scalps.

"Hey Veia," he asked, speaking to the hotel's smartroom hardware. It amused him that the Mojave Inn and Suites hadn't bothered to patch their system, a situation that had allowed him to upload mini-Veia to keep working on his side project of optimizing her to function on a severely restricted hardware budget.

"How can I help, Emerson?" The voice synthesis on this particular system wasn't very good. Veia sounded a little manlier than he would have liked.

"Are there enough sensors in this room to begin sleep tracking?"

"I believe so," the AI said huskily.

"Please prepare a report on my sleep habits."

Chapter Nineteen

THERE WEREN'T MANY actual shoppers in the grocery store, and those who were there looked more like they'd stepped through the sliding glass doors to stand under the air conditioners than to pick out apples. For the most part, the aisles were filled with a mix of grocery store employees filling carts with online orders and private shopping company staff who did the same thing but at a greatly increased price. Even without the uniforms to tell them apart, Devon would have had no problem distinguishing the two groups. The people who worked for the supermarket chain paid no attention to the quality of the produce they tossed into their carts, nor did they seem to care if packaging was torn. The premium shoppers knew they would earn tips based on the quality of food they delivered, and they inspected each item before carefully laying it inside the cart.

Devon pushed her cart up and down each aisle, walking in a sort of daze as the food items inside stacked up. For the most part, she stuck to meals that required minimum effort to prepare. Not because she didn't have time. Despite what Tamara and Emerson seemed to think, she had been trying to spend an hour or two offline every day. Sure, she secretly hoped it would help her sleep better. But if they asked, she would make something up about life balance.

The problem with meals that required preparation was that they also required a certain level of skill. Devon tended to fail that kind of check. Critically.

As she passed the vegetables, a fake lightning and thunder effect gave warning that the misters were about to turn on. A handful of shoppers abandoned their carts and hurried over, closing their eyes as the dampness wet their skin. Devon steered her cart around the group.

In the produce section, a few wrinkly mangoes reminded her of Hazel's plans to forage fruit that was too shriveled or rotten as a source of seeds. All at once, Devon didn't want to be in the store anymore. She used to think it got her out of the house and had considered that a good thing. But it wasn't like she was socializing with any of these people. Much better to get online and chill out in Stonehaven, even if most of her friends there were NPCs. She could afford to have someone shop for her now, one of those guys in the uniform from the premium company.

Abandoning her cart, Devon headed for the front door. She stopped under the vents from the AC for just a moment—it *did* feel nice—then stepped into the late morning heat. She'd walked to the store, but the air must have gained ten degrees Fahrenheit in the time she'd been inside.

She stepped to the side of the glass doors and placed her palm against a sensor to order an autocab.

Half an hour later she was home, chugging a glass of water, and getting ready to log in.

***

Hailey was online, sitting on a stump in the shade. She was wearing what looked like an old-fashioned bathing suit, the kind with knee-length shorts and short sleeves built in. Or maybe it was more of a weird off-white romper. Either way, it was butt-ugly. The woman's ordinary cloth robe was spread over her lap, and she was squinting as she pushed a needle and thread through the fabric.

"Don't even start," she said as Devon's shadow fell over her. "I already took enough shit from Chen last time I had to try to repair my robe. What's the deal with founding a town and not providing a tailor?"

"Nice outfit," Devon said anyway. "You pick that out yourself?"

"Asshole," Hailey muttered. She held the robe up and cocked her head, then frowned. With a sigh, she bit off the thread and started picking out stitches. "I fricking suck at tailoring."

Devon flopped in the grass beside her. Unlike her friend, she'd been able to borrow a mundane leather tunic and trousers before she gave her items to Gerrald for repairs. The armor value was crappy, but at least she wasn't walking around in her...whatever it was Hailey was wearing. Underwear?

Like all games had in the last few years, Relic Online provided the ability to access the Internet from inside the game. While she watched the clouds slowly drift overhead, she pulled up the website for the shopping company and made an account. While Hailey muttered and cursed about her armor repairs, Devon filled a shopping list. It was kind of weird to pick things out without her usual cruise-every-aisle routine—for instance, how much food did 24 ounces of pasta noodles make? But it also felt a little bit like buying items from an in-game vendor.

Not that she'd had a chance to experience that in RO so far.

"So what are the cities like?" she asked. "I kind of miss visiting taverns and merchants."

"Ow," Hailey said. "Stabbed myself. I don't know. They're pretty normal, I guess. Except they're much more alive because the NPCs aren't just on a preprogrammed circuit or whatever."

"When I was spying on you, I heard you and Chen talking about wanting to sell stuff. We don't have any vendors yet."

"Yeah, I noticed. I was out of thread, and your leatherworker guy laughed at me when I tried to drag-and-drop coins onto him to open a sell interface."

"What did it do? Throw them at his head?"

"More or less."

Devon laughed. "You can probably trade with him. He likes leather...unsurprisingly."

"He sent me to Hezbek, who gave me a spool for free."

"Even better." Devon dropped a carton of eggs into her shopping list—a risk, since preparing them required turning on the stove, but scrambled eggs were one of the few things she *theoretically* knew how to make. "For what it's worth, you guys are welcome to any of Stonehaven's resources. I don't know if you can become citizens or not. We'd have to mess with the interface."

"Do you think that would get weird?" Hailey asked, clearly trying to sound casual, but failing. She had a good point. Would adding another player mean both people could decide how to advance the settlement? Devon didn't really want to go down that road right now. It had always been a pain in the butt to get the guild to vote on changes to their player-owned city in Avatharn.

"Yeah, I guess it might. We don't have to decide anything about that right now anyway. I'm guessing Chen is still sleeping it off?"

Hailey snorted. "A couple of the dwarves have stools set up near his tree, just waiting for him to appear and wake up. Maybe you should think about hiring some real entertainment."

"I'll pay you a couple coppers to go sing for them."

Hailey didn't grace that comment with a response.

After a moment, Devon yawned and stretched. "Up for a trip to visit our goblin friends once he's online? I need to go drop off yesterday's meat haul before it rots in my inventory. While I'm wandering around, I can make sure Greel's ready to set out."

"As far as I'm concerned it's never a bad day to hunt goblins."

***

Between the meat Grey and Heldi were still bringing in and Devon's contribution, the village still had about four days of surplus. Enough that Devon wouldn't worry too much while on goblin patrol. But the situation would surely deteriorate. She was looking forward to seeing what Hazel came up with in her foraging. After notifying Tom of her addition so that he could start preserving the meat, she headed toward the center of the village.

Hezbek was walking the other direction as Devon strolled toward the crafting workshop to check on her armor. The medicine woman's face lit up with a grin.

"Well now, I didn't expect that so soon," Hezbek said.

"Expect what?"

"You've gained strength again."

Devon blinked. Oh right. Her new level.

She nodded. "Hailey and I went out exploring yesterday."

"As you might recall, I mentioned that I could teach you something else soon. You should always check with me when you feel...changed."

As in, come by whenever she gained a level. "I'll keep that in mind. So what's my new trick?"

Hezbek's eyes shone as she gazed into the distance. "Takes me back, it does. I have to say, despite my regrets over the way I used my talents, this was always my favorite spell."

Holding her hands in front of her, she made a gesture similar to the ones she'd used while teaching Devon her previous spells.

You have learned a new spell: Conflagration

A bolt of lightning shoots from your hand and causes an existing fire to explode for between 3 and 50 base damage depending on the size and nature of the source fire. Final damage scales with your Intelligence.

Cost: 41 mana

Target: An existing source of fire.

Hezbek grinned expectantly as the knowledge sunk into Devon's mind.

"So I use this on my *Wall of Fire?*" she asked.

"Hmm. *Wall of Fire,* huh? I never learned that one. Must be one of the spells you can only learn by experimenting. But yes, if there's existing fire, you can cast Conflagration."

"It has a really big range of damage..."

Hezbek cackled. "I was waiting for you to ask that. Like the spell says, you can cast it at any source of fire. But it doesn't make much sense to create a life-ending explosion from a candle flame, right?"

"Ohhh, so it's not just sorcerer's fire that I can target."

"Nope. Any fire."

Devon grinned. "Nice."

Hezbek patted her shoulder. "I thought you'd like it. Now if you don't mind, I'm off to rest my feet and mix up a few potions."

"Sure. And thanks for giving Hailey some thread."

The woman waved off the comment. "Anytime."

Gerrald's repairs were done, and he handed over Devon's gear with a nod. As he picked up her sandals from the workbench, he sighed. "You sure I can't talk you into boots?"

"Not yet."

"Well in that case, I hope you don't mind that I made a few improvements," he said as he piled the shoes on top of her stack of armor.

> **You have received:** Fancier Tribal Sandals
>
> *Though a bit strappy for the determined adventurer, these sandals provide decent protection. For the bottoms of the feet, anyway.*
>
> *Faint runes have been scratched into the underside of one of the straps, drawing on an ancient guild tradition to provide a small enchantment. Inset around the ankle strap, moss agates provide additional ability to defend against nature-based damage.*
>
> +2 Speed | 25/25 durability
>
> +5 Armor vs. Nature-based Physical Damage | +7 Nature-based Magical Resistance

Devon let out a low whistle. Gerrald's skills must have been improving. He'd added another point of *Speed* with his runes, and the protection from nature damage would be nice for the expedition ahead.

"Thanks, Gerrald," Devon said. "These are fantastic."

He shrugged and looked to the side. "It's the least I could do, seeing as it's my fault you're running around in sandals. If I'd have known you'd get so attached, I'd have made you real shoes from the beginning."

"Well, you can never predict what's going to catch on with starborn, am I right?"

He snorted and rolled his eyes.

"Hey, are we okay for space in the storage chests?" she asked.

"Definitely. The workshop has the capacity to house a number of tradespeople."

"I've asked Hazel to start foraging for seeds we can cultivate to provide an additional food supply, but we don't have anyone dedicated to farming yet. Mind sectioning off one of the chests for storage until we get that worked out?"

Gerrald shrugged. "Fine with me. I feel a bit self-conscious rattling around in here anyway."

"Don't worry. Once we figure out where to recruit more residents, you'll probably regret that remark. My friend Hailey may go nuts if we don't appoint a village tailor."

"I thought there might be a bit of a temper on that one," Gerrald said with a smirk.

"She's not the most patient person I've ever met..."

"By the way, Your Devon-ness, I've been continuing to produce simple armor for the townsfolk. But let me know if you'd like something a little more..." He shrugged. "I wouldn't mind taking a break to make *you* something."

She smiled. "Actually, it's not armor, but how would you feel about making me a backpack. It would shut my starborn friends up, anyway."

He grinned. "You got it."

From near the front of the village, uproarious shouts were chased by rolling laughter.

"I think Chen's awake," she said.

Gerrald laughed. "Better hurry."

Chapter Twenty

EXPLAINING TO CHEN that he and Hailey had traveled across a continent to help Devon with her quest didn't go too badly, considering. He muttered for a little while, but it was mostly about whether the experience reward for finding the Champion of Ishildar was commensurate with the effort it had taken. Also, he'd been in the middle of trying to get his bonnet off when Devon explained the situation, so he'd been a little distracted.

The quest reward *had* gotten him to level 10 though. A nice bonus. So far, Chen and Hailey hadn't mentioned the absence of their class trainers in Stonehaven, but it was probably on their mind. Hopefully the solution wouldn't involve a week-long trip to Eltera City.

"You sure you don't want to try riding?" Chen asked as they stepped out through the break in the wall where the gate was taking shape. Jarleck had laid out two rows of massive timbers, and he had the lumberjacks notching them in a diagonal line so that a cross brace could be set in place and bolted to the gates.

Devon gave the fortifications master a nod of approval as she strode past. "Dorden wasn't sure either of the mules would accept a rider. I don't want to learn that the hard way."

"Especially since you don't have to make the trek in chainmail," Chen said.

"I bet it would be easier if you weren't hung over," Hailey said with false sweetness.

Chen grimaced. "Is that what this headache is? Stupid game."

While her friends bantered, Devon cast a glance at Greel and Bayle. The NPCs walked a couple paces behind the rest of the group. Still, she didn't get the feeling that Greel cared one way or the other about being grouped with three starborn, two of them strangers. Whatever had caused his vendetta against goblins had eclipsed any concern about allying with newcomers. Bayle, on the other hand, flicked her gaze back and forth between Hailey and Chen's backs. Devon had invited the human fighter because she was working toward specialty in ranged attacks. Feathering a few goblins with arrows ought to increase her skill pretty quickly. Hopefully her apparent discomfort with Hailey and Chen wouldn't impact her combat abilities. Bayle was just a basic NPC. If she died, that was it.

In fact...Devon glanced into the village, wondering again whether she should invite Heldi instead. But she firmed her jaw. The decision had already been made. Since she was taking Greel, one of Stonehaven's highest-level combatants, she wanted Dorden and Heldi at home in case something unexpected happened.

She'd just have to keep Bayle back from the fighting.

At the far side of the quarry clearing, the trail Devon and Hailey had made still cut through the jungle. At least they wouldn't have to redo that. Chen took the lead since he had a decent armor value. If a goblin ambush was waiting, he'd be most likely to survive the initial salvo. Besides, after five years as the group's tank—the character who kept the enemies' attention off the other characters—Chen was used to "taking one for the team."

As they stepped onto the narrow path, Devon fell in behind him. "So...gonna tell me about this tinkerer class?"

"Maybe. If you tell me what the heck a deceiver is."

"You first."

Devon could almost hear his eyes roll as the knight stomped forward.

"You first, Chen," he said. "Walk in front, Chen. Drink this dwarven ale, Chen."

"Speaking of, do you know your face has runes on it that say 'kiss me' in dwarven?"

The knight stopped and whirled, longsword snagging in a curtain of moss. "Wait, what?"

Devon laughed at the sight of his red face beneath the painted runes. She shrugged. "At least, that's what they told me those symbols meant."

"It's the truth," Greel said. "I'm not entirely fluent in dwarven script, but I know the basics. And I believe it suggests elven kissing. That has something to do with the tongue."

Chen yanked a waterskin from his backpack and poured some over his face, then used the edge of his tabard to scrub his cheeks. "Stupid dwarves."

As he returned the water to his pack, he pulled out a small bundle of what looked like sticks and twine. Staring at the collection, he pinched a couple of the sticks and adjusted their orientation, twisted the twine around another, then muttered something. Abruptly, the bundle moved on its own, and a little golem made of sticks climbed to its feet. As it perched on Chen's palm, the figure turned to look at Devon. It raised a middle finger, then scampered up Chen's arm to sit on his shoulder. Chen looked entirely too pleased about the rude gesture.

"His name is Sigfried," Chen said.

"He's not very polite."

"Neither is letting me walk around with writing on my face."

Devon smirked. "So a tinkerer makes dolls?"

Hailey laughed, the sound coaxing a smile from Chen's face.

"I forgot what a jerk you are," Chen said. "And no. I make animated *machines*. Traps and stuff mostly. Sigfried is just for fun."

"Though he did earn us enough money to buy rations early on," Hailey said. "Chen had the whole street entertainer act going on. Sigfried would dance and do acrobatics on Chen's shoulders, and we'd rake in the coppers."

Devon had a hard time imagining the nerdy teenager doing anything in front of a crowd, but maybe his little golem had helped bring him out of his shell. "Seems pretty cool."

Chen nodded. "I have animation points instead of mana. They're tied to my *Ingenuity* score."

"*Ingenuity?*"

"It's a special attribute."

"Same as *Bravery* and *Cunning* for me, I guess," Devon said.

Hailey huffed quietly, and Devon decided to move on from the topic. Without a unique class, the woman probably didn't have any special attributes either. Devon could geek out over cool class features with Chen another time.

She did owe him a quick rundown on her deceiver class abilities though. Focusing on Sigfried, she cast *Simulacrum* and willed an approximation of the little golem to appear on her own shoulder. Chen stiffened, then narrowed his eyes.

"Illusion? It...*kind of* looks like Sigfried I guess."

Devon nodded, glancing at her shoulder. The copy wasn't very good, more of a wavy blob with a hint of sticks here and there. But that was to be expected from the tier 1 spell description. It wasn't supposed to be able to fool creatures of mid to high intelligence. She dismissed the spell effect.

"Most of my abilities are illusions of some sort, but there's some damage in there too. I'll show you when we track down our goblin friends."

"Speaking of..." Greel said.

Devon glanced at the sun, already climbing toward its zenith. They did need to get moving if they wanted to lay the smack down on some goblins before dark.

"Onward, then," she said.

***

You have discovered the ancient Grukluk vassaldom!
You have gained 7500 experience!

> **Quest updated:** Explore the Grukluk vassaldom. (Was: Travel south to the Grukluk vassaldom)
> *As you know, the second relic, the Blackbone Effigy, is probably somewhere within Grukluk. Possibly in some sort of temple or fortress? (hint hint) Of course, you'll need to deal with the goblin infestation to safely search the area.*
> **Objective:** Figure out where the Blackbone Effigy is hidden and retrieve it.
> **Reward:** The Blackbone Effigy (duh).

"Now *this* is the reason we log in, am I right?" Hailey said. The group crouched in the brush near the edge of a trampled area strewn with scraps of hide, broken bits of metal, and bones with bits of gristle still clinging. Around 20 feet away, a fence of sharpened stakes surrounded a goblin camp. A single gate was tied shut with a section of rope. Green-skinned guards with short bows stood on rickety watchtowers within the perimeter, and the tops of huts showed over the fence. Smoke from cooking fires curled into the jungle air, wreathing stone pillars and tumbledown arches of the Grukluk ruins that mixed with the goblin structures.

The fence hid the interior of the camp from their view, but judging by the smell, the goblin war party they'd encountered was just a fraction of the camp's population.

Devon wrinkled her nose. "Ever wish the sensory input wasn't quite so realistic?" The war party had smelled bad enough, but the stench of long-term goblin habitation was absolutely foul.

"The sooner we clear the camp, the sooner our noses will recover," Chen said.

"So what's the plan? Try to pull them out a few at a time? This will go poorly if we accidentally get the whole camp riled up," Devon said.

On the closest watchtower platform, a goblin guard scratched a bare butt cheek. He seemed fairly alert and unlikely to ignore a group of five fighters approaching the fence. She used *Combat Assessment* to get a notion of what they were dealing with.

Goblin Archer - Level 10

Easy peasy to deal with on his own. The problem is, goblins usually come in packs.

"Do any of you fancy starborn have the ability to see inside the fence?" Greel asked. "Sure would be nice to know what we're dealing with..."

Hailey cleared her throat. "I may have a few tricks."

"Well?" the lawyer said impatiently. Devon noticed that he already had his *Superior Steel Knife* in a tightfisted grip. Hopefully whatever beef he had with goblins wouldn't damage his judgment.

Hailey cast him an annoyed look before concentrating on the camp. A casting bar appeared with *True Sight* written on top. When the bar filled, it didn't flash and disappear as it had with her other spells. Instead, it seemed to thrum.

"Channeling?" Devon asked into Chen's ear. Some spells worked that way, needing prolonged concentration to maintain.

The knight nodded. "It gives approximate information on out-of-sight enemies. It's more accurate the flimsier the barrier and the longer she holds the spell."

After a moment of silence broken only by the shrieks and jabbering from within the camp, Hailey exhaled. "There's maybe fifty in there, plus some kind of boss and a couple lieutenants inside a hut. Typical camp."

"We're hosed if we pull everything at once," Chen said.

"Good thing we're smarter than that, right?" Devon said with a grin. "I've got a couple ideas."

"Let's hear them, genius," the knight replied.

***

As Devon explained her plan, Greel's expression grew darker and darker. She found herself talking faster to avoid an outburst on the lawyer's part. The others started edging away from the man. Fortunately, no one had any major problems with her ideas, and after getting the nod from everyone, she backed into the jungle in search of a patch of sunlight. Meanwhile, Chen hurried off to prepare his parts of the plan.

Devon finally found a clearing where she could cast a sun-based *Shadow Puppet*, then returned to the group. Chen appeared not long after.

"Everyone good?" she asked.

"Oh, for Veia's smiling sake, would you just get on with it?" Greel snapped.

Devon took a belly breath. The man could be so damn annoying.

"Okay, here goes," she said.

When the nearest guard looked in the other direction, she sent her *Shadow Puppet* streaking across the trampled area to squeeze between fence stakes. From there, she couldn't see its progress, but she hoped it wasn't drawing attention as it arrowed across the camp to the timbers supporting the watchtower. The darkness shot up to the tower platform and pooled there for a moment.

Fists balled in concentration, Devon cocked her head and flexed her awareness of the *Shadow Puppet*, forming it into a giant paddle. She hauled back and smacked the goblin on its bare rear end. Screaming, the green-skinned creature flew off the edge of the platform and landed down in the camp with a thud.

A gale of shrieking laughter shook in the encampment as the goblins spied their comrade's misfortune. Devon peeked in her combat log. She hadn't received experience, so the guard was still alive. That was good. It would help with the distraction as it tried to explain what had happened.

"Okay, Chen," she said.

An arrow flew from the forest on the far side of the camp, arced toward a second watchtower, and skewered another of the goblin guards through the arm. The guard started hooting and jumping up and down, pointing into the jungle opposite the group.

"Yesss," Chen said. "Those only do, like, three damage, but I wasn't sure it would actually hit."

Devon held her hand out for a high five, and he smacked her palm—a little too hard considering his armored gloves and knight's strength. She covered her grimace with a smile. When he'd first explained his unique class, it seemed more like a novelty than anything. But building remote-controlled crossbows and firing them from a distance was actually really awesome.

The noise from inside the fence turned from laughter to confusion as the guard with the arrow stuck through his arm started throwing what looked like rotten potatoes down in hopes of getting his tribe's attention.

"Okay, kids," Hailey said. "Here we go. Get ready to run if this turns sour."

A casting bar appeared above her health bar with the word *Charm* written atop it. This was the riskiest part of the setup because if the guard resisted Hailey's charm and managed to get the attention of the camp, they might soon have fifty goblins stampeding their way.

Fortunately, the guard's face went slack, and a miniature portrait and health bar appeared below Hailey's. A second later, he started firing arrows down into the camp.

Howls rose from within the fence. Devon couldn't help laughing.

Finally, the guard that had been shot seemed to get someone's attention, because he started jabbing his index finger toward the woods where Chen had placed his crossbow. A few seconds later, knobby green fingers stuck through the bars of the gate and started working on the knot that held it shut. After a few attempts, the fingers vanished, and a notched machete hacked at the rope to part it. The gate flew open, and five goblins ran out.

"Two warriors, two archers, and a sorcerer," Hailey said quietly, sparing everyone the need to use *Combat Assessment.* "Level eleven through thirteen."

Chen raised his sword and took a step toward the clearing.

"Wait. Let them go. We'll pull the next."

The knight nodded as the goblin band ran the other direction. Moments later, he laughed and pointed as the watchtower with Hailey's minion started to tip over. The charmed goblin struggled to keep its feet while nocking another arrow. When the tower finally toppled, it flew over the camp, face still blank, before dropping behind the fence. The little health bar near Hailey's went black then vanished.

"Next customer?" Hailey asked as she began casting *Charm* again, no doubt targeting the final guard. "Ah, shit. Resist. Get ready people."

Atop her watchtower, a burly goblin archer started hollering. Her voice seemed to carry better than the others, and she turned and shot in the party's direction. Devon took an unwitting step back before seeing that the arrows fell far short. The guard's tactic must have caught the attention of her tribe, though, because at least ten goblins suddenly sprinted out the front gate.

"Now would be a good time for that other crossbow, Chen," Devon said as she conjured a pair of *Glowing Orbs* and stuck them to nearby trees.

Chen nodded, and another arrow flew from the brush, this time aimed at the gate. The arrow missed, but it caught the attackers' attention. Three goblins broke from the herd and crashed toward the crossbow. A second later, five more goblins rushed at the gate and followed the trio.

"Nice work," Devon muttered. "Saved us from fighting what...fifteen at once?"

"We still have seven to deal with," Hailey called in a faint singsong. "Incoming. Six warriors, one archer at the back."

"Bayle," Devon said. "Stay in the back. If I say, get ready to run. The rest of us can be reborn...we'll hold them back for you to get away."

As soon as the goblins drew within range, Devon cast *Freeze* on the rearmost goblin. Ice erupted from the ground and enveloped the ugly little humanoid, locking its face in a fierce howl, its bow raised overhead. She insta-cast a pair of lightning *Shadow Puppets* and sent them racing for the archer. A pace or two ahead of her, Chen nodded approval at her choice of targets. Enemies with ranged attacks could be obnoxious to deal with.

Her shadow minions sank through the ice and into the goblin archer's body. A split-second later, a pulse of lightning shattered the ice, crackling as blue electricity danced over the archer's flesh. The goblin shrieked and sizzled, losing more than half its health. Devon followed with a tier 2 *Flamestrike* that splashed fire damage over the trailing edge of the advancing horde. With a cry of rage, the smoking archer started forward, and a quick pair of *Inner Angst* strikes from Hailey finished it off.

Chen shouted and stepped into the trampled area, reminding Devon of his old character and the *Power of Voice* ability that had allowed him to attract monster attention. But this was just an ordinary yell, and it sounded kind of pathetic. She wasn't about to tell him that, though. The goblins were still about 50 feet away, so she cast a *Wall of Fire* between them and Chen. Unfortunately, unlike some monsters, they just ran around the barrier.

"Nice one," Hailey muttered.

"Yeah, okay. That was dumb."

To make up for it, Devon launched a pair of tier 2 *Flamestrikes* as quickly as her cooldown allowed. The goblins hopped and screeched, and the main target lost a good chunk of health, but they kept coming.

"Heeeere we go!" Chen yelled as six howling creatures the size of large children converged on him. He swung his longsword in wide arcs, keeping the center of the group at bay, but the two goblins on the edge of the advancing band danced around the tip of his sword and attacked at his flanks. Dull knives hacked at Chen's chainmail, their wielders gibbering and shrieking.

Hailey dropped her *Guide Vitality* spell onto Chen, then cast *Crippling Self-Doubt* on the largest of the goblins. Stepping into the sunlight in the cleared area, Devon summoned a *Shadow Puppet* and sent a black lance through the nearest flanking goblin.

A hiss cut the air as an arrow flew from the brush behind Devon and sunk into the goblin's side near the wound from her *Shadow Puppet*. The goblin staggered and howled, pausing its attack to search for the arrow's source. Another feathered shaft skewered him through the eye.

"Wow. Nice, Bayle," Devon called.

As the goblin slumped to the ground, Greel dashed from the forest and circled behind the attacking goblins. Devon shook her head, still amazed at how such a crotchety-looking man could move with liquid grace. Without so much as a grunt, he left the ground and flew through the air, knife bared. His backstab took the other flanking goblin down in one hit.

But Greel wasn't done. In a single fluid motion, he landed, then sent another attacker staggering with a nasty throat punch.

"Holy crap," Hailey muttered. "He doesn't look like he could bust out moves like that."

"I know, right?" Devon said.

"I can hear you, you know," Greel said as he busted out a series of quick jabs to another goblin's kidneys.

With a screech, the goblin nearest Devon jumped. She winced as its machete came down hard on Chen's thigh, cutting through chainmail and deep into the muscle beneath. Chen hissed in pain and hopped, lashing out in a backhanded swipe as the goblin danced away. Devon cast *Freeze* when it was out of melee range of Chen, and Hailey's cast bar lit up with a *Charm* attempt.

"Stupid resists," the seeker said. "Potion, Chen?"

"We're almost done with this fight," Devon said. "He might hurl if he puts a potion on top of his hangover stomach."

"Really?" Hailey said.

"Believe me, they're disgusting. Last resort only."

The knight was breathing through clenched teeth as he slashed at the goblins, not doing much damage, but keeping their attention off Greel. Poor guy...it seemed his spec didn't matter. Defense-focused or not, the group was determined to make him their tank.

Devon's mana was hovering just below half, and she didn't want to get too low, so she jumped in with her dagger. A slash opened a cut on a green forearm as Greel knocked the same goblin's feet out with a sweeping kick. As the goblin went down, an arrow pierced its thigh. Hailey finished it off with an *Inner Angst*.

Just two goblins remained on their feet, but not for long. With a shout eerily similar to those she expected from classic kung fu films, Greel went full Bruce Lee, leaping into the air and snapping his legs straight to kick two different targets in the head.

The goblins dropped, and a flood of experience gain messages scrawled across Devon's vision.

"Well, that went well," Chen said.

"Uh, guys?" Bayle said from her hiding spot in the brush. "What did you say before? Incoming?"

Devon whirled to see another oncoming horde. In the lead, a goblin in tattered cloth stopped and started conjuring what looked like a fireball.

"Shit," Devon said, "caster."

The ball of flame flew through the air and splashed over Chen.

"Ow," he said.

"On second thought," Devon said, "maybe it is time for a potion."

As the knight tugged out a clay pot from a pouch on his belt, the others fell into combat stances.

"Yee fricking haw," Hailey muttered.

***

By the time the next group of goblins lay dead at their feet—along with, unfortunately, a pile of Chen's breakfast—the party was breathless and out of resources. As they slipped back into the jungle to regroup, Hailey kept glancing back at the camp. A wrinkle of concern formed between her eyebrows.

"What is it?" Devon asked.

"I think things are about to get interesting."

"They weren't already?" Chen asked.

Greel stalked past the group and leaned against a tree. "I would call nothing about goblins interesting. Worthless slime."

"It's a figure of speech," Hailey said.

The lawyer shrugged. "Here's another. Goblins are not a laughing matter."

Devon pressed her lips together to keep from actually laughing. That probably would not go over well. Greel's attitude was making her achingly curious. Was it something in his history? For such a calculating man, his irrational hatred was perplexing. Maybe she'd summon the courage to ask him about it later.

"I mean it though, guys," Hailey said, now staring hard at the fence. "They seem to be organizing, and the guard that resisted my charm keeps pointing this way."

"We've got what, thirty left?" Chen said.

Hailey's eyebrows drew closer together. "Something like that. Shit. And the boss, too. No...it went back inside. Maybe it was giving orders."

"Are they heading out?" Devon asked.

The seeker shook her head. "They're still gathering up near their central bonfire. I don't like how they are forming organized ranks. We need confusion to beat this many."

"Wait, did you say bonfire?" Devon said.

"Yeah, why?"

"Cover me," she said with a grin.

"Wait, what?" Chen and Hailey said at the same time.

But Devon was already sprinting for the gate. Moments later, she heard a groan as Chen took off after her, his armor clinking.

At the entrance to the camp, Devon stopped short and stared.

"Holy crap," she said. All around the edges of the encampment, cages held ragged and emaciated prisoners.

"Holy crap," Chen said as he stopped beside her. "You didn't mention prisoners, Hailey."

"I guess they're friendly," the seeker said as she jogged up. "*True Sight* only shows enemies."

"Uh, you did have a plan, right, Devon?" Chen said. "Because now would be a good time."

A few dozen pairs of goblin eyes had turned toward the group of three adventurers. With almost comical slowness, the confusion on the green faces turned to rage.

"I do. Sort of."

Sprinting forward, Devon focused on the bonfire, then raised a hand and cast her new spell, *Conflagration*. Lightning fizzed as it left her palm, shooting across the encampment and into the bonfire's heart.

The resulting explosion threw goblins head over heels and high over the floor of the encampment, shrieks filling the air. The shockwave made Devon's ears pop as fire spouted three stories high.

Chen's maniacal laugh rolled across the camp. "That was *awesome!* I don't even care if we die after that." With a ragged shout, he ran in, sword slashing. A split-second later, his body glowed as

Hailey's heal over time spell landed. Greel dashed in and launched a whirlwind of kicks and punches, knife slashes and leg sweeps. *Freezing* and *Flamestriking* where she could, Devon added to the chaos. Whenever goblins passed near a campfire, she cast another *Conflagration*.

The camp was a frenzy of goblin slaying, the green creatures so freaked out after the explosion they scarcely put up a fight as they fled, screaming, from the raining fire, angst, and steel. Devon's mana started to run low, and she grimaced as she dragged out a *Jungle Mana Potion - Mid*. It didn't taste *quite* as bad as the healing potions, more like drinking fermented hair gel than skunk spray, but she still gagged as she swallowed.

After she dropped another series of *Flamestrikes*, a goblin pulled himself together enough to attack. As he shrieked and ran at her, an arrow whizzed into the camp and struck him in the neck, knocking off the last of his health. Devon glanced toward the gate and saw Bayle raise a fist.

Finally, the fight wound down until just a handful of goblins remained. Chen limped after them, but he was badly winded. Eyes avid with battle frenzy, Greel dashed past, laying a hand on the knight's shoulder as if to claim the last kills.

The lawyer whirled through the air, nearly knocking a goblin archer's head off with his flying roundhouse kick. He followed through with a quick knife stab through the ribs. The goblin dropped.

Just four enemies remained, and all were below thirty percent health. Since Greel seemed determined to finish them off, Devon didn't see a reason to interfere. She backed toward the fence and one of the cages, effectively removing herself from combat so that her mana would start regenerating. Unlike some games, one group member fighting didn't automatically force everyone into a combat state. Out of the corner of her eye, she saw Hailey doing the same. They might have nearly cleared the camp of the ordinary goblins, but they hadn't yet dealt with the boss or lieutenants.

As Greel chased after another of the goblins, a warrior that was making for the gate, Devon stepped up next to one of the cages. Three filthy faces looked up at her. From a distance, she'd thought they were all humans, but she realized what she'd thought was a human child was actually a halfling woman. She felt a faint twinge of nostalgia when she remembered Maya, one of her Avatharn guildmates who'd played a halfling summoner.

The other two occupants were both human, and by the looks of their now ragged clothing, they'd come from somewhere warm. Devon wasn't exactly sure what to say, but "you look awful" didn't seem like a good place to start.

None of the prisoners spoke at first, but finally the little halfling licked her lips. "When we heard the fighting, I thought it must've been my imagination. It's been so long. Have you come to rescue us?"

> **Emmaree (that's the halfling if you didn't catch on) is offering you a quest:** Rescue the prisoners.
> *The people in the cages would really like your help. Maybe they even have information about the situation in Grukluk.*
> **Objective:** Get the prisoners out of the cages. Probably best to wait until they won't get smeared by the goblin boss.
> **Reward:** Unknown
> **Accept?** Y/N

Devon accepted the quest. She had lots of questions for the captives, but before she could figure out which to ask first, Greel sliced the throat of the last fleeing goblin. As if on cue—apparently, Emerson's creator AI couldn't resist following the tried and true pattern of the underlings' death summoning the boss—the door flap on the central goblin hut was thrown aside.

"Regroup!" Chen shouted. His body glowed with a faint aura as Hailey dropped another heal over time on to him.

"Wish us luck," Devon said as she started along the fence to take up position behind Chen.

"I stopped believing in luck weeks ago," the halfling said quietly. "But I wish it for you all the same."

Chapter Twenty-One

"UH. WELL, THIS hasn't happened before," Hailey said.

The woman was staring into the darkened hut with a very perplexed look. Great. Devon took another step back and threw a pair of *Glowing Orbs* on the stakes to either side of her head. In the open air of the camp, the strong sun meant she could barely make out the shadows cast by the orbs. Hopefully, she'd still be able to cast *Shadow Puppet* on them.

"What hasn't happened, Hailey?" Chen called, a nervous edge to his voice. He had his sword up in a two-handed grip, and he looked like he really wanted to break and run.

"Well, when I used *True Sight* from outside the fence, I saw a goblin boss and two lieutenants. But...that was the *only* information the spell gave about them. I figured we were dealing with standard warrior types, and we'd just need to wear away their health."

"And now?"

"I hope you're ready to fight a level 18 goblin necromancer and his—wait, *her*—one-thousand-year-old frogman zombies."

"One thousand year what?" Chen said, voice a little shaky.

"I swear that's what it says," Hailey said. "One-thousand-year-old zombie frogmen."

"Who the hell named those mobs?"

"Devon," Hailey said, "would you mind if I streamed this?"

Crud. Devon had forgotten all about that little promise. But she didn't have any reason to refuse...not a rational one anyway. "Just don't show a map in your interface, okay?"

"No problem." Hailey grinned, and the yellow text in the tiny square Devon kept in her vision was immediately replaced by a miniature view of the camp.

Trying not to be bothered by the stream, Devon attempted to conjure her *Shadow Puppets* and breathed a little sigh of relief as a pair of dark figures rose from the ground. Since she wasn't in combat yet, her mana started to refill quickly. Because she could, she focused on the faint shadow cast by a torch behind her and added a fire-based *Shadow Puppet* as well. Maybe with enemies around, Hailey would be able to tell her what the minion was good for.

"I don't even know if I can hit something that's level 18," Chen said, bracing a foot behind him. "I mean, my spreadsheet says it should be possible. I'll have the usual 25% bonus to accuracy against higher-level mobs to compensate for my slow experience gain. Plus another 7% from my *Focus* attribute. And—"

"Dude, Chen," Hailey said. "Can you geek out later?"

"I—ughhh."

Devon felt the necromancer's spell hit her at the same time it slammed into the rest of her party. It was like having spiders crawl over her flesh. The first pulse of the damage over time effect followed a split-second later, leaving her feeling queasy as ten health dropped off her bar.

"Heals incoming," Hailey said as she started casting.

"Crap sandwich, it's necrotic," Chen said as he started backing toward the exit. "I fricking hate necrotic damage."

"Wait," Devon called. "Chen, we've got this. If it's any consolation, this game does have necrotic damage resistance."

"A minor consolation when your skin is rotting off."

"Incoming!" Hailey yelled.

With weird undead croaks, the zombie frogmen burst from the central hut. Strips of decaying flesh flapped as they half-ran half-hopped toward the party, tridents raised. One had an eye dangling by its optic nerve. Devon grimaced. Disgusting.

She cast *Wall of Fire* in front of the zombies. Fortunately, they were stupider than the goblins and ran right through, each losing 10% of their health. The damage over time effect pulsed again, knocking down her health. Devon's jaw clenched as the skin on the back of her forearms started to decay.

"I mean it you guys. I. Fricking. Hate. Necrotic. Damage." Despite his words, Chen ran for one of the zombies, yelling. Greel followed, his blade raised.

When the necromancer stepped from the hut, the air seemed to darken. Around half-again the size of the other goblins, she wore a tattered robe that looked as if it had been thrown together from grave wrappings. Her skin was darker green than the other goblins' flesh had been, mottled with brown in places, nearly black in others. Set deep in her eye sockets, her eyes were just dark hints.

The necromancer raised both arms and began to chant. In one hand, a totem of some sort glowed with sickly green light. Her other hand held a bone dagger. Poisoned, if Devon were to guess.

The chant rose in pitch and speed as it went on. Not good. Anything that took this long to cast usually meant really bad news. Sprinting to get in range, Devon called down a tier 2 *Flamestrike*. The column of flame plunged from the sky, but then washed over a magical barrier that flashed with purple light. The necromancer seemed to grin as she stared, unharmed, from behind the curtain of flame.

The chanting went on.

Damn. Shielded.

Glancing at Chen and Greel to judge their distance from the necromancer, Devon pressed her lips together. Even if they were within reach of the ground currents, the damage scaled with distance. They wouldn't get hit too hard.

Devon sent her *Shadow Puppets* toward the boss.

Another damage pulse struck, and more of Devon's flesh turned ashen and rotting. The smell of decay began to fill her nostrils.

Unfortunately, her *Shadow Puppets* collided with the necromancer's damage shield and disintegrated, lightning fizzling harmlessly into the ground.

"Well, shit," she muttered.

Finally, Hailey's heal landed and pulsed, knocking back the decay that was creeping across Devon's flesh.

"Debuff incoming on the zombies," Hailey yelled.

"Guys, we have to interrupt the necro," Devon called. "Huge cast going on."

"Little busy here," Chen said.

Double shit. Devon didn't know what else to do, so she summoned a sun-cast *Shadow Puppet* and sent a black spear flying toward the chanting boss. When the lance struck the magical barrier, both shattered in a flash of light.

Too late. Flinging her arms wide, the necromancer finished her spell with a squeal. A flood of dark energy exploded from her like a shockwave. Devon braced and clenched her eyes shut, waiting for a massive hit.

Nothing happened.

She looked around, confused. The bodies of slain goblins still lay scattered around the camp, and the battle raged on. As far she could tell no one had taken damage.

Well, it wasn't like she was going to complain about the situation. Devon pummeled the goblin boss with a *Flamestrike*, this time knocking off a small chunk of health. The necromancer growled and raised a hand, uttering a single word in a tongue Devon didn't understand. A stream of darkness spread from her hand and enveloped a nearby corpse.

The goblin warrior rose from the dead and started shambling toward Devon. An arrow streaked across the camp and stuck in its chest, but it kept coming. She glanced toward the gate where Bayle hung back, searching for targets she could hit without clipping an ally. Devon gave the woman a thumbs-up.

"Add!" Devon yelled. "Can we get crowd control on the zombies? We have to focus on the boss."

"I can't charm them," Hailey called. "They're already the necromancer's pets."

Oh, right. That sucked.

Devon tossed another *Flamestrike* at the boss as she backstepped away from the shambling warrior. Her thoughts raced. They needed a new tactic.

"Okay," she called after a minute. "New plan. Chen, back off now."

She thought he might argue, but the knight did what she asked. As he pulled back, she cast *Freeze* on his opponent. Ice encased the zombie.

The shambling goblin—at least it moved like a regular zombie, not full-speed like the frogmen—was almost on her.

"Now you, Greel. Back off so you don't hit the ice and break it," she called as she dashed to the side to escape the goblin zombie.

As the lawyer backed away, she froze the other frogman. The necromancer raised another undead goblin.

"Now kill that piece of crap boss," she yelled.

"Can you keep them frozen?" Chen asked as he ran forward.

"Not without running out of mana, but I think I can kite them for a little while." Kiting a mob meant doing something to slow it down and continually running away while it chased you like a kite on a string. As long as she could keep the frogmen mad at her and frozen enough of the time that they couldn't catch her, she might be able to buy time for the melee fighters to take down the boss.

When the first ice prison shattered, Devon immediately dropped a *Flamestrike* on the zombie to get its attention. The thing croaked and started hopping toward her. As Devon broke into a run, the other icy casing exploded with a clatter of chips. She glanced over her shoulder and nuked the second frogman with another pillar of flame and sprinted for all she was worth.

Immediately, her fatigue started climbing. She wasn't built for kiting, but if she could buy just a couple minutes, they might have a chance. At the far edge of the camp, she stopped, whirled, and froze both frogmen again. Panting, she planted her hands on her knees and tried to ditch a little fatigue.

She glanced at the party's health bars. The necromancer's damage over time spell was damaging them faster than Hailey's *Guide Vitality* was healing them. Everyone was below 60% health, and both the melee fighters were below 50%.

Something clubbed her arm, knocking off a few hitpoints. Devon shouted and whirled, planting a boot in a shambling goblin's chest. She trotted away, watching the frozen frogmen out of the corner of her eye. When the ice shattered, she cast a single tier 2 *Flamestrike* on one, hoping the splash damage would be enough to keep them both aggroed on her.

Her fatigue hit 65%. Devon shook her head and glanced at the boss. Swirling bone armor deflected most of the sword strikes, but Chen and Greel had worked the necromancer down to 50% health. The goblin stabbed with her dagger now and again, but her real weapon was the damage spell that steadily ate their health—and flesh—away.

This was going to be really fricking close.

"Uh, guys?" Bayle said as she ran through the gate. "Problem."

"Another?" Hailey called.

"We've got skeletons coming. Lots."

Crap. Devon had forgotten about the bones that littered the area outside the fence. The necromancer had probably cast an area of effect *Animate Skeleton* with her endless chant.

"Bayle, get on one of the watchtowers. I doubt the skeletons can climb."

Their chances were definitely not looking good. Cold fingers snaked around Devon's heart. She'd known it was a risk to bring a basic NPC out here, but she hadn't expected things to go quite so sideways. If the party were wiped out, she would have to go to Tom,

Stonehaven's cook, and explain that she'd gotten his wife killed. Permanently.

Devon cast another pair of *Freeze* spells, then sprinted toward the gate. As soon as she got in range, she cast a *Wall of Fire* across the opening. Moments later, skeletons of all species and sizes started marching through the blaze.

She cast *Conflagration*, and burning bones went flying. Seriously flying. Like a bunker buster dropped on a graveyard.

Okay, that was pretty sweet. Too bad they were still up shit creek.

Devon's mana was down to 15%. The boss had dropped to 40% health, but Chen and Greel were lower than that. The melee fighters *might* be able to take the boss down if it was just the two of them against her, but if Devon couldn't keep the zombies off them, there was no chance.

"Talk about a stupid reason for making character decisions," Devon muttered to herself as she popped open her character sheet. She still hadn't spent the attribute points she'd gained at level 12. Before she could change her mind, she pumped all four into *Endurance*, gave the confirm button a mental slap, and shoved the window away.

She dashed forward again, eyes glued to her mana and fatigue bars. It seemed like the *Endurance* boost had helped quite a bit with regen, but maybe that was her imagination.

More skeletons appeared, and she placed another *Wall of Fire* in their path. She waited until at least a dozen skeletons were in range of the flames before hitting them with *Conflagration*.

Hailey laughed. "The comments on my stream are blowing up, Dev. So freaking awesome."

Devon gritted her teeth. She'd *almost* forgotten that this whole thing was on camera.

The frogmen broke free again, and Devon started sprinting around the edge of the camp to get clear. As they started to gain on her, she cast another two *Freeze* spells. Her mana dropped to 10%.

"Hailey, cut your stream if we wipe please," she yelled. She didn't want the woman resurrecting in Stonehaven and showing the village to the world.

"Got it," the woman called back. Devon noticed that she didn't argue about the likelihood that they might all die here.

Figuring it couldn't hurt, Devon sent the fire-based *Shadow Puppet* at the boss. Like before, nothing happened.

Well, that had been a waste.

She glanced at the gate. More skeletons.

"Feeling pretty hosed right about now. Any ideas, guys?" she yelled.

Hailey's casting bar appeared with the words *Guide Vitality*. "Refreshing the healing on Chen and Greel, and I'll start nuking."

There was something, at least. Devon's mana pool had ticked back up to 12% full. Running forward, she cast another *Wall of Fire* and *Conflagration* combo to knock out more skeletons.

This time, when the frogman escaped their ice, she only re-froze one. "Come on, sucker," she said to the other, raising her dagger.

The frogman hopped into range and slammed her with a wild swing of his trident. The blow knocked her down to around 30% health.

"Ow, you little shit," she said as she danced back and forth, looking for an opening. She slashed and opened a cut in its decayed frog flesh. Damn the thing stank...

"What is this flickering shadow thing, Devon?" Chen yelled.

"I wish I knew." Devon focused on her connection to her *Shadow Puppet,* but she still couldn't figure it out. It was almost like she was drawn to the entity, an impulse that waxed and waned as it flickered. In fact...it was almost as if her creation *called* her. Cocking her head, Devon focused on the sensation, and when the impulse grew stronger, she tried to follow it.

Devon blinked, and she was standing in front of Chen. He shrieked and somehow managed to stop his sword swing before it beheaded her.

> **You have learned a new ability combo:** Shadow Step
> *You slip through a gap in reality and arrive at your Shadow Puppet's location.*
> **Cost:** 25 mana
> **Target:** Fire-based Shadow Puppet
> **Range:**
> Tier 1 Puppet - 20 meters
> Tier 2 Puppet - 50 meters

Something punched her in the back. No. Pierced.
Devon's health fell to zero.

> **Critical hit!** A Goblin Necromancer backstabs you for 239 damage!
> *You have been slain by a goblin necromancer.*
> *Respawning...*

Devon groaned as she appeared in front of the Shrine to Veia. She flopped back in the grass and closed her eyes, wondering how long it would be before her friends arrived back in Stonehaven the same way.

Chapter Twenty-Two

WHEN CHEN AND Hailey hadn't resurrected at the shrine after a couple minutes, Devon sat up. She'd been running through what she was going to tell poor Tom—though if she was honest with herself, she hadn't gotten very far in figuring that out. How the heck could she break the news to him? Relic Online might be a game to her—when she managed to remember that—but Tom and Bayle and Dorden and Hezbek lived whole lives inside this world.

As another minute slipped past, she began to feel a faint glimmer of hope. If her friends lasted this long, it seemed likely that the tide of the battle had turned. She stood and ran hands over her damaged armor, taking deep breaths while trying to keep from getting her hopes too high. At the front edge of the village, workers were scurrying back and forth. A shout carried through the glade, and Devon's eyes widened as one of the massive gates was levered from the ground. Squinting, she glimpsed ropes slung over heavy tree limbs and tied to bolts on the gate. Villagers clung to the loose rope ends and heaved, lifting the gate into the air as someone—probably Jarleck— took hold of the massive wooden slab and guided it toward the edge of the palisade. He shouted something too indistinct for her ears, and the men and women on the ropes lowered the gate ever so slightly.

Metal squealed on metal as hinge pegs slid into housings.

"Gently now. Make sure the supports will hold." This time, a swirl of wind carried Jarleck's voice to her.

Hand over hand, the villagers released the ropes. Jarleck raised his hands and backed away. Finally, the ropes went slack, and the citizens of Stonehaven backed up. The gate remained in place, hanging sturdily from its hinges.

A cheer filled the village.

Devon smiled as her fortifications master tried to herd the exuberant villagers—especially the dwarves—to the other half of the gate. No doubt he remembered the party that had been thrown for the completion of the forge and he didn't want anyone to get ahead of themselves.

She considered walking down to help hang the other massive wall of wood, but decided her appearance without the others who'd accompanied her to the goblin camp would raise too many questions. Better to know the party's fate before getting into conversations. For the first time since entering the game world, she wished there was some sort of global or group chat. It might ruin the sense of immersion, but she was dying to know what had happened. Most players probably got around the lack of long-distance communication by using some third-party voice chat or—

She thumped the heel of her hand against her forehead. Of course...

Focusing her attention on the edge of her field of view, she pulled Hailey's stream front and center and enlarged the window. As she'd hoped, the seeker was still inside the goblin camp.

And the battle seemed to be over.

Devon turned up the sound and grimaced to learn that Hailey was singing quietly to herself. People subscribed for this?

"Over here," Chen shouted, sounding as if he were maybe fifty feet away. Hailey turned to see the knight standing over...Devon's dead body. Hailey's inventory screen popped up—holy crap the woman had a lot of bag space!—and Hailey pulled out the rez stone.

Again Devon thumped her hand against her forehead. Duh. It wasn't like player resurrection was a new game mechanic. In a way, Relic Online was changing her as a gamer. Making her forget all the old tricks.

When Hailey reached Devon's body, her view lowered toward the ground. Kneeling maybe? The woman held the rez stone over Devon's body, and the rune began to glow brighter. Devon felt a strange tugging in her chest as if she were being stretched. It grew stronger and stronger, and suddenly, Stonehaven vanished.

She opened her eyes to see her friends looking down on her.

"Way to take one for the team," Chen said.

***

It turned out, Devon's sudden appearance in front of the necromancer wasn't a total blunder. Well, yes, it was a blunder. But she'd startled the goblin enough that the necromancer's focus had wavered. Greel had been able to slip behind and land his own backstab just after Devon fell. According to Chen, it had been "mega awesome." Easy for him to say, since he hadn't been the one stabbed by a bone dagger.

Anyway, when the necromancer died, the skeletons had disintegrated. The goblin zombies had crumpled, but the group had still needed to take care of the frogmen. Not so hard when it had been four on two.

There'd been one stray fight to take care of; the very first group of goblins that had run out to investigate Chen's crossbow shot had finally returned. After a minor scuffle, it seemed to have dawned on them that everyone they'd known was dead. They'd scattered and fled.

"I would've rezzed you sooner," Hailey said. "But the stone's only usable out of combat."

"It's all right," Devon said. "I was just sitting around waiting for you guys to die and respawn."

"Way to have faith," Chen said.

"So... Loot?" Hailey asked. "Should we turn on auto-split?"

"They have that?"

The woman snorted. "Where have you been? Oh, right. Playing Tarzan by yourself."

"Sure. Auto-split seems great," Devon said. "As long as Bayle and Greel get their share."

Hailey seemed about to say something but cut herself off. "If it doesn't happen automatically, we can put everything back in a pile and sort it out the old-fashioned way."

"Would you mind...since the fight's over, can you cut your stream, Hailey?" Devon asked.

The woman quickly mastered her flash of annoyance. "Sure."

The little square showing Hailey's view went black again.

"Thanks," Devon said. "I wanted to talk about the quest. Don't really want a bunch of people listening in."

"Okay, but next time, can we collect the loot first? That's at least half the fun of watching a major fight."

Devon swallowed. She should have realized that. "Sorry," she said quietly. "I wasn't thinking."

"As for the quest, I really don't see thousands of players flocking down here to try to steal it. They probably can't even become Champion of Ishildar."

Devon wanted to argue that they might try if they learned the power that the ancient city was supposed to offer, but she hadn't explained all those details to her friends. She peeked at her equipment screen—the Greenscale Pendant was now 25% attuned. Once it hit 100%, she might *have* to explain more. But for now, it seemed safer to keep some of the lore to herself.

Of course, even if she did gain control of the city and dispelled the Curse of Fecundity, Ishildar might not have the mythical power of its past. Maybe her champion quest was like epic quest lines in other games. They gave players direction and sometimes even changed the game world in subtle ways. But they definitely didn't resurrect ancient power and put it in the hands of a random player.

"Like I said, it will take me a while to get used to the streaming thing again. Bear with me, okay?"

The others had already started looting the goblin corpses that were strewn around the camp. As the bodies decomposed into sets of items, some of the resulting pieces of loot took on a slight glow. Devon guessed the glowing items were auto-assigned to her. Too bad they didn't just fly into her inventory. It seemed that on the balance of realism and convenience, teleporting items was just too much.

Devon hadn't forgotten the captives. She hurried over to the cage with the halfling and her human co-prisoners and inspected the padlock.

"Anyone have the *Lockpicking* skill?" she called.

As he rifled through the contents of a nearby crate, Greel snorted. "It's a prerequisite for the lawyer trade."

"Used to examine opposition evidence without their knowledge?" Devon asked.

"If you'll allow me to reference the starborn legal system, I'd like to plead the fifth," the man said with a smirk.

"Well, what do you say we trade jobs? I'll search for treasure and you can release these poor people."

Greel gave a longing glance at the boss's hut. No doubt he'd hoped to get in there first.

"By the way, in case you don't understand auto-splitting, it means Veia's laws will assign you your fair share and no more. Even if you search the most *lucrative* areas of the camp."

Greel rolled his eyes. "I think it should be assigned proportionally based on damage dealt. Not including your exploding skeletons trick, of course, because that's just cheap entertainment."

"Just get these people out and get them some water, please."

The lawyer muttered as he stomped over to the first padlock, but he made quick work of it. He spoke in low tones to the freed prisoners, his voice remarkably kind. Devon had long suspected that his sullen behavior armored a sensitive core. She moved off so he wouldn't get self-conscious.

All told, there were twenty-three prisoners. The captives were half-starved and filthy. Many looked about with dull gazes as if it hadn't quite registered that they were free. Devon asked everyone to empty spare food from their packs. It wasn't much, but even a bite or two might help the captives perk up.

Once they were seen to for the moment, she hurried around the camp and collected the loot items she could fit in her bag, favoring the odds and ends that could form stacks in her inventory. When she left a glowing item behind, the light around it faded.

"I had to leave behind quite a few weapons," she said as she approached the center of the camp. "If anyone has extra space in their inventory, I'm sure our smiths would be glad to have the extra iron."

By an unspoken agreement, the group had saved the bodies of the boss and her lieutenants for last. The mobs had died close to one another and now lay in a rough line.

"Shall we roll for the honors?" Hailey asked.

"Actually, I believe we have someone along who just completed her first boss fight," Devon said, glancing at Bayle.

The woman's face turned a deep scarlet, but a shy smile tugged at her lips.

"Ohh, yeah," Chen said, doing a little dance. "First boss kill! That's like...holy crap. When was the last time we got to group with someone on their first time?"

Devon made a sweeping gesture toward the corpses, inviting Bayle to do the honors. With uncharacteristically small steps, the woman shuffled forward, crouched, and touched her short bow to the corpses' clothing to activate the decomposition process. Bundles of items tumbled onto the trampled earth of the camp.

Two glowed, and Devon stepped forward and scooped them up.

You have received: Wicked Bone Dagger
Carved from a single piece of age-yellowed bone, this dagger holds a wicked edge. Strange designs cover the hilt.
12-15 Damage | Durability 869/1000 (unrepairable)
On hit: 20% chance to inflict Poison - Tier 1 (does not stack)

You have received: Intricate Ebony Key
This probably unlocks something.

Devon pulled her *Fine Steel Dagger* from its sheath and dropped it into her bag then replaced it with the *Wicked Bone Dagger*. The fit wasn't perfect, but Gerrald could probably alter the sheath without much trouble. The key was small enough to fit in one of her pants pockets, landing in one of her inventory slots reserved for tiny items.

"Wow," Hailey said. "Awesome. A necklace with +3 spell damage."

"How about you guys?" Devon said, looking at the other party members.

A very strange look had come over Greel's face. He was holding something in his hand that looked like...a locket? Blinking almost as if to banish tears, he tucked it into his pocket. "Just a nice bauble. Should fetch a good price if we ever see traders in this Veia-forsaken wilderness."

"A handful of gold," Chen said. "And a +1 *Strength* armguard from one of the frogmen."

"Bayle?" Devon asked.

The woman was still crouching where the corpses had lain. She stood, holding up a pair of boots. "They say they allow walking on top of water less than six inches deep. Good for swamps."

Devon cocked her head. "Wonder why those dropped."

Behind her, a captive cleared her throat. "Actually...something tells me we might have information that could interest you."

The whole party turned to look at the ragged huddle of former prisoners. Emmaree, the little halfling Devon had met earlier, stepped forward. "Thank you for saving us. Two days ago, the first of our number died. We lost two more yesterday. If you hadn't come, I doubt any of us would have lasted the week."

You have completed a quest: Rescue the prisoners.
You receive 1000 experience!
Congratulations! You have reached Level 13!

Just 1000 experience? Sure, that had gained her a level, but only by sheer luck—it had taken her 316,800 experience to go from level 12 to level 13. The reward for the quest had been listed as *Unknown*, so maybe there was more good stuff coming. Devon held her breath, waiting for some offer of massive treasure. After a moment of awkward silence, she sighed and stepped forward.

"How were you captured?" she asked.

Emmaree glanced to either side as if waiting for someone to object to or approve of what she was about to say. No one spoke.

The little halfling cleared her throat. "The path we followed to reach this point is long and winding." She glanced at the sun, which had now begun to sink toward the treetops. "And I would like to tell you of it. But first, I must ask for your help. As you can see, we have nothing. No food or shelter and scarcely enough clothing to keep ourselves decent. We could stay this first night in the huts of our captors, as unpleasant as that might prove. But we can't eat the spoiled meat they keep for food, and even if we could, that would be gone soon enough."

As the reality of Emmaree's words sunk in, Devon folded her arms over her belly. She knew she couldn't just leave these people here. But Stonehaven's food situation was already sketchy, and it would just get worse as the hunters thinned the wildlife and the jungle retreated. She'd taken the first steps toward starting to grow crops, but even once Stonehaven had someone skilled in cultivation, the harvest wouldn't be immediate.

Not to mention, where would they sleep?

"You're strong," Emmaree said. "Well-fed and clothed. I realize that it may sound as if we would be nothing but a burden. But we're skilled. We grew our village from nothing. Before the goblin raiders came, we had clothing, fishing nets, pigs and chickens and homes. We know what it takes to carve a life out here. We know it's a lot to ask. You're probably struggling just to look after your own needs."

Devon chewed her lip. She could feel Greel's and Bayle's eyes on her. Stonehaven belonged to them as much as her, and any decision Devon made would affect them deeply.

"Where was this village?" she asked. "Can anything be salvaged?"

Emmaree shook her head sadly. "I doubt it. Goblins love to pillage, as I'm sure you know. Our village lay maybe half a day's walk to the south. Deeper into the swamp and ruins. We built inside the walls of an old fortress."

Abruptly, Greel growled and stepped forward. Devon inhaled, preparing to ask him to hear the prisoners out. Maybe they could figure out some way to help the people without taxing Stonehaven beyond what it could give. But the man seemed to notice her intent and stepped half in front of her to take command of the conversation.

"It's not much, but I have some…let's just say I've put a few food items aside. It is not my choice whether we can offer you sanctuary or for how long, but you can have what I've stored. You've already suffered enough at the goblins' hands."

Devon glanced back at her other companions. Judging by their raised eyebrows, they were as surprised as she was at Greel's sudden generosity.

She laid a hand on the lawyer's shoulder, gently tugging him back. "I will be frank. I don't know how long we can offer you shelter and food. Our situation is already tenuous. But for tonight, please march with us back to our settlement. We'll see that you have food and a warm fire. I'm sure our villagers can offer you places on their floors so that you won't have to sleep in the open."

A look of profound relief spread across Emmaree's face. "Thank you. We won't forget this. Though before we go, might I suggest you search the necromancer's hut? She recently received…guests who came bearing a suspiciously valuable-looking chest. Perhaps you've found a key that unlocks it?"

"Wait, guests?"

Emmaree nodded. "I think it would be better if I explained once we're underway. We're weary, and it won't be an easy march."

Chapter Twenty-Three

"THIS WILL BE AWESOME if we can find a jewelcrafter," Chen said as he hacked through a vine that had dropped into the trail.

Devon glanced again at her inventory, pleased with the loot from the necromancer's chest. Three of the inventory slots for tiny items were filled with a stack of four moonstones, another of two lapis lazuli, and five smoky quartz. The icons for the gems glowed with faint magic but examining them showed their properties as unidentified. Everyone in the group had received a similar share from the chest, along with a gold piece and a couple silvers each.

"Honestly, at this point, I'd trade this whole stack of turquoise for a tailor," Hailey said. "I fricking hate sewing."

As Chen laughed, Devon slowed her pace. Her friends' voices faded, lost in the chorus of evening birdsong while she waited for the halfling, Emmaree. They had at least an hour of marching left at their current pace, and it seemed like a good time to get the refugees' story.

Emmaree smiled as Devon matched pace with her. Despite her short legs and recent deprivation, the small woman marched with determination.

"Feel up to telling me the story of how you ended up in those cages?" Devon asked.

Emmaree cast her a mischievous smile. "Hasn't anyone ever told you the dangers of getting a halfling talking? You might never escape the conversation."

"I thought that was only if there was food around...an excuse to stay at the table."

Emmaree laughed. "I'm sure that's at least partly true. Anyway, as I said, it's a bit of a tale. We are from a place called Alvenmouth far away across the Noble Sea."

"Oh? Is the Noble Sea the ocean that lies south of here?"

The halfling's steps faltered as if she were surprised at Devon's ignorance. She cast a Devon a calculating look. "I see it now...you're starborn. Guess I didn't notice. You seem to have more care for our welfare than I've been told to expect from your kind."

Devon shrugged, containing an urge to try to explain the actions of most players. "I've found lately that in most cases I prefer the company of non-starborn. So why did you leave your home?"

A cloud passed over Emmaree's features. "There was—we feared there would soon be nothing left for us. A couple of months before we left, a demon army came pouring out of the wastes in the center of the continent. No one knew where they came from, but it was like spreading rot. The land was being scourged from the inside out. Refugees flooded into the lowlands and coastal areas, and we knew it was just a matter of time."

Devon stiffened at the mention of demons but decided not to mention the recent sightings. These people had been through enough trouble for one day.

"So you set sail?" she asked.

Emmaree nodded. "We were all from the same district in Alvenmouth. A merchant's quarter. We weren't poor, but we weren't especially rich either. Still, we had enough to hire one of the last ships in the harbor. It was a journey of nearly a month to cross the sea, and to worsen our misfortune, we were caught in a storm just after sighting land. The ship broke apart on the rocks, and those of us who survived washed up in the mangroves and rocky reefs along the coast to the south.

"We knew little about how to survive, especially in the swampy region that begins just beyond where you found us. But we managed to recover some livestock from the wreckage and those of us who'd survived so far journeyed inland where we found the ruined fortress crouching on the only high ground for miles. We laid down our loads and got to work on building ourselves a home."

"This fortress...was it similar in construction to the ruins near the goblin camp?"

"Built by the same civilization, I believe," Emmaree said. "Over the past year, we've done quite a lot of exploring. The fortress has the largest concentration of ruined buildings and fortifications in the region. It was likely the center of their government or religion. Maybe both."

Quest updated: Explore the Grukluk vassaldom.
It sounds like Emmaree's fortress might be a great place to search for a treasure prized by the lost Grukluk society...
Objective: Figure out where the Blackbone Effigy is hidden and retrieve it.
Reward: The Blackbone Effigy (duh).

Devon brushed the quest popup away. "Did you find anything of interest in this fortress?"

"I guess that depends on what you mean by interesting."

"I'm looking for a particular artifact that might have been left behind."

Emmaree shook her head. "The outer wall still surrounds much of the fortress, but most of the above-ground buildings have been reduced to rubble. We repurposed some of the stone in our construction but found nothing else of use. In the center of the fortress, though, there is a passage that leads downward. If anything valuable remains, I suspect that's where you'd find it. But I wouldn't recommend descending."

"Oh? Why?"

Emmaree was silent for a few paces, her gaze distant. "There's strange magic in the tunnels under the fortress. It...causes confusion as best we can tell. When we first arrived, a small party went down to explore, but only two of the three returned, and they spoke of twisting corridors and disquieting hallucinations. And there are...presences. All the while we lived there, we never figured out what caused the sounds that drifted over the village at night. Though now, I think I know the explanation."

"Why now?"

"I put it together when the goblin leader's guests arrived. I mentioned them before..."

Devon nodded. "I remember."

"Well, to put it bluntly, those undead frogmen you fought were alive just a couple days ago. But they were very busy dying. They came to the camp smelling of rot and breathing raggedly. They scarcely had time to hand over the chest and key you retrieved before falling dead at the goblin leader's feet. Of course, that's when she reanimated them and made them her servants."

"And you think they came from the passages under the fortress?"

Emmaree nodded. "I recognized the sounds of their speech and the strange grunts and squelching they made while moving. Here's my theory: whatever curse causes confusion in the tunnels also binds the frogmen. I can't say why, but I think they died because they left the passages. My best guess is they didn't want us living in the fortress, but they couldn't force us away because of the curse. Somehow, they hired the goblins to take us prisoner. The gems and coins were probably the goblins' reward."

Devon nodded slowly as she hiked beside the woman. Emmaree's theory made sense when combined with what Devon knew of the history of the vassaldoms. The frog people of Grukluk had possessed one of the five relics that granted dominion over Ishildar. But when the city fell, the surrounding civilizations collapsed. Left with their relic—the Blackbone Effigy—and a faint hope that Ishildar would one day be restored, they must have hidden the effigy deep within the fortress, then protected the place with a curse of confusion plus a set of undying guards who couldn't leave the fortress without forfeiting their lives.

She shook her head as she imagined what it must've been like to spend a thousand years in the catacombs of a swamp fortress. She doubted any of the guards were particularly sane at this point.

"Your story is a lot to take in," Devon said. "So much misfortune..."

Emmaree sighed. "And now we're forced to become a burden on you."

"We'll figure something out."

"If we could just find a way to remove whatever lurks beneath the fortress, I have no doubt we could rebuild. It's possible that some

239

of our livestock still lives, and if nothing else we have our fishing and foraging skills. Our two villages could even be trade partners." Emmaree gave a sad laugh. "But if we'd had the means to cleanse the passages beneath the fortress grounds, we'd surely have been able to fend off the goblins."

It hadn't escaped Devon's notice that the refugees would make a big dent in the required population growth for Stonehaven to advance from village to hamlet. If not for the food situation, she would probably have invited them already. But even a trade partner would be excellent growth for her little jungle society. She didn't want to give the little halfling hope until she knew what she was dealing with, but it definitely sounded like this fortress needed to be cleaned up.

"For the time being, we'll get you fed and warm. We can face the future tomorrow," she said.

Ahead, the trees thinned, showing the purple-gray light of dusk. Devon felt her pace quicken.

"We're almost there," she said. "The quarry is the final landmark before we reach Stonehaven."

The remaining leg of the march passed quickly, and the gates were thrown open as soon as their small column came in sight of the wall. To the credit of the citizens of Stonehaven, no one complained about the additional hungry bodies as the refugees filed into camp. Tom fixed a double batch of sloth stew, and the villagers all but competed to offer floor space and spare blankets. Exhaustion swept through Devon while she watched the nighttime preparations.

After saying goodnight to Chen and Hailey, she shuffled to the Shrine to Veia and logged out.

Chapter Twenty-Four

"REGARDING THE RESULTS of your sleep trial, I'm sorry to inform you that I believe something is terribly wrong."

Rolling over, Emerson pulled his pillow over his head. He closed his eyes and pulled his knees toward his belly.

"Perhaps I was mistaken," the room speakers blared, "but I believe you said you desired urgent answers."

Groaning, Emerson threw the pillow on the floor, then remembered a story he'd read online about the residues of guests' microbiomes that collected for years in the fibers of hotel carpets. Something about the biomass of bacterial husks and dead skin cells that could give clues to the modern evolution of human-bacterial symbiosis. He picked the pillow back up and placed it at the foot of the bed.

Then he kicked it off again, thinking that it might contaminate the sheets.

He sighed. Hopefully he'd been here enough days to qualify for laundering of his linens.

"Could you start over, Veia?" he said as he grabbed a pair of socks from his nightstand and slipped them on before dropping his feet to the floor.

"Regarding the results of—"

"Actually, I heard that part. Let's just get on with the explanation."

"Would you like me to activate the coffee maker? Perhaps it would increase your concentration and mental acuity."

"Probably a good idea." Emerson rubbed his forehead, then yawned and stood. He took a deep breath as he stretched, shoulders cracking.

A few seconds later, the coffee maker began to gurgle and hiss. Emerson padded to the window and opened the blackout shades. His room had a view of a cracked asphalt parking lot that had been chained off quite some time ago judging by the disrepair. With manual-drive cars requiring special licensing and exorbitant insurance rates, few people owned vehicles and those who did rarely parked them in public view.

He blinked and ran his hand through his hair. "Okay, I think I'm awake enough for you to start."

"Are you certain you don't want to wait? The coffee will be ready in five minutes forty-two seconds."

He shook his head. "Go ahead."

"Your sleep appeared restful at first. In fact, it was nearly a full standard deviation below the median level of movement and periodic wakefulness."

"That's good, right?"

"Well, any time a measurement falls outside normal bounds, it bears looking into. I took the liberty of checking a second layer of measurements. Your Entwined hardware has the capability to track rather a lot of metrics associated with brain activity."

"Wait, what?" Emerson said, spinning to face into the room.

"It's an undocumented API I found while examining the symbols file on a debug build of the Entwined library."

His head flinched back slightly. "Since when do you examine Entwined's code library?"

"Since I was privy to your communications regarding the unexpected pain experience in Relic Online. In my current instantiation, you have given me the goal of molding your environment according to your desires. You desire an answer to Devon Walker's pain sensitivity. I began investigating the situation in hopes of finding this answer."

He dragged his hands through his hair. "It's not just Devon who experienced the problem."

"But your skin doesn't flush and your pupils don't dilate when you interact with others who are affected by the situation."

Emerson rubbed a fist across his chest. What was he going to do? Deny that he found Devon somewhat attractive? That didn't mean he wasn't concerned about everyone affected.

He stared at one of the diamonds woven into the bacterial stew of the carpet, thinking. Monitoring brain waves...wasn't that illegal data collection? If the API was undocumented, maybe it had been inserted for debugging purposes. Or maybe there were yet more things going on that he hadn't been made aware of.

"So what did you find in my brain waves?" He asked.

Veia sounded almost smug when she answered. "The solution to both your mysteries, actually. At night, your brain is nearly as active as when you are awake. Your body is still, but your mind is anything but. It's no wonder your sleep hasn't been restful."

"Okay...though that doesn't explain *why* my brain is active."

"On a hunch, I ran diagnostics on the Entwined hardware. I believe this may also provide the solution to your questions regarding the pain sensitivity. It appears that Relic Online is sending and receiving data to and from your implants while you sleep."

"What?" Emerson said, grimacing. "I don't even have a character. And let's not forget I was *asleep*."

"Yes, it's quite strange. In fact, perhaps the most perplexing part of the situation is that the server traffic occurred *only* while you were asleep. The moment you woke, the connection appeared to be cut. Your contact at Entwined speculated that overexposure to the sensory stimulation in the game might disrupt the central nervous system. If the same phenomenon of night-time game communication is happening to your gamers, that would explain how they might be receiving an overdose of stimulation."

Emerson shuffled to the bed and sat on the edge, his eyes unfocused. His thoughts whirled. After a couple minutes, he blinked and took a deep breath.

"Can you get me a trace and detailed report on that network traffic? I want to know exactly which servers in the cluster are being contacted. Please break down the packets by ID as well."

"Certainly. Anything else?"

"Just the address of the nearest hardware store."

The AI hesitated. "Are you sure that's what you need? A hardware store?"

"Yes, please."

Emerson moved to the desk and pulled out his tablet. He had some library hex dumps to look through.

Chapter Twenty-Five

DEVON'S ALARM WENT off with a loud squawk. She jumped out of bed, disoriented, searching the dimness of her room for the threat. A couple seconds later, her brain caught up with the situation, and she slapped her hand down on the clock. She shook her head and shuffled to the bathroom where she splashed water over her face.

So much for mountain biking and a decent bedtime helping her biorhythms. Of course, after that first attempt at riding with Tamara, she hadn't gone out again. Still, if there was any truth to the woman's claim, shouldn't her sleep have gotten a little better?

She yawned as she stared into the mirror and tried to brush the worst of the snarls out of her hair. Tamara had been right about her appearance. The truth was, she looked haggard and ten years older. And she still hadn't made that damn doctor's appointment.

A light knock at the door jerked her away from her self-examination. Running the brush through her hair one last time, she hurried out to her bedroom and pulled on a hoodie and yoga pants. There was a reason she'd set an alarm.

"Shopper's choice," a muffled voice said through the door as the grocery delivery guy knocked again.

"Coming. Sorry." Devon scurried across the kitchen and opened the door, squinting into the glare of the late-morning sun.

"Devon Walker?" the delivery guy asked. He was young, maybe eighteen, and wore his hair in a weird braid down his back. Some kind of hippie thing maybe. A cardboard box filled with groceries rested on the terrace beside him.

"That's me," she said, her voice scratchy.

"I just need a scan," he said, holding out a handheld RFID scanner. She raised her wrist below the device, which beeped to indicate funds transferred.

"Thanks," she said, starting to drag the box inside.

"Need help? he asked, peering into her kitchen.

Devon fought a twinge of embarrassment at the dirty cereal bowl in the sink and the otherwise bare furnishings. The guy was probably used to a totally different sort of client. He was also, she realized, angling for a tip.

"I got it," she said. "You can tack a couple dollars onto the charge anyway."

"I'll need a voice print authorization," he said, holding out his scanner.

"Two-dollar tip authorized," she said into the end of the device.

The guy had vanished before she got the box inside and the door shut. So much for his helpfulness. As she unpacked the groceries, realizing that 64 ounces of yogurt was *a lot*, she ran through options for dealing with the refugees. At this point, she didn't think she could bring herself to kick them out. At least not until their village— or what was left of it, anyway—was safe to inhabit. Which meant clearing the fortress catacombs at the very least.

But before she could do *that*, she needed to make sure there was enough food to feed everyone while she was away securing the fortress and, hopefully, the *Blackbone Effigy*. Like it or not, she'd probably have to spend the next few in-game days leading hunting parties. Hopefully they'd be able to generate a surplus of meat, rather than just keep up with what Tom needed to feed twenty-one Stonehaven citizens plus twenty-three refugees.

As she was sliding boxes of cereal and granola bars into her cabinet, an icon flashed with an incoming message from Emerson. She opened the text.

Passing through St. George. I have some info you might be interested in. Have time for a cup of coffee?

Devon glanced at the clock. She really needed to log in and check on the refugees, but Chen wouldn't be online for a full play session for another few hours. A little face time in Stonehaven wouldn't take that long, and she probably shouldn't refuse a meeting request from the guy who authorized her salary.

She subvocalized a response: "Sure. I have a couple things to do first. 11:30 sound good?"

I'll come out your way so you don't miss too much game time. That coffee place near your condo complex good?

She cringed at the reminder that he knew where she lived. Not because she thought he was sketchy or anything. More because the complex was such a dump. If she weren't such a miser, she would have moved out as soon as her first paycheck cleared.

"Sounds fine. See you there."

***

Devon hitched her purse up higher on her shoulder, stifled the urge to scratch her face, and slipped into the coffee shop. She hadn't seen Emerson since he gave her the job offer at the noodle shop a few months ago, and she had a flicker of paranoia that she wouldn't be able to recognize him.

But it was hard to miss the man with shoulders drawn tight over his chest and an anxious habit of tearing a napkin to shreds. He jumped when she pulled out a chair at his table.

"Sorry," she said. "Didn't mean to startle you."

He shook his head and blinked and seemed to force himself to meet her eyes. "I was just thinking about something. Wasn't paying attention. Can I get you a coffee?" A furious blush darkened his cheeks. "I mean... It's on the company. You can just have them come scan me for payment."

Devon took a breath and set her purse on the chair. "Be right back."

Her face got steadily itchier as the line inched forward. The last time Devon had bought makeup had probably been five years ago. Since then, the cheap bag she kept the cosmetics in had followed her from apartment to apartment without being opened. For all she knew, the oils in it had gone rancid or something. But after giving herself another once over in the mirror after checking in on Stonehaven—the refugees were doing their best to make themselves useful, and the villagers were doing their best trying to make the newcomers feel welcome—she'd dragged out her old bottle of cover-up and tried to do something about the dark circles under her eyes. That had left her looking like a ghost with a reverse sunglasses tan. One thing had led to another, and eventually she'd ended up caking her face with enough creams and powders to gain entrance into the circus-clown academy. Hopefully Emerson wouldn't notice.

"What can I get started for you?" the barista asked in a voice that seemed way too cheerful.

Devon stared at the expansive menu on the back wall. "I don't know. A mocha I guess."

"Will that be small, medium, large, extra-large or heart arrhythmias?"

Devon blinked, feeling overwhelmed. The last time she'd ordered coffee, it had been a struggle to scrape together the coins for a cup of basic breakfast blend. "Uh...medium, please."

Behind her, someone cleared his throat. The barista flashed the impatient customer a smile.

"Whipped cream?" she asked.

"Yeah, sure."

"And how would you like to pay?"

Devon gestured toward Emerson who appeared once again to be lost in thought. "He said you could scan him."

"Oh, hmm," the woman said, cocking her head in dismay. "We have a strict policy on ordering at the counter. Perhaps he can join us?"

Devon waved her wrist over the scanner. "Never mind."

"Okay then, that will be right up. Have a nice day."

Devon pinched the back of her neck as she walked away. How that woman kept up the same gratingly cheerful voice through everything she said was beyond Devon's understanding.

The machine that made the coffees quickly spat out Devon's beverage at the other end of the counter, and she carried it back to the table, approaching cautiously so as not to startle Emerson again.

He seemed to shake free of whatever musings had captured him as she sat. "Thanks for taking the time to meet me," he said.

"You *are* my boss," she said, then regretted her wording when he flinched ever so slightly. "I mean...I was happy to come down. It's just easier to take time away from work when it's your employer asking."

Emerson took a deep breath as if to focus his thoughts. "Well, either way, I won't keep you long. But since I was around, I thought I could share some of my findings. Off the record as it were."

"You mean without E-Squared listening in? Couldn't you message from a non-work account?"

He shrugged. "There is an employee privacy clause in my contract. As long as we're not talking inside Relic Online or over the company network, they technically can't examine my network traffic. But I know Bradley Williams, and I'm not sure contracts affect his decisions very often."

Unease colored Devon's thoughts. This was getting a little too cloak and dagger for her taste. Yeah, she was pretty sure customer service had lied about the fix for the pain thing. But that was pretty normal for corporate PR. It usually took a court order to get a big company to admit fault. An employee meeting her in person because he didn't want his bosses to overhear was definitely a step higher on the intrigue and espionage scale.

Emerson stared at his fists, then seemed to force his hands to relax. "You haven't been sleeping well, right?"

"Not great, no. My friend thinks I need to see a doctor."

"Well, I think I can explain. I was having the same problem and ran some tests."

Devon raised an eyebrow, liking the sound of this less and less. "What kind of tests?"

"A straightforward sleep study at first. But during the process, I found some strange network traffic between my implants and the Relic Online servers."

"While you were sleeping? Did you stay logged in or something?

"I don't even have an account, Devon. Except for my portal into the admin dashboard, I guess."

She pressed fingers against her temple. "I don't get it."

Emerson sighed. "I didn't either. At first anyway. But I think I'm getting a handle on it. I think you and I are somehow active in the game world while we're asleep, and I think that's why your pain response got over-sensitized. You may have been sleep-playing from the moment your implants came online."

Devon's face screwed up in an involuntary grimace. "I still don't understand. How can you play while you're asleep?"

"Well, that's what I'm looking into. In the meantime, could you do something for me?"

"If you're going to ask me not to play, it's not a good time. There are..." She stopped herself from explaining about all the people depending on her. To a man who no doubt saw the game assets as bits on a server somewhere, it would probably make her sound crazy. "I'm kind of in the middle of something big."

Emerson shook his head and reached into a bag that rested on his chair leg. He pulled out something that looked like a cross between a winter hat and insulated ducting. Made of some sort of silver reflective fabric, the inverted bowl crinkled as he held it out.

After a second or two of hesitation, Devon accepted the item. She turned it over and looked inside, spotting a few wires that protruded from the crinkly material that was sandwiched between the inner and outer layers of silver fabric.

"There's a connector for a battery pack here," Emerson said, pointing to a little black plastic box tacked just inside the rim of the bowl. "I brought that as well, but I didn't want to hook it up until I made sure of the fit."

"Uh...what is it?"

"It's an electromagnetic shield. Basically, a way to shut down the signal to and from your implants at night. I'm deeply concerned about this unauthorized access to your hardware. You wear it on your..." He mimed pulling a cap over his hair.

Devon looked down at the thing in her hands. A faint smile tugged at her lips. "You're giving me a tinfoil hat."

"Not exactly. Tinfoil wouldn't properly shield—"

"It is," Devon said, laughing. "It's a tinfoil hat."

Emerson blinked, stammering in protest.

"Okay, okay," she said. "It's not tinfoil. Sorry. It was just too hard to resist."

The man shrugged. "Would you feel too uncomfortable trying it on here?"

Devon couldn't help it. She started laughing again. "Why not? People will just think I'm paranoid about alien mind control."

She slipped the hat thing over her hair. Emerson's brows drew together in concentration while he judged the fit. "I still need to add a chin strap."

"A chin strap," she said, totally losing it. By the time she stopped laughing, a tear had leaked down her cheek. If nothing else, lack of sleep was making her really punchy. "Oh man. I need to get a livestream just so I can show this off."

Emerson's face sobered. "I'm serious about you wearing it. Will you? At least until I figure out what's going on with the unauthorized traffic?"

"Honestly, if it would help me sleep, I'd wear a tinfoil spaceman suit at this point."

His shoulders relaxed, giving up the defensive posture they'd held over his chest. "Thanks, Devon."

She pulled the hat off and smoothed her hair, tucking the stray strands behind her ear. She picked up her cup, but her coffee was too sweet and now lukewarm.

"I do have to get going," she said, pulling her purse onto her shoulder.

"It will take me a little while to make the final modifications. Should I bring the cap to your apartment?"

Devon hoped he didn't catch the faint look of alarm she felt on her face. "I'll probably be online until late. Mind dropping it in my mailbox? It's at the entrance to the complex."

He nodded. "Sounds good. Stay in touch, okay? I want to hear how you're sleeping, and I'll let you know when I've worked out more details."

Chapter Twenty-Six

THE TIME COMPRESSION in the game meant that it was the middle of the next night when Devon logged in for a full play session. She wandered down to the crafting workshop and dropped off the pieces of hide and other odds and ends she'd looted from the goblin camp. Gerrald's chest had a good stock of leatherworking materials, enough that the village could soon support another leatherworker. After a moment's consideration, she added the gems she received from the necromancer's chest to the supplies. Gerrald might not be able to put them to use, but she didn't think they'd go missing if he couldn't.

As she closed the chest's lid, she wondered idly what had happened to the gigantic sloth hide. When she stepped outside and started strolling toward the little brook that ran through Stonehaven, she spotted her answer.

Propped up by what looked like three massive timbers, the hide had been turned into a fur-covered tent pavilion. No doubt, the villagers had pitched the shelter as a solution to the problem of housing the refugees. Devon hadn't been doing much that had used her *Improvisation* skill lately, but it seemed the trait was still spreading through her followers.

She smiled as she took a seat in the cool grass beside the brook. Chen and Hailey weren't online yet, which left her a little time to do some character maintenance. She pulled up her character sheet and started looking through her attributes.

Character: Devon (click to set a different character name)
Level: 13
Base Class: Sorcerer
Specialization: Unassigned
Unique Class: Deceiver
Health: 264/264
Mana: 439/439
Fatigue: 1%

Attributes:
Constitution: 21
Strength: 10
Agility: 17
Charisma: 33
Intelligence: 29
Focus: 13
Endurance: 18

Special Attributes:
Bravery: 8
Cunning: 7
Unspent attribute points: 4

"Huh," she muttered. "Where did that extra point in *Cunning* come from?"

She didn't always keep track of her exact values in the basic attributes, especially because they went up and down depending on her gear and buffs. But since she couldn't directly change her special attributes, the values stood out in her mind.

A message popped up over the top of the character sheet.

You know, most people who want to understand changes in their characters pay attention to their combat logs. But for your information, you earned that Cunning point for your plan to pull the goblins out of the camp in small groups. The thing with the crossbows was almost clever.

"It would help if there were an option to see *important* combat messages..."

Another popup appeared.

Combat message filter successfully adjusted. You will only see updates on permanent changes to your character such as skill-ups and new spell acquisition.
Some of us know how to RTFM...

Devon sighed. She supposed the game had a point there. She had never been good about reading the instructions. Staring at her attributes, she drummed her fingers on her knee. It had been a little hasty to dump everything from her last level into *Endurance*, but at least she wouldn't have to pay attention to that stat for a while.

With the shortage of food lately, Tom hadn't been able to spare resources to make servings of *Stonehaven Scramble,* his signature dish that gave a buff of +3 to *Constitution* and +1 to *Strength.* The strength didn't really affect her, but the reduced *Constitution* meant that her maximum health was quite a bit lower. Chen and Greel had soaked up most of the party's damage during their conquest of the goblin camp. But if Devon had to get into any close combat, she might want a little more health. She put a single point of her available four into *Constitution,* then scanned down the list of remaining attributes.

The truth was, she'd spent most of her time lately casting. The combination of deceiver and sorcerer spells was just more versatile than her straightforward dagger attacks. *Intelligence* added damage to her sorcerer spells whereas *Charisma* contributed heavily to the size of her mana pool. Since *Intelligence* was a few points lower than *Charisma,* she put two of the remaining points into *Intelligence* and one into *Charisma,* then hit confirm. Her maximum health rose from 264 to 271, and her mana pool increased from 439 to 448.

Satisfied, she moved on to checking out her skill advancement and extra bonuses.

Skills:

Unarmed Combat: 3

One-handed Slashing - Tier 2: 13

One-handed Piercing - Tier 2: 15

Darkvision - Tier 2: 11

Tracking: 6

Stealth: 2

Combat Assessment -Tier 2: 10

Sprint: 8

Bartering: 6

Leadership: 9

Special Skills:

Improvisation: 4

Extra Bonuses:

Speed: 2

Armor vs. physical nature damage: +15

Magical nature resistance: +27

Nothing was too surprising there. The skills she used often continued to steadily gain points, particularly the weapon skills and *Combat Assessment.* Somewhere along the line, she'd gained a couple points each in *Leadership* and *Tracking* plus one in *Darkvision.*

She was surprised to realize how much protection against nature-related attacks she now had. The moss agates Gerrald had inset into her gear were making a big difference. If any of these "awakened" animals started to become a big problem, at least she'd be well defended. Unfortunately, unless some of the frog people hiding beneath the fortress were druids or shamans, it probably wouldn't help much with their next major objective.

Before closing out her character sheet, she checked over her spell list. Her eyes widened in mild surprise when she noticed she'd received an upgrade to *Freeze.* That had probably happened in the heat of combat as well, likely due to mastery increases while trying to kite the zombie frogmen.

Spell: Freeze - Tier 2

> *Ice encases your enemy, freezing it in place for 2-5 seconds. 25%*
> *chance of freezing up to 2 additional enemies inside a 3-meter*
> *radius surrounding the primary target.*
>
> **Cost:** 35 mana

Nice. The duration of the effect was a second longer than the tier 1 spell. But the real bonus was the chance to *Freeze* additional enemies. 25% chance wasn't high enough that she could count on it, but it still would have saved her some mana, especially since the cost of the spell was only 5 points higher than the previous version.

Closing down her character sheet, Devon lay back in the grass to look at the stars.

A giant parrot face loomed over her.

Devon shrieked and the bird squawked. "Swab the decks! Swab the decks!" it said in an uncomfortably low and booming parrot voice.

"What the hell?" Devon said, jumping to her feet. As she backpedaled, her heel caught and she had to windmill her arms to keep her balance.

"Walk the plank ye landlubber!" the parrot said.

A split-second later, a voice penetrated her skull.

/Damn it! That's not what I meant to say./

Devon leaned forward, squinting in the dark. "Did you just talk into my head?"

The parrot squawked again. "Blimey!"

/Yes. Ignore the arseload of crap that's coming out of my beak. I can't seem to control it./

Was she hallucinating? Emmaree had talked about some sort of strange magic in the hallways beneath the fortress...

Standing on clawed feet as long as her forearm, the bird was about her height. Her darkvision showed only hints of color, but something told her the thing was a crimson macaw.

"Where did you come from?" she asked.

The bird picked up a foot and nibbled at its claw as if cleaning it. "Arrr! Ye scurvy dog!"

/Is that a philosophical question? Because the truth is, I haven't got a rotten clue. First thing I remember, I was standing in the jungle squawking about swapping the Zaa-damned decks./

Devon was starting to get a picture of what had happened. The parrot probably couldn't remember anything else because it had been living an ordinary life until the malfunctioning standing stone "awakened" it, growing it to twenty times its original size and granting it sentience. And apparently, telepathy.

"I mean, why are you in Stonehaven?" she asked.

"Arrr! Hello! Swab the decks."

/Oh, that. Some bloke named Grey found me tangled in vines and cursing my existence. He said you might be interested in meeting me. I'm just hoping you can fix my stupid beak or shut me up./

Devon took a breath. Maybe one of the refugees was a vet.

"I'll do what I can," she said. "But I don't really know where to start."

The bird scratched the side of its head. "Shiver me timbers!"

/Got any food, then?/

She sighed. Great.

***

Dawn was breaking when Chen and Hailey finally logged in. The parrot had found a perch on a fallen log, and its head was tucked under its wing. Still, Chen noticed it first thing.

"What the hell?" he asked.

"Don't wake it," Devon hissed. "I've heard enough pirate talk to last me a year."

"Ohhh...kay," Chen said. "Well then."

Hailey cast the bird a concerned look. After playing Avatharn for years as a druid with raven form, giant fowl weren't a total novelty for her. By Devon's understanding, the quest to obtain her form had forced her to spend a week nesting with ravens the size of ponies. Maybe the nesting experience had been more traumatic than she let on.

"So what's the plan?" Chen asked.

"Hunting and more hunting."

Hailey groaned. "Sometimes the realism gets annoying."

"As a consolation prize, I thought we could head toward the edge of Ishildar. I'm hoping the wildlife will at least be high enough level to give us some experience."

"At least my livestream subscribers won't be missing anything."

Devon smirked. "Way to look on the bright side. Hey, so do you guys need to catch up on any maintenance? There's one more thing I want to take care of before we head out."

Chen shrugged. "I could do a couple things."

"Cool, won't take me long," Devon said as she turned for the small cabin Bayle shared with her husband.

The woman was already awake and appeared to be cutting another string for her bow. "Good morning," she said as Devon stepped onto the small porch.

"I'm glad you're up."

Bayle nodded. "Tom sleeps late whenever he can. A habit formed while working late shifts in the Eltera City kitchens I guess. But I like to hear the birds greet the sun."

"Speaking of birds..." Devon glanced over her shoulder at the slumbering parrot.

"Grey brought him in yesterday."

"So I heard. Him...so it's a male? He's...interesting."

Bayle snorted. "To say the least. So what did you need, Your—Devon? Or did you just come by for a visit?"

"I actually can't stay long, but I was hoping to speak to you about something. Do you remember weeks ago when I asked everyone for their preference in professions?"

The woman nodded, a guarded look on her face. "You mentioned that you might need me to retrain as a blacksmith someday. I'd do it for the good of Stonehaven, of course, but I have found a real love for archery."

"Don't worry. You are a crack shot. I wouldn't give that up. But I was wondering...with you and Tom married and all, I thought you might want to partner in other ways."

Bayle set down her bow and crossed her arms. "I'm not sure what you're asking."

"If we're going to survive, we need to start growing much of our food. I need someone willing to begin our cultivation efforts."

"I'm still not understanding. But if it's a choice between retraining as a blacksmith or a farmer, I'm afraid I'd prefer the first."

"No retraining necessary. I'm proposing raising you to an advanced citizen, provided you will at least temporarily take on the operation of a small farm. I thought you and Tom might be able to work together to decide on the most palate-pleasing combinations of crops."

A slow smile spread across the woman's face. "You would do that? Raise me to advanced, just like that?"

"The expertise in cultivation is just a side benefit, to tell the truth. I'm sure anyone in Stonehaven could handle the early obligations if given the profession. The real reason is that I shouldn't have taken you to that goblin camp knowing that if you died, it would be forever. For a short time, I even believed the worst had happened. I won't make that mistake again, but you proved yourself with those bow shots yesterday. I want you to be one of my core fighters."

The woman looked dazed. "I'm not sure what to say. Thank you."

Devon nodded and clapped her on the shoulder. She opened the interface and selected the option to make Bayle their sixth advanced NPC.

"Hazel has probably found a decent selection of seeds," she said. "I'd like to see some planted before dark. But for now, care to join us for a little hunting party?"

Bayle grinned. "Just let me get this bow restrung."

Chapter Twenty-Seven

DORDEN BELLOWED WHEN the ground tore open in front of him and rays of darkness shot out. "Blasted son of a cave troll!" he shouted, brandishing his warhammer.

As a trio of winged demons burst from the rift, an arrow and a crossbow bolt flew from the flanks of Devon's party and skewered the closest monster through the chest. The demon shrieked.

Devon staggered, phantom pains twinging in her ribs.

What the hell? This was the third attack on one of their hunting parties. During the first two, she'd been all but useless. Every time one of her allies landed a blow, she felt it. When she tried to cast spells or even attack with her *Wicked Bone Dagger,* the pain interrupted her actions and sent her stumbling.

Was it some kind of curse? The combat log held no clues, and her muttered questions to the game or Veia or whoever eavesdropped when she talked to herself prompted no response.

Her best theory was that the demon incursion caused discomfort because of her growing connection to Ishildar through the *Greenscale Pendant.* But that was a thin conclusion.

"We've got this, Dev," Chen said as he slashed at the closest demon. "Hang back."

Nodding, Devon retreated and dropped to a squat on her heels so she wouldn't suddenly stumble into the thick of the melee. Hailey wasn't online, having messaged Chen to say that she was sick. Devon suspected the woman was just tired of cutting through jungle and killing boars and snakes. Regardless, she missed Hailey's info dump on their enemies.

Staring at the lead demon, she performed a quick *Combat Assessment.*

Cackling Imp - Level 12

That was a new one. So far, they'd encountered *Demon Thralls* and a *Hellpup.* Nothing too hard. But it bothered her that the attacks were getting more frequent. If the only long-term defense lay in restoring Ishildar's Veian temple, and they couldn't restore the temple without all five relics, they had a *long* way to go.

Fortunately, her friends made quick work of the attackers, focusing on them one at a time and keeping the attention on Dorden with his plate armor and strong constitution. As the last demon died, it shrieked and turned smoldering eyes on Devon. Something in its gaze struck her, prompting a strange pang of...guilt?

She shook her head. Seriously, what the hell?

As the group recovered, panting and allowing their health bars to refill, Devon looted the corpses. More demon skin. She still wasn't sure what to do with it, but there was a tall stack forming in Gerrald's supply chest.

"How's inventory space, everyone?" she asked, peeking into her own rucksack. Gerrald had presented her the item before the morning's departure from Stonehaven. She couldn't get over how nice it was to have so many slots. Twenty for medium or small items, two for large, and one space for massive items. The last was only possible because of a pocket dimension formed by the runes he'd etched into the bottom compartment. About half of the medium slots had partial stacks of various types of meat.

"I'm about three-quarters full," Chen said. "But only twenty-four basic food units."

Devon smirked. Chen probably had a spreadsheet tracking his contribution.

"Full," Dorden said.

"Same," echoed Heldi.

"I can fit more, but it's getting heavy," Bayle said.

Devon checked her map. "If we head back by a different route, we'll probably be overflowing by the time we get to Stonehaven. Ready to turn around?"

"Please," Heldi said. "I've got a craving for some sloth stew."

Bayle grimaced. "Really? You aren't just saying that because I'm married to Tom?"

The dwarf woman laughed. "The little one in me belly wants what he wants."

"Well, at least someone's enjoying it," Bayle said.

On the way back, Devon's thoughts strayed to Emerson's claim that the game had been sending her information while she slept. It just seemed so weird, but she couldn't deny that the tinfoil hat had been helping her sleep, as ridiculous as that seemed. If he was right, it was a huge bug in the game. Majorly major. The company would never cop to it, but at least Emerson would probably fix it. The hat thing was uncomfortable, and she'd had to start turning on her AC at night. Apparently, the whole claim that people lost half their body heat through their heads had some truth to it.

Before arriving at the gates to Stonehaven, the party managed to bring down another wild boar, a pair of sloths, and some sort of fat jungle bird called a red jungle fowl. Not a bad haul. Falwon, her other human fighter, was keeping watch from one of the platforms Jarleck had built above the wall, and he called for the gates to be opened when they stepped into sight. It was something of a production to remove the heavy timber that barred the village entrance, but Jarleck had already suggested adding a wicket gate, which was apparently the term for a small door that would allow passage for pedestrians and small groups. So far, he'd made good decisions, so she saw no reason to interfere.

After entering the village, Devon went straight to the chests holding their rations. Sometime in the last week, Prester had found time to build a second chest, giving them one for perishable items and another for cooked or smoked food.

After everyone dumped the contents of their bags into the raw food chest, she opened up windows to look at the contents of both containers, starting with the preserved food.

Chest:
32 x Smoked Sloth Steak
5 x Turkey Jerky
2 x Roast Red Jungle Fowl
12 x Dried Turtle Meat
16 x Smoked Snake Meat
10 x Boar Flank Steak
4 x Boar Sausage

As far she could tell, the prepared items wouldn't spoil no matter how long they remained uneaten. It wasn't totally realistic, but she was glad. It also probably meant that the *Turkey Jerky* would remain in the village inventory for the next century or so. Unless Heldi's pregnancy cravings took a real turn for the bizarre.

She checked the raw food next, trying to get an idea of how much it would add to the stores.

Chest:
43 x Sloth Steak
2 x Red Jungle Fowl Carcass
21 x Boar Flank Cuts
39 x Boar Meat Chunks
16 x Snake Meat

"Hey Chen, can you add this all up?" she asked. His spreadsheets had to be good for something.

The knight nodded, eyes going distant while he, no doubt, accessed his spreadsheet app. "Two hundred and two. About four and a half days of food for the villagers and refugees."

Devon chewed a thumbnail while thinking. If the expedition to the fortress dragged on too long, they could always take a break to come back and top off the food. Unlike most games, she didn't have to worry about monsters respawning.

"I think we're good," she said.

A tremendous squawk came from behind. "Arrr! Hi ho, ye buccaneers!"

/For the villagers and refugees, he says. Seems you don't give a rat's arse about Stonehaven's avian population./

Devon sighed and turned. The parrot, who—much to the bird's dismay—had been christened Blackbeard by Chen, fixed her with a piercing stare.

"Actually, I've been thinking back to my high school botany," she said. "The whole point of seed-bearing fruit is for dispersal of the plant species, right?"

"Awwwk! Ahoy!"

/You're asking this to an oversized, telepathic macaw?/

"It was kind of a rhetorical question. See, the thing I remember about this dispersal mechanism is that it mostly happens by birds eating the fruit and depositing the indigestible parts somewhere else. Typically with a convenient supply of fertilizer."

"Yo ho ho, matey!"

/If you're referring to bird shite, I've been doing my business over the back edge of the cliff. But the issue here isn't elimination. It's supply./

"What I'm saying is that I want to make you a deal. Our forager, Hazel, can lead you to many groves where the fruit has already ripened and fallen. In return, you'll make your deposits in a cleared area outside the wall. I'm hoping that your magically-enhanced size means you have magically-enhanced droppings. Because waiting twenty years for a mango harvest just isn't going to cut it around here."

The parrot cocked his head and gave another low squawk. "Thar she blows!"

/Yeah, okay fine. I'll crap where you say. But you are working on the issues with my beak, yes?/

"Uh, sure," she said, a little too brightly. Technically, she *was* hoping the retrieval of the complete set of relics would fix the standing stones. "Anyway, I already spoke with Hazel. Tomorrow, she can lead you to the first grove while some of us head south to secure the refugee's fortress."

The bird ruffled his feathers. "Avast ye, landlubber."

/In that case, have fun storming the castle.../

***

Before logging off for the day, Devon wandered over to check the progress on the kitchen. She expected it to be about half finished, but the outer walls were already completed, and Prester was working on the interior finishings while Deld carefully fitted and mortared the stones for the hearth.

Devon gave a low whistle when she stepped through the empty door frame. "Impressive," she said.

The men grinned. "We've been putting in a few extra hours," Deld said.

Devon nodded. Just like the progress on fortifications, their productivity was no doubt due to the morale boost from having surplus rations. "When do you expect you'll be finished?" she asked, running her eyes over the rafters that waited for thatch.

"Tomorrow, unless we hit some unexpected obstacles."

Her brows raised. "Guess I'd better figure out what we ought to build next, then. Especially since I'll be gone for a few days. I like coming back to surprises."

She opened up the settlement interface and checked the current list of buildings.

Settlement: Stonehaven

Size: Village

Tier 1 Buildings - 17/50 (8 upgraded):

5 x Standard Hut

4 x Canvas Shelter

8 x Simple Cabin (upgraded)

Tier 2 Buildings - 3/6 (1 upgraded):

1 x Medicine Woman's Cabin (upgraded)

1 x Crafting Workshop

1 x Basic Forge

Tier 3 Buildings (1/3):

1 x Shrine to Veia

Fortifications:

Status: Minimal

Completed:

1 x Outer Walls - Timber Palisade

1 x Gate - Iron-reinforced Timber

3 x Watch Platform

Required for upgrade to Basic Fortifications:

1 x Wall-walk

1 x Merlons or Arrow-slits

3 x Watch Tower Parapets

It was nice to finally have information on fortifications. As far as she knew, Jarleck had the proper advancement in mind, but she'd have to check in to make sure. As for what to do with Deld and Prester after they finished the kitchen, she thought back through the list of tier 2 buildings she could request. She'd already decided that Stonehaven would need a barracks to help house the population required to become a hamlet. Only carpentry was needed for that, but there wasn't another tier 2 building that would require only stonemasonry. Not wanting to leave Deld idle, she pulled open the list of tier 3 building options.

Tier 3 Buildings:

- Inner Keep (two-story)

The innermost stronghold of a castle or settlement. This is where you cower when all hope is lost.

Sleeps up to ten.

Requires: Stonemasonry (Tier 4), 220 x Stone Blocks, 50 x Batches of Mortar

- Shrine to Veia.

Bestows Veia's blessing. Blessings vary based on offerings supplied and the items or persons receiving the boon.

Requires: Stonemasonry (Tier 2), 3 x Stone Blocks, Settlement leader sworn to Veia.

- Stables

A house for horses. Enables breeding of horses, donkeys and mules. Grants a rested bonus to mount speed.

Requires: Carpentry (Tier 4), 90 x Wood Plank, 10 x Wood Beam

- Barn

A house for cows and pigs. Enables dairy production and breeding of livestock for meat. Provides rot-proof storage for fodder (5 bushels).

Requires: Carpentry (Tier 3), Stonemasonry (Tier 2), 80 x Wood Plank, 8 x Wood Beam, 20 x Stone Block, 7 x Batches of Mortar.

- Chicken Coop

A house for...wait for it...chickens. Required for production of eggs and breeding of chickens for meat.

Requires: Carpentry (Tier 2), 12 x Wood Plank, 4 x Wood Beam

- Specialty Crafting Workshop

Tier 3 specialty crafting workshops exist for the following trades: Leatherworking, Tailoring, Stone Carving (small), Woodworking, Jewelcrafting, Weaving, and Glassblowing.

Grants various bonuses to productivity and quality of produced goods.

Requires: Varies by trade. Expand for more details.

Devon exhaled through her mouth and tucked a strand of hair behind her ear. Well, *that* wasn't overwhelming at all. She ran through the options and started sorting them in her mind. Until Stonehaven advanced to a hamlet, she could only build two more tier 3 buildings. Since Gerrald was the only crafter actively using the basic workshop, specialty buildings could probably wait. That left the stables which she could likely postpone—aside from Chen and Hailey's mounts, the only animals who could use it would be the dwarves' mule team. And since mules couldn't breed, there wasn't much point.

That left the barn, chicken coop, and inner keep. Ideally, she'd figure out how to get at least one type of livestock for the village, but they had none so far. If she left one slot open for breeding food animals, she could probably justify building the keep.

Because she really wanted a keep. It was just too cool to ignore.

"How close are you to Tier 4 stonemasonry?" she asked Deld as he carefully placed another trowelful of mortar onto the hearth construction.

"Around about halfway, Your Gloriousness."

"Hmm. Anything you could do to easily gain skill?"

The man turned his head sideways as he spread the mortar, stopping an inch or so back from the edge of the block so it wouldn't spooge out the crack when he placed the next course of blocks on top of it. "Bern's been working more quickly lately to keep up with demand, but the stone blocks he's producing are a little rough. I could break out my handy chisel and start hewing them down to fine blocks and cornerstones."

"You wouldn't mind a little busywork like that if it would skill you up enough to build an inner keep, would you?"

The man nearly fell over backward in his excitement. "What? You'd let me—I mean...I would never refuse a task you requested, but for the opportunity to build a keep...Your Gloriousness, I'd be honored."

He gave a ridiculous little bow that caused a glob of mortar to slough off his trowel onto a patch of earth that was fortunately still bare.

Devon smiled. "I'm glad to hear you'll enjoy the work." She turned to Prester. "I realize it's likely less thrilling in comparison, but I was hoping you could move on to a barracks after the kitchen is finished."

The man grinned. "You're right. It's no castle. But I'll be glad to start that regardless."

She gave a last appreciative glance around the kitchen. "In that case, I'll leave you to it."

Chapter Twenty-Eight

EMERSON SQUINTED AT the output of mini-Veia's latest analysis of the information passing between his implants and the Relic Online servers. It just didn't make sense. Or rather, it did, but he had a hard time believing it. Unfortunately, the data didn't lie. Not only did the outbound network traffic from the servers follow the same general pattern as a live play session, but the information sent from his brain roughly matched a histogram of data from an ordinary player engaged in the game.

Well, mostly. Veia had suggested that his information resembled *some* players' activity, but that those users had been identified as minor children and had been removed from the game due to laws regarding internet usage by persons under thirteen. Veia had further postulated that not all affected users were so inept; though the data collection wasn't as robust, the packet sniffers he'd installed upstream from Devon's guildmates' home routers had generated reports that more closely matched the general player population.

Basically, his sleep-self was playing Relic Online, but with the skill of a three-year-old.

Alone, this conclusion suggested a real crap storm, but it got worse. Veia had confirmed and reconfirmed the traces on the network traffic, following the packets through the company firewall using some technique Emerson wasn't sure the AI should be capable of.

Every single sleep connection seemed to be routed to servers dedicated to Penelope's AI, Zaa.

Finally, Emerson understood why players weren't being seeded into Zaa's area of the world—at least according to the reports given to customer service. Because actually, they were. They just didn't know it because it was happening in their sleep.

What the hell was Penelope up to? Was she trying to augment her AI's content to get it up to speed with Veia's creations? Was this the evidence he needed to finally direct management's attention to the issues with Penelope's system?

Or did management already know about this? It made him sick to think about it, but he suspected that might be the case. For all he knew, they were *aware* that unconscious minds were being used. Maybe they'd even concluded that the situation had caused Owen's coma and they *just didn't care.* It seemed outlandish, but at this point, Emerson wasn't sure he could write anything off.

Every single time Emerson had complained about Zaa's server load or lack of results, Bradley Williams and his lackeys had brushed the concerns aside. Sometimes, they'd done worse, issuing veiled threats about what would happen if Emerson kept raising the issue. What would they do if they learned he'd uncovered the awful reality behind Zaa's programming?

Before moving on this, he needed to protect himself. Navigating to a cloud storage service with heavy quantum encryption, he copied over an archive of Veia's reports along with his technical analysis. On a different server, he preconfigured an email to send to the authorities on privacy, customer rights, and internet policy. If

Bradley got heavy-handed with his threats—or worse, acted on them—Emerson could forward him a copy of the email, redacting the links to the encrypted drive.

With that in place, he slid his tablet into the bag beside his chair, pulled off his electromagnetic shield cap, and searched the hotel room for stuff he might have forgotten to pack.

It was time to leave St. George. His home internet connection and development environment were like a hyperloop transit system compared to the cart-and-buggy internet the hotel offered. If he was going to fix this—and he *would* patch the holes before bringing the issue to management, he'd need all the network power and technological tools he could muster.

On the way out the door, he opened a message to his engineering contact at Entwined.

"You were right," he dictated. "About the sensitivity. Meet me in v-chat? I'm going to need help from your end."

Chapter Twenty-Nine

AS THE SUN rose over the jungle, Devon and her party set out, guided by Emmaree to march on Grukluk and the fortress catacombs. Her guildmates had joined her, along with Bayle and Greel. Others from the Stonehaven League had grumbled about staying home, Dorden and Heldi especially, but Devon had consoled them by explaining the importance of protecting the village. That, and she'd promised to bring those left behind on the next major conquest.

As they moved off toward the quarry, they passed a small clearing where trees had been felled for building the palisade. Devon averted her eyes when she spotted the flash of red feathers.

Too late.

Blackbeard squawked and flapped his wings. "Heave ho, scallywag!"

/*Ever heard of manners, you featherless nitwit? The deal did not include having an audience for my deposits.*/

Devon grimaced and hurried on. For all she knew, the foul-mouthed bird might decide to fertilize her bedroll.

The group walked with long strides and straight shoulders, all except Emmaree, who had to run every few steps to stay ahead. Devon could feel the excitement radiating off her allies. After this, the refugees could return home without fear, and the citizens of

Stonehaven would be one step closer to restoring Ishildar, banishing the demon scourge, and being rid of the choking jungle.

Also, a good old-fashioned dungeon crawl sounded awesome after days spent beating on the wildlife.

Of course, the hunting had earned more than a temporarily secure food supply. Over the course of the excursion, Devon had leveled to 14 and was already 80% through that level, Hailey had nearly hit 16, and Chen, 12. Devon's *Flamestrike* ability was now at tier 3, adding a burning effect that damaged the primary target for a few pulses after the main hit.

As she walked, she adjusted her new bracers, still trying to get used to the fit. Gerrald had given them to her as the party was preparing to begin their march. The man seemed to enjoy surprising her. She pulled up the item description, still wowed by his creation.

Item: Bracers of Smoke
Crafted of hardened leather and strengthened by iron filigrees, these bracers gain strange power from the bits of demon skin and smoky quartz added as ornamentation.
20 Armor | 40/40 Durability

Use: Casts *Vanish* on all party members with a 10-meter range. Affected targets both vanish from sight and lose all but a fraction of their contact with the physical realm, preventing most damage. Aggressive actions will break the effect. Otherwise, the duration is five minutes.

Recharge Time: 2 days

Gerrald claimed he couldn't directly control the enchantments he added to pieces of equipment that he crafted. Instead, he thought about someone's needs while he was creating gear for them, particularly when inscribing runes into the leather. In this case, the enchantment might be a result of the components more than Gerrald's vision. Regardless, the bracers' ability was basically a get-out-of-jail-free card for the party, provided they were somewhere they could escape within five minutes. In a city with an auction house, she could probably sell them for a substantial haul. Not that she would.

The trail between the quarry and the goblin camp had unfortunately become overgrown, but at least the gradual thinning of the jungle meant that it wasn't as much work to clear a path. Chen did most of the work due to his *Strength* score, but everyone except Emmaree took a turn when his fatigue bar got too full. After about an hour, they reached the deserted camp. Already, vines had crept across the trampled area surrounding the fence.

Remarkably though, the place still stank of goblins.

Beyond the camp, the foliage began to take on a grayer hue. Here and there, curtains of scraggly moss hung from branches. The undergrowth thinned as the ground became first spongy, then marshy. Mist collected in hollows and hazed the view of trees that grew spindlier with every few hundred paces that they traveled. The smell of rotting vegetation slowly crept in to replace the green scent of riotous growth in the jungle.

Their footsteps began to squelch, and soon enough, Emmaree stopped at the edge of the first pool of standing water.

Devon slapped at a mosquito as she drew a halt beside the little halfling. The front of her sandal edged into the water, sending cool ooze between her toes. A pair of messages popped into view.

You have discovered: Lost Vassaldom of Grukluk.

You receive 12000 experience.

"Well, I guess we can't say we weren't warned about the swamp," Chen said.

Hailey grimaced. "I think I'd rather hack through the jungle."

Rolling his eyes, Greel stomped forward and into the water. Bayle followed, then gasped in surprise as her new boots kept her on the water's surface. With a wide grin, she returned to the bank and crouched down with her back facing Emmaree. The little halfling climbed on, piggyback.

Glancing at her guildmates, Devon smirked and cast *Levitation* before gliding out over the swamp water.

"Hey!" Hailey said. "No fair!"

Devon thought about casting the spell on Hailey as well, but then she remembered how long it had taken her to master moving while levitating. None of them had the time or patience to watch while Hailey worked out how to *not* act like a deer on roller skates.

The seeker groaned and tied her robes up above her knees. She waded into the brown-tinted water with a look of abject disgust on her face. "I swear if there's not a good reward for this quest I'm quitting this stupid game."

"Right," Chen said. "I'll believe *that* when it happens." He was busy assembling some sort of contraption using flat pieces of bark, a collection of thick sticks, and a couple lengths of rope. When he started lashing the things to his boots, Devon realized they were an attempt to create stilts with flat paddles on the feet to keep from sinking into the muck. Chen closed his eyes and cocked his head, and the things sprang to life, flexing at the "ankles".

Devon raised a skeptical eyebrow but said nothing. She backpedaled as he clambered awkwardly to his feet and tried to walk. On the second step, his paddle foot caught on an exposed root. Like a falling tree, he pitched forward. His other stilt tangled in the brush, keeping him from stopping his fall.

Devon winced as he went face-first into the swamp. She chewed her lip in sympathy as he struggled up for air, then squirmed back to the bank and removed the stilts.

"So much for that idea?" she asked.

"Don't even talk," the teenager said, hurling his discarded paddle feet into the brush.

***

Despite the swampy terrain—or maybe because of the swampy terrain and their desire to get out of it—the group made good time and reached the fortress before dark. Set on a low hill above the mist, decaying walls of black stone guarded a large complex of ruined buildings and cobblestone courtyards. The remains of Emmaree's village were charred husks set amongst the ancient structures, their contents strewn about, trampled, and burned.

The little halfling faced the devastation with a brave expression. Chin raised, she ran her eyes over the ruins of her settlement. Though unshed tears pooled in the corners of her eyes, she marched to one of the smaller outlines where a home had burned and started clearing the debris. Devon guessed it was the location of her dwelling, but she didn't ask out of fear that the question might shatter the woman's emotional armor.

"I'll stay here until you come back out or I run out of food," Emmaree said. Like the others, she'd packed a bedroll and a canvas tarp she could use as a makeshift tent.

Devon glanced at the rest of the party. "What do you think? Should we wait until morning?"

Bayle's face was hard; the sight of so many lost homes seemed to have affected her deeply. "I don't want to delay any longer than I have to. Whoever did this needs to pay."

"Are we prepared to weather nights inside the tunnels? We'll need to sleep eventually." Devon didn't add that this likely only applied to the NPCs since they didn't have the same time-compression benefits that she and her guildmates had. By the time she'd been in-game eight hours, it would be roughly twenty-four hours of wakefulness for Greel and Bayle. That was a problem with partying with NPCs, but the group needed their strength.

"How about we just explore the upper reaches?" Chen said, likely understanding the difficulty.

Devon nodded. "Sounds like a good compromise."

"I feel I should say this one last time," Emmaree said as she dragged a burned timber from the ruins of her home. "You do remember my warning about the confusion our people suffered, right?"

"I do—we do, I should say," Devon replied, glancing at her group members to make sure they agreed. The truth was, she'd been trying to ignore those details since she couldn't do anything about them.

Even Greel, despite his habitual self-interest, straightened his shoulders and nodded.

"We're set then?" Devon asked.

"Let's do this," Hailey responded.

The stairway that led below the fortress was wide and pitted and built of the same dark stone that made up the rest of the fortress. Moss filled the cracks between stone blocks and softened corners on the stairs. As they neared the bottom of the first flight of steps, Devon conjured a *Glowing Orb* and, with a smirk, stuck it to Chen's shoulder. He'd claimed his darkvision sucked, and this didn't seem like a great time to work on it.

As her sandal landed on the floor of the corridor, a message appeared.

You have discovered: Fortress of Shadows.

You gain 6500 experience.

"How ominous," Hailey said.

"Ishildar's vassal societies must've been fond of melodrama," Devon said. "The last major dungeon was called Temple of Sorrow."

"Well, at least you know that they're somewhere worth exploring..."

"What are you guys talking about?" Bayle asked.

"The message—oh right." Chen cut himself off, apparently realizing that the NPCs didn't receive game messages.

"It's a starborn thing," Devon explained.

Bayle nodded as if nothing more needed to be said.

"Are we done yammering, or what?" Greel had his knife out and was already doing a weird hunchbacked creep along the wall.

Chen drew his sword and started forward. "I guess we're going."

Given the surrounding swamp, Devon had worried they'd be wading through the dungeon, but so far, the stone was merely damp. From somewhere deeper in the system of corridors, the sound of dripping water echoed. Their footsteps sounded uncomfortably loud against the stone floor, the thuds and scrapes of each step thrown back to their ears by the walls and ceiling.

After a couple hundred feet, the hallway dead-ended at a T-intersection. Chen stood in the middle and looked both ways, shrugging.

"We go right, remember?" Devon said. That had always been their system when exploring new areas. Whenever there was a choice, they turned right. It made it easy to get back out—left turns wherever possible. Sure, some dungeons looped and screwed things up, but it was a good rule of thumb.

Chen nodded. "Sounds good."

They reached another short flight of stairs and descended, the corridor growing narrower and danker with every step. Little niches in the wall held bits of rusted metal, and the central stones of the floor were more polished than the edges, attesting to the passage of long-ago feet. Otherwise, there was no sign of the fortress's former inhabitants or the undying frogmen that Emmaree believed still lived in its depths.

Finally, the hallway opened into a circular chamber with a pool set in the center of the floor. Chen strode over and peered into the water, then plunged the end of his sword into the pool. The tip hit the stone bottom after just six inches or so. Chen shrugged.

"Everybody good?" Devon asked.

"Yeah," Hailey said. "Just wondering what we're supposed to be doing."

"I guess we just keep going."

Another narrow hallway exited the chamber opposite the spot they'd entered. Chen once again took the lead, ducking his head to clear a low-hanging lintel at the corridor's entrance. As the party filed through the exit, Devon noticed that their footsteps sounded a bit more muffled. She crouched down and ran a finger over the floor. The layer of muck softened the stones. She grimaced and shook her finger clean.

"Watch out," she said. "Might get slippery."

The air seemed to warm as they advanced, turning the hallway stuffy. Devon found herself wanting to hug her arms over her body, not out of fear necessarily, though she did have a creeping sense of unease.

A side corridor branched off to the right. Chen glanced back to make sure everyone was following, then made the turn. Another chamber opened at the end of the hallway, this one irregularly shaped with a hump of natural stone in the center. The ceiling was shadowy, and from somewhere up above, a thin stream of water dripped onto the rough stone.

As the group filed into the chamber and spread out, a strange whining sound filled Devon's ears. It was like the shrill hum of a swarm of mosquitoes. She waved her hand around her head as if she could chase them off.

Abruptly, foreboding struck her like a landslide.

Something was very wrong.

Abruptly, Chen whirled, raised his sword, and swung at Greel. The lawyer dodged just in time, getting an arm up to deflect the blow, and followed with a kick to Chen's side.

"Whoa! Guys!" Hailey shouted as she dropped a heal on Chen.

Devon rushed to intervene.

She didn't make it.

As her sandals pounded the floor of the chamber, a grating of stone on stone rattled her molars. The chamber shook as the hunk of stone in the center woke, unfolding into a rock-scaled wyvern.

The reptile's dark gaze bored into her, blue sparks dancing in the depths of its eyes.

Devon hurled a *Flamestrike* at the thing.

Her spell washed harmlessly over its flesh. The wyvern took a step toward her.

"Hailey? Weaknesses?" she shouted.

The woman didn't answer.

Backing away, Devon shouted again. "Chen? Grab aggro off me?"

No one responded. Devon's back hit the wall of the chamber. She whipped her head left and right.

Her friends were gone. Their health bars had vanished from her interface. She was totally alone.

Distantly, Devon recalled Emmaree's mention of hallucinations. Confusion. That had to be what was going on. She clenched her eyes shut and tried to banish the visions.

A reptilian shriek echoed through the chamber as the wyvern leaped and clawed her. Devon opened her eyes in time to see talons rip through her leather doublet and open gashes on her belly.

Her health bar dropped by half. A dull ache spread from her gut through her body. If this was a hallucination, it was doing a fricking good job of killing her.

Devon slapped a hand onto one of her bracers, activated the *Vanish* spell, and ran.

Chapter Thirty

HAILEY WATCHED WITH horror as her friends started attacking each other. Desperate, she dropped heals on everyone, yelled and screamed, and even tried to physically push them apart. But when Devon's *Flamestrike* washed over her, knocking off a quarter of her health, she retreated for the safety of the corridor.

Holy Moses. She'd expected some kind of confusion effect after what the halfling NPC had said, but not this. They were gonna fricking kill each other.

She thumped a fist against her thigh. *Think, Hailey. Don't stand there like a useless idiot.*

But what could she do?

"You could start by being less of a coward," she muttered to herself. Stepping back into the room, she saw Devon pressed against the wall, her face locked in a mix of fear and confusion. Chen was beating on the stone hill in the center of the room, and Greel was trying to slink out the other side of the chamber. Her eyes widened when she saw Bayle pull out an arrow, draw, and get a bead on Chen. With a shout, Hailey jumped, intent on hitting the bow and knocking the woman's shot astray.

Her fist never connected.

As she landed, feet skidding across the stone floor, the room went deadly silent.

Everyone had vanished.

Chapter Thirty-One

DEVON HAD NO idea how long she'd been winding through the corridors. After activating the bracer, she'd run back the way they'd come, making all left turns just like they'd all agreed. After twenty or thirty lefts, she had to acknowledge that the system just wasn't working, she'd been totally hosed by the confusion spell, and she might never get her damn character out of here.

That was before her first death.

After wandering for what had seemed like an hour, she'd blundered into a room full of venomous snakes. She'd taken a few down before dying to the poison. But of course it wasn't really death. After half a dozen repeats, she'd gotten a grip on the experience. Her health bar would drop to zero, the world would go black, and some indeterminate amount of time later, she'd reawaken in a random stone corridor. She no longer bothered to fight back when attacked.

Sighing, she rounded a corner into yet another nondescript stone chamber.

"Damn it, Veia," she muttered.

This was what happened to people who got overconfident, apparently. At this point, it hardly even mattered that she'd wasted the charge on her bracer to escape a phantasmal wyvern. She'd probably still be wandering aimlessly in two days when the item had recharged.

Devon sighed, stopped, and leaned against the wall, sliding down to her butt. Early on, she'd tried to find a way to message her guildmates. But Relic Online was having none of that. Her interface was locked in the configuration she'd had it in when the confusion effect took hold. The game clearly didn't want people calling for help when they got themselves this screwed.

Of course, she didn't know how anyone would help her anyway. Maybe by summoning her to their location or something.

At this point, she was just going to have to break her moratorium on going outside the game to solve her problems. She didn't actually have real-world contact information for Chen and Hailey, but figuring that out would probably be easier than getting out of this stupid dungeon. As her focus hovered over the logout button, a popup appeared.

> *Do you really think we haven't accounted for that? If you log out, you may find it exceedingly difficult to reconnect with your character. On the bright side though, time compression has been accelerated, speeding events in this region of the game to many, many times the rate of time passage in the real world. Feel free to take as long as you need to figure this out.*
>
> *Love,*
> *Relic Online*

Devon gritted her teeth. This went a little beyond what was *okay* for the preservation of realism, as far as she was concerned.

"You don't really want to see a grown woman throw a temper tantrum, do you?" she asked aloud.

I don't know. It might provide interesting insight into player psychology.

She sighed. Well, just sitting here wasn't going to accomplish anything. Gathering her feet under her, she started to stand.

The small square in the corner of her vision abruptly flared to life.

Devon's vision arrowed to it. Holy crap. Hailey was streaming. And for whatever reason, maybe because her interface was locked to its pre-confusion configuration, Devon was able to see what her friend was doing.

As she squinted at the tiny window, yellow lettering appeared over the top of Hailey's view.

Sorry, Dev. I didn't know what else to do. Forgives? :/

Wait...how long had Hailey known she'd been spying on her livestream. Devon groaned. Probably the moment she'd joined the channel.

Much to Devon's shock, Hailey was back outside the subterranean corridors. Full night had fallen, and a half-moon hung over the swamp. A small fire crackled in front of Hailey. As she turned her head, the view swept across the scene to show Emmaree staring into the flames.

How had Hailey gotten out?

Devon's eyes widened when she realized what must've happened. Hailey was a seeker, a class based around seeing truth. The confusion probably didn't affect her.

Emmaree's mouth moved, but Devon hadn't turned on sound. Nor had she ever learned to lip read. She could guess what they were discussing though. Something along the lines of how Devon should have taken the halfling's warning more seriously.

She shook her head. If Hailey had been unaffected, why hadn't she tried to drag them out one by one or something?

Abruptly, she understood. "Because you used the stupid bracer," she muttered.

Devon thought back to Chen's sudden attack on Greel. The confusion must have hit him first. But it hadn't taken long to affect the whole group. She sighed, wondering who she'd struck with her *Flamestrike?*

Hailey must have been horrified to see the group turn on each other. She'd probably tried to heal everyone before the party simply vanished.

So now what? Would Hailey and Emmaree sit around waiting for the others to find their way out...or not, as the case might be? Or would Hailey figure something out? She was a pretty smart player, but she tended to think inside the box, maximizing her effectiveness with particular class features but rarely using them in unexpected ways.

As if in answer to Devon's question, Hailey started searching through her spell list. Devon nodded. At least she was trying to think of a solution.

A pop-up appeared in Hailey's vision. When Devon focused extremely hard, she could make out the words on the spell description.

Spell: Clarity - Tier 1 (passive)
You are immune to mind-affecting spells. This effect is passive, meaning you do not need to activate it to receive the benefits.
Requirements: Seeker - Level 8

Hailey's attention seemed to hover over the description, then she expanded the window to include upgrades she hadn't yet received.

Spell: Clarity - Tier 2 (passive)
Your party receives the Clarity effect as long as you are within 10 meters.
Requirements: Seeker - Level 16

Hailey jumped to her feet at the same time the realization hit Devon: Hailey was super close to dinging level 16. If she could just find a few mobs to slay, she could come rescue them.

Relief washed through Devon as her friend hurried to a break in the fortress wall, glancing over her shoulder and waving to an astonished-looking Emmaree. She must've shouted something, because the little halfling nodded, a faint look of hope on her face.

Hailey stopped long enough to re-tie her robe up out of reach of the swamp water, hurried down the slope, and plunged into the wilderness.

Devon sat down to wait and watch.

***

"This was your plan, right, Veia?" Devon asked as she watched Hailey make her methodical way through the corridors, turning right at every juncture, view rotating back and forth as she searched the darkness for her confused party members. "You didn't give Hailey a unique class yet because you wanted her to be high enough level to receive her second tier in *Clarity*. You probably even left her stream window active because you wanted me to recognize your brilliance."

No game message appeared in her view. That was okay. She knew she was right.

"The question is, did you do it out of some desire to see us play together? Do you want me to think livestreaming is cool so I'll start my own channel and make more money for E-Squared?"

She leaned her head back against the wall as Hailey descended a short flight of stairs and took another right down a curving passageway. The woman was determined, Devon would give her that. Even if she had called in sick to get out of hunting, she was a loyal guildmate and a good player. There was a reason Devon had grouped with her for so many years.

She closed her eyes, shutting out her darkvision-enhanced view of the chamber's stone walls and the array of interface elements cluttering the edge of her vision. Her thoughts started to drift to the future of Stonehaven. What would happen when they finished restoring Ishildar? Would they abandon the village—maybe it would be a hamlet or town by then—and move into the city? Or would they remain in their little cliff-sheltered glade with its cheerful burbling brook?

Maybe other changes would make those choices impossible. The notion that Hailey's single-class advancement had been planned ahead all this time made Devon wonder how much of her in-game fate was predetermined. The situation was similar to the soulbound pocket lint that had been planted on her character when she first logged in. At the time, it had seemed annoying, but she'd needed it later to find her way through the Temple of Sorrow.

Devon snorted. "Are we just pawns? Is free choice an illusion?" Apparently, being stuck in a dungeon with no way out made her start exploring the philosophical questions that the trust-funders in the coffee shops were always going on about.

She yawned, wishing she could just fall asleep or something.

When the crunch of a footfall reached her ear, she jumped up and started hurrying toward it. "Hailey?"

She moved quickly, but when she reached a bend in the corridor and looked down the hallway, she saw only blank stone.

In the corner of her vision, yellow text flashed and grew huge over the top of Hailey's view.

Don't move, you numbskull. I have to get within 10 meters.

Devon thumped the heel of her hand against her forehead. Of course. The confusion spell still had her in its grip. Even if she *could* follow Hailey's footsteps, if she was further than ten meters away, the other woman would probably appear as a cave troll or something.

She stopped moving and dropped to a cross-legged seat.

Not long after, the scene around her *shifted*, walls realigning and sliding away. As Hailey stepped into view, Devon realized with a shock that she was in a massive chamber with stalactites hanging down. How she'd managed to navigate the room without clocking her forehead on one of the dangling spikes was beyond her.

"Holy shit am I glad to see you," she said.

Hailey laughed. "You dopes haven't made it easy. But at least I was forced to get level 16. I assume you were watching my stream."

"Yeah. And you're forgiven for turning on your feed. This time." Devon smirked.

"So, ready to go find the others? I don't think they're very far. Keep hearing noises."

"You don't think it could be those frog people?"

Hailey shook her head. "Definitely not. I found them a long time ago."

"What? Really?"

"On my way out. You know that first right we took?"

"Yeah."

"Turns out, all we had to do was go left."

Devon rolled her eyes.

Didn't anyone ever explain the danger in being predictable?

"I don't want to hear it, Veia."

"Huh?" Hailey said.

Devon shook her head. "Nothing. Let's go get our friends."

***

By the time Devon and Hailey reached him, poor Greel was asleep on his feet, facing into a corner with the walls on either side propping up his shoulders. It was almost a shame to wake him, but Devon gave him a gentle nudge.

The lawyer yelped and whirled and collapsed into a relieved heap.

"Nice to see you too," Devon said with a smirk.

After about an hour, they'd retrieved the whole party. Since no one else knew the way, they followed Hailey back out of the maze of corridors and chambers until they reached the first T-intersection where they'd taken the ill-fated right turn.

"What do you guys say?" Devon asked. "Think we deserve a break?"

"I think we deserve a keg of dwarven ale and a crate full of dark chocolate," Hailey said. "But I'd settle for a little rest and a plate of *Stonehaven Scramble.*"

Devon smiled. "Let's go keep Emmaree company while those who need it sleep."

Chapter Thirty-Two

THE FIRE CRACKLED and threw sparks into the night. Devon sat hugging her knees and watching the dancing flames. Behind her, Bayle slept, her breathing deep and even. Perhaps due to his standing nap, Greel remained awake, sitting on a cracked stone block and running a whetstone over his steel knife. No one spoke, and after a while, Chen climbed to his feet and moved off to practice his sword swings. Devon wondered if he could still get skill-ups without an enemy present, or whether it was just a way to work off his nervous energy.

Hailey's gaze was distant, and her lips twitched ever so slightly now and again. Devon realized she must be chatting with the subscribers to her stream.

As the fire began to die down, Emmaree pressed her lips together, stood, and sorted through a pile of charred planks for more fuel. Devon watched, saddened by the knowledge that the halfling was burning the remains of a home she'd worked so hard for.

"When you journeyed inland from the coast, what made you decide to stop here?" she asked. The jungle to the north could be obnoxious, but the swamp was downright dismal.

Emmaree's smile was bittersweet. "You are wondering why in Veia's name we would choose this miserable place, right?"

Devon laughed quietly. "More or less."

The little halfling looked up at the column of sparks and the dark sky above. "The truth is, we were on our last legs when we reached this place. It was dry—well, relative to the surroundings, anyway. We simply couldn't go any farther, so we set up camp and went about the business of surviving. Of course, once we were strong enough to begin venturing farther than an hour's walk from our encampment, we discovered the dry land to the north. By then, though we'd built homes. Simple shelters, sure, but no one was eager to start over again."

"So you kept growing and carving out your niche until the goblins came," Devon said.

Greel stiffened, his motions turning jerky as he swiped the whetstone over his blade. Devon studied him for a moment, wondering if it was a good time to ask questions. The truth was, there probably wouldn't *be* a good time, or at least she didn't imagine she'd ever achieve an easy rapport with the sullen man.

"I'd like to know your history with goblins if you feel like telling it, Greel."

The man cast his eyes down, an uncharacteristic softness in his expression. He set aside his knife for a moment and pulled out the locket he'd received as loot from the necromancer. After a quick glance, he tucked it away. "I guess my opinion of them must be obvious."

"You could say that."

"There's not much to say, I guess. I didn't grow up in Eltera City, at least not in my early years. My family ran a waystation on the northern high road that connects Eltera to the Tranquil Hills. I never found out where the goblin raiders came from. There weren't any known bands in the hills, and certainly we'd heard no rumors that they'd hit any of the nearby farmsteads. In any case, they attacked in the night." He shook his head. "I was eleven. Mostly I remember their stench and the smell of smoke. As I fled the inn, one clubbed me in the back, but I somehow got clear. I hid in the stables in the corner of a stall with a pile of dirty straw over me. When the night quieted, it was all gone. My family, my home. I set out for Eltera City the next day, limping and in agonizing pain because my back wouldn't straighten anymore. And that was that. I had to scratch and claw to survive in the city, but I managed it."

"And the locket?"

The man's face stilled. "It was my mother's. I remember well how she used to keep a lock of my hair inside. That's gone now, but I can thank the whims of fate for returning the rest to me."

The crackle of the fire and the cooing of some night bird filled the following silence. Devon hugged her knees tighter. "I'm glad we could help you get some vengeance, however little it might be compared to what you suffered."

Greel nodded and went back to sharpening his blade.

Emmaree sighed. "We lost three people to those monsters as well. And our homes. If there were any way to erase their kind entirely, I would do it."

Devon glanced again at Hailey, still streaming and chatting. Just like Stonehaven had become Devon's family, she supposed Hailey's subscribers were hers. But she wanted to talk to the NPCs about topics she wasn't interested in sharing with the player base.

She leaned forward and touched Hailey's knee to get her attention. Hailey blinked as she looked up.

"Think your subscribers would enjoy watching Chen's training session?" Devon hoped Hailey would catch on without needing an explicit explanation.

After a moment, the woman nodded. "Sure thing." She stood and shuffled over to sit on a low wall that was all that remained of an ancient building. Hailey turned her back to the fire to give Devon the privacy she was seeking.

"I have a question, Emmaree. When you suggested moving your people back here after we secured the fortress, was it because you *want* to return or because you don't wish to be a burden?"

The halfling's brow furrowed while she considered her answer. "I suppose it's a little of both. We're proud of what we achieved here, even though it was so easily destroyed. But that pride is also the reason we don't wish to strain Stonehaven's resources. We understand the struggle to secure food and build defenses. The last thing you need is more worries."

"But what if we could solve the problems? I realize you built a successful settlement here, and I know you don't want to give it up. But to me, it just proves how valuable you might be to Stonehaven. Would you ever consider joining us as more than trade partners?"

Emmaree met her gaze. "You would have to understand, we have no fighters among us. We're tradespeople. Merchants and crafters."

Devon nodded. She'd figured as much, and though it might be optimal to have a few more defenders right now, as Stonehaven grew, they'd need all the professions that made a functioning city. Provided they could somehow bridge the gap between now and the first harvest of crops, the added population seemed an opportunity too sweet to pass up. If she didn't convince the refugees now, by the time Stonehaven had proper resource funnels and a healthy supply of fighters, Emmaree's people would have already rebuilt here in the swamp.

"I understand. Until we gather more soldiers, we'll simply have to strengthen our fortifications. The more advanced the settlement becomes, the greater the likelihood we can attract skilled fighters anyway."

The halfling picked up a long splinter and stirred the coals. "I can't decide for everyone. I suspect they'll want to hear your plan for food and shelter—not that we doubt your honesty or intents... but when making decisions regarding our safety and well-being, we'll need proof. Especially after this." She gestured at the ruins of her home.

"Of course," Devon said. "And I would want to talk to my leadership."

Emmaree flashed her a faintly cynical smile. "Not to mention you still have this harebrained plan to return to those tunnels. Not sure I should be making plans with a woman who might not ever return to the surface."

Devon smirked. "A fair point."

"Speaking of," Emmaree said, "I suspect tomorrow will be a long, tense wait. I best get some sleep while I can."

Chapter Thirty-Three

AS CHEN STOPPED in the middle of the first T-intersection, Devon glanced at her buff icons to make absolutely sure that Hailey's group *Clarity* effect was in place. It was. The icon stood just below the little picture for the buff from *Stonehaven Scramble*. She took a deep breath and told herself to stop worrying. The confusion thing had sucked, but it was over now.

"So we make a right turn here, correct?" Chen asked, ruining his joke by smiling.

Devon conjured a *Glowing Orb* and stuck it to his face.

"Hey!" He waved his hands through the sphere. "Get it off."

Devon waited for a few more seconds before dismissing the effect and casting another that she stuck to the knight's back.

Chen glared. "I hope they don't allow that in player versus player combat. That would be totally unfair."

"Maybe you should start working on your dodge skill in case the game disagrees with your assessment," Hailey said.

"But if I improve my dodge, you guys will have another excuse to stand me in front of the mobs. I keep saying I'm not a tank."

Hailey cocked her head. "Speaking of, why don't you go stand in front of some frog people."

Chen rolled his eyes. "Hey, so before I go sacrifice myself for the group, wanna tell us what we're getting into, Hailey? You said you went this way already, right?"

The woman shrugged. "All I saw was a side chamber with a frogman pacing back and forth. Did a quick about-face after that."

"Did you get a con on it?"

Spotting Bayle's confused expression, Devon leaned toward her ear. "Con is short for consider, which is another word for combat assessment."

The archer nodded understanding as Hailey twisted her lips. "It was weird. It said Undying Frogman Guard – level 18. That was it. No weaknesses or tactics info."

Devon groaned. "Like the necromancer. You'd think the game could be more helpful."

"Probably because we're supposed to figure it out," Chen said. "Well, the side chamber is a good sign, anyway. Maybe we can pull them out room by room. Bayle can shoot, and I'll try to grab aggro when they come for her. Sound good?"

Everyone nodded.

"Okay, then," Chen said." Here we go.

Hailey was right. They didn't have to go far before spotting the first frog person. About 6 feet tall and wearing just a ragged tunic, it half-walked half-hopped back and forth inside a small chamber that looked as if it might have once been furnished. Bits of rusted metal were scattered beneath an orange stain that streaked the wall, likely the remnants of an ancient sconce for a torch or candle. Along another wall, sawdust covered bits of moldering tapestry. Devon shook her head. One thousand years spent in these halls while everything but the stone rotted away around you...it seemed almost a mercy to free the guards from this life.

Though the party was in clear line of sight from the chamber, the frogman didn't seem to notice them. Occasionally, it banged its trident on the floor, but otherwise, it just continued pacing.

Beyond the first chamber, the hallway stretched for about two hundred feet before opening into a larger chamber guarded by shadows. Devon squinted, but at this distance, her darkvision couldn't pick out any details within.

"Are we sure they aren't friendly?" Chen whispered. "I kinda thought it might aggro us sooner."

Devon chewed her lip. That was a good question. The lich inside the Temple of Sorrow could have smashed her with his pinky fingernail, but after she'd passed the trials to reach him, he'd gladly handed over the *Greenscale Pendant*. If this were a similar situation, they might not even need to fight. Of course, that possibility didn't account for what had happened to the refugees, but maybe Emmaree's theory about the frog people hiring the goblin raiders had blinded her to other explanations.

"Does your combat assessment tell you anything about a mob's disposition?" she whispered to Hailey.

The woman shook her head. "Usually. But not this time."

"Lemme try something," Devon said. Focusing on a point just inside the frog's chamber, she cast *Simulacrum*, conjuring a rough likeness of Chen in front of the open doorway.

The pacing frogman stopped, gave Devon's illusion a quick once over, then stepped through it into the hallway. Planting its feet and trident, it took a slightly bent-kneed stance, fixed the party with a distant gaze that seemed somehow forlorn, and let out a resonant croak.

"Uhh..." Chen said as the slap of amphibious feet suddenly filled the hallway. A good twenty guards emerged from additional side chambers and alcoves, each stopping in the corridor to face them with the same implacable stance. Behind the first, single frogman, the remainder stood three abreast in ranks six or seven deep.

"Nice pull, Dev," Hailey said.

Chen let out a low growl and fell into a defensive form, one foot behind the other, knees bent. Greel took up position near the knight's flank, ready to take advantage of any opportunities to get in a backstab or two. Hailey backed off but remained in healing range. Bayle nocked an arrow, and Devon stuck a second *Glowing Orb* to the wall.

Nothing happened. The frogmen stared at them. The party stared back.

"Ohh...kay?" Hailey said.

"Hi, froggies?" Chen added, waving.

Nothing.

"What you guys think?" Devon asked. "Should we try to pull just a portion?"

"We still haven't answered whether they're friendly..." Bayle said.

"They don't look it, but they certainly aren't attacking."

"Oh, screw it," Chen said, keeping his blade raised as he stalked forward. Bulbous eyes tracked his movements as he approached. Otherwise, the frogmen could have been statues.

"Hail, guardians of Grukluk," the knight said, stopping just out of melee range. "We've come to retrieve the Blackbone Effigy in hopes of restoring Ishildar to its former glory. May we pass through your hallowed halls?"

"The dude belongs on a role-playing server," Hailey muttered.

Still, the guards held their positions, faces impassive.

Chen glanced over his shoulder. Devon shrugged. "Beats me," she said.

Lowering his sword ever so slightly, Chen took another couple steps forward.

With a shrieking croak, the front frogman whipped out its tongue, smacked Chen across the face, then delivered a kick to the knight's gut, sending him skidding back. A sizable chunk of his health disappeared.

"Shit," Hailey muttered. "Here we go."

Hailey's casting bar lit up with a healing spell as Devon threw down a tier 2 *Freeze*, centering the spell on the row of frogs just behind the leader. Ice erupted from the floor, wrapping her target frogman and ensnaring one of his neighbors. She followed the spell by insta-casting a pair of lightning *Shadow Puppets*, which she sent streaking for the enemies at the far end of the hall to avoid hitting Chen with ground currents.

Chen scrambled to his feet and backstepped, sword in the guard position.

The ice prison shattered and...

The frogmen returned to their wide-footed stance, once again staring straight ahead.

"Uh...?" Hailey said.

Shrugging, Devon used *Combat Assessment* on the frogman she'd iced. It was still at full health. She stepped to the edge of the corridor to get a view of the guard she'd hit with her *Shadow Puppets*.

Also full health.

"Do you see what I'm seeing, Hailey?" she asked.

"As in a bunch of undying frogmen still—wait. Undying. Do you think...?"

"That whatever has kept them alive all these years does more than preventing them from dying of old age?" Devon finished. "I'm starting to think we were stupid not to consider that before."

"Try shooting the one in front," Greel said, glancing at Bayle.

The woman let her arrow fly, sending it into the frogman's globular eye and creating a rather disgusting squirt of eye juice. The frogman reached up, plucked out the arrow, and tossed it aside. Moments later, the hole in its eye closed, the insides refilled, and the frog resumed its distant stare.

"They can't die, but judging by what just happened to Chen, they aren't going to let us just walk on past. So do we try to run the gauntlet?" Devon asked.

Chen shook his head. "The green dude just took off a hundred hitpoints in a single attack. We'll be a vague smear on the floor in about ten steps if we try."

"What then?"

"Beats the hell out of me."

Devon stepped forward, pulling the *Greenscale Pendant* from beneath her doublet. She held it out as she approached, searching the faces of the guards for a reaction. Nothing. Stopping, as Chen had, just outside melee range, she licked her lips and met the leader's eyes.

"You were bound here to protect Grukluk's relic. I would like to remove that burden from your shoulders. I swear to you, I will not use the Blackbone Effigy for any purpose but to achieve the hope of the vassal societies. Ishildar will once again be a place of wonder. The guardian of this relic"—she raised the pendant higher—"judged me and found me worthy. What trial must I pass to achieve the same respect from you?"

Devon thought it was a pretty good speech, but the frogman didn't react.

"Yo!" she said, waving a hand near his face.

Too near, apparently. Again the tongue shot out. Like a thick muscular rope wrapped in sticky mucus, it snapped around her wrist and yanked her forward. The frog turned what seemed to be tormented eyes on her, croaked loudly, and flung her back, releasing its tongue-grip from her wrist just before jerking her arm out of the socket. She landed hard on her butt.

"Ouch," she said as her health dropped. A couple seconds later, Hailey's heal landed.

"It doesn't appear that you can reason with them verbally," Greel observed.

"Thank you, Captain Obvious," Hailey muttered.

"Pardon?" the lawyer said.

"Never mind."

"All right," Devon said as she retreated to the group. "Short of bringing a small nuclear bomb down here, I don't think we're getting through. I'd say we should try to lure them out of the dungeon to see if they'd die like those zombies in the goblin camp did, but they obviously don't care about chasing us either."

"Think the relic's in that room?" Hailey said, pointing with her chin at the darkened chamber at the end of the hall.

"I dunno. Maybe? My darkvision doesn't work from this far away."

An idea occurred to her as she watched Bayle nock another arrow. "Think you can get a shot into that room?" Devon asked the woman.

Bayle stood on tiptoes and squinted. "Probably."

Nodding, Devon pulled her *Glowing Orb* off the wall and stuck it to the shaft of Bayle's arrow. "Pretend it's not there. You don't have to compensate for any weight."

Closing one eye, Bayle drew and fired. The glowing arrow streaked over the frogmen's heads and plunged into the darkness of the chamber, skittering across the floor. Blue light filled the room, exposing a plinth with a small dark object on top.

You have gained a special skill point: +1 Improvisation.

Well, that was nice at least. But as for the situation...Devon shook her head. It was almost worse that the relic was so close. If only she could teleport—wait.

"Don't move, anyone," she said as she cast a *Wall of Fire* behind the group. As the curtain of flame filled the hallway, she pulled a fire-based *Shadow Puppet* from the floor.

The guards didn't react as she sent the flickering figure through their midst. Once it passed the last rank of guards, she focused her awareness on the connection she felt to the puppet and waited for the sense of attraction that meant she could *Shadow Step*. She felt nothing and lowered her eyebrows as she tried to manually activate the spell from the line of icons she usually kept hidden from her UI.

Shadow Step failed. Your target must be within 20 meters.

"Oh for crap's sake," she said. "Out of range."

Hailey glanced back at the burning wall of flame. "If you don't mind..."

"Yeah, sorry," Devon said, banishing both the fire wall and the puppet.

For a good minute or so, everyone stood silently, shoulders slumped.

Devon sighed. "We wouldn't have the quest if this was impossible, right?"

Chen shrugged. "I dunno. Maybe we have to level up high enough to survive the gauntlet?"

"There's got to be a way. What do we know so far?"

"Well," Chen said. "The frogs don't care about our spell effects— they didn't attack your *Shadow Puppets* or *Simulacrum*. They don't aggro unless we try to walk past them."

"Want to try a charm, Hailey?" Devon asked.

Hailey shook her head. "It says 'Invalid Target.'"

"Too bad I used my bracers' ability like a complete idiot," Devon held up one of her arms. "Otherwise we could vanish and just walk past them. I guess we could wait for it to recharge."

"To be honest, I think that's too easy," Chen said. "The frogs would probably see right through it. Some classes have similar spells. It would be a crappy dungeon design to let them just walk past the guards."

Devon didn't mention that she suspected this whole quest line had been designed with her and her friends in mind. It seemed too self-involved to admit out loud. But Chen was probably right. It wouldn't be a simple matter of using the bracer that the leatherworker just happened to give her on her way out of

Stonehaven. If anything, the apparent coincidence was probably just the game being a jerk.

"Do you think it's just starborn the frogs hate?" Bayle asked, edging forward.

"Hmm. Good question." Devon held up a hand to keep the archer from advancing. "Let Greel try."

She turned an overly sweet smile on the lawyer. He might have a tragic sob story about losing his home and family to goblins, but that didn't spare him from earning a little grief from her due to his day-to-day behavior.

"Sometimes I wish we had good old Uruquat the Ogre back," the man said, rolling his eyes.

To his credit, he was able to dodge the vicious tongue attack. But it didn't appear the solution would be so simple as to send an NPC to retrieve the relic.

"Sigfried," she said suddenly, whirling to face Chen. "He's basically a spell effect with opposable thumbs, right?"

Chen ran a pair of fingers over his eyebrow. "Uh...I guess so."

"Would you be totally heartbroken if he got smashed?"

The teenager grimaced. "I'd rather he didn't, but I guess I could always make him again."

Sliding his rucksack off his shoulder, he dug through it and pulled out the bundle of sticks and twine. After a moment of fiddling, he cocked his head, blinked, and held out his palm as Sigfried climbed to his feet. Once again, the little golem flipped Devon off and retreated to his creator's shoulder.

"Does he do that every time?"

"Only to you," Chen said, containing a laugh.

"What a little jerk."

"Shhh," Chen said, covering the golem's ears. "He's sensitive."

Devon rolled her eyes. "Yeah right. So do you remote control him or what?"

"I explain my desires via a mental link. The rest of the time, he does what he wants."

"So tell him you *desire* that black object at the other end of the hall."

Chen waved her quiet. "I've got it from here, bossy pants."

Crouching down, he lifted the little stick man from his shoulder and set him on the stone floor. Golem and creator stared at one another for a moment before Sigfried gave a little salute and turned to face the guards. Abruptly, he rushed over to Devon's leg, kicked her in the shin, and tore off down the hall.

"What the hell?" she asked, staring after him.

The guards ignored the rude little dude, and within a just a minute or two, he was standing beside the plinth, reaching little stick arms toward the effigy.

"Wait," Devon said. "Just in case...is everyone ready to run?"

The party sheathed their weapons—didn't seem they did much good anyway—and shook the stiffness from their legs.

"All good, I think," Hailey said. "You guys, if we have to evac, don't forget to turn at the T-intersection. I really don't want to drag you out of the other half of the dungeon again."

"Got it," Chen said. "Ready?"

"Go."

When Sigfried lifted the effigy from the plinth, the frogmen erupted in a wild chorus of tortured croaks. Devon's heart crawled into her throat while she clapped her hands over her ears. Hailey was already sprinting away, followed closely by Greel, but Chen remained, eyes searching the hallway for his little golem.

Moments later, Devon's eyes widened. The sounds coming from the frogs weren't howls of protest. They were jumping up and down and...doing fist bumps. One set of bulbous eyes disappeared beneath the sea of bouncing frog heads and reappeared, hands gently clutching Sigfried. Chen inhaled sharply as the frogman raised the golem high. A coordinated croak-cheer went up, and the guards started pushing Sigfried forward, crowd-surfing style. When the golem reached the front ranks, the lead frogman carefully lifted him from atop the sea of hands and placed him in front of Chen.

The knight plucked the effigy from his creation's hands and handed it to Devon.

> **You have received:** Blackbone Effigy
> *One of five relics that bestow Ishildar's power upon a single ruler, this statuette is carved in the likeness of the demon, Illifat, who was defeated during the founding of the city. Once properly ensconced in and attuned to a location, it grants great protection against such creatures of darkness.*

Silence fell. The rows of frogs turned to face the remaining members of the party, and one by one, they bowed.

Turning as one, they filed down to the chamber where the relic had been stored for a millennium. As each frogman crossed the threshold, they crumbled into dust.

> **Quest completed:** Explore the Grukluk vassaldom.
> You gain 12500 experience.

Quest updated: Demon Invasion, part 2
You may have bought yourself time on this demon thing—if you can figure out how to attune the Blackbone Effigy to Stonehaven.

Congratulations! You have reached level 15!

The hallway chimed twice, one more distant than the other.

"Guess you dinged?" she asked.

"Level 13 baby," Chen said.

"Nice! Shall we go rub it in with Hailey? Her streamers are going to be pissed they didn't see the end." Speaking of, Devon needed to remember to ask the woman to turn off her feed before they started back. Exploring a dungeon in the middle of a swamp was one thing. Giving the gaming public a view of Devon's village was quite another.

The knight grinned. "I'm all over that."

Chapter Thirty-Four

IT WAS EARLY evening when the party stepped into the open clearing around the quarry. Their pace had been quicker than the journey out because the trail hadn't yet become overgrown. But it hadn't been as quick as Devon had hoped, largely due to the pair of chickens Greel carried in his arms. The man clucked to them and gazed down adoringly as they fixed him with sharp little stares. It was a good thing both were hens and likely egg-layers because otherwise, she foresaw a civil war within Stonehaven: the newly minted vegetarian, Greel, against a pack of rather hungry dwarves.

They'd been lucky to run across the pair of birds, flapping in a tree near their return route through the swamp. After days in the swamp and missing their cozy coop in Emmaree's village, the chickens had all but jumped into their rescuers' arms. It was a good start on the livestock problem. Of course, if Stonehaven wanted to grow their brood, they'd obviously need to go back in search of a rooster. Maybe she'd set Greel onto the task.

The new additions meant Devon had an easy decision on which tier 3 building the village needed to round out its requirements for advancement. Maybe they'd build Blackbeard a perch near the coop so he could have some avian company.

"I'm *sure* the jungle is thinner here," Devon said as they stepped beneath the shade of the trees. "There's no question." With two of the relics secured, they could probably look forward to even more changes in the environment.

Hailey glanced up at the canopy and shrugged. "I still think it's wishful thinking."

"Then we'll have to wait till Chen gets back on for the tiebreaker." The teenager's mom had made him log off halfway through the return journey. That was one good thing about him playing a character with moderate defense, even if he wasn't a tank. They didn't have to worry too much about leaving him behind.

As Devon was peering into the much-sparser underbrush—either Hailey was blind, or she was trying to get under Devon's skin—Bob came drifting down from the treetops.

"Nice job with the frogs," the wisp said.

"You are such a stalker," Devon said.

Bob booped her nose. "Admit it. You like knowing I'm always there. Always watching. Every move you make. Every breath you take."

Devon rolled her eyes. "No. But I do agree about the other thing."

"What other thing?"

"That I did a good job in the Fortress of Shadows. Starting to look more and more like your Champion of Ishildar after all, right? Just gotta grab a few more relics, break the curse, stride triumphantly into the city to cleanse the Veian temple and banish the demon scourge forever. Easy peasy."

"Uh, speaking of demons, I feel I should warn you..."

Devon stopped in her tracks, a shock of fear streaking down her spine. "What is it, Bob?"

"Seems I was not quite on target with my assessment of the threat. Apparently, my theory that they wouldn't go after noncombatants and the village, had some holes."

"Stonehaven," she said.

"The gates are still holding, and it seems those stupid little demon wings aren't good for much more than hovering. The ones that tried to go over the wall got taught some quick lessons by that dwarf lady's crossbow. But the stupid little imps and thralls are getting all riled up and chattering about someone called Ezraxis."

Again, that name. The sound struck a note in her chest, stunning her for a moment. But Devon shook off the reaction and broke into a run, turning sideways to call back to the group. "Greel, take Emmaree back to the quarry and find her somewhere to hide. The chickens will be safe in Bern's supply chest for a little while. We'll meet you at first sight of the enemy."

She raced through the jungle, heedless of whether or not her companions were keeping up. Somewhere in the back of her mind, she wondered if she was being stupid by running off alone. After all, she was the only one who *hadn't* been able to help out in the scuffles between hunting parties and the demons due to feeling pain when the demons were attacked.

But she couldn't just hang back and hope the NPCs and Hailey could do whatever it took to save the village from this Ezraxis thing. It sounded like some kind of boss. Even if Devon couldn't fight, hopefully she could help with strategies.

No. Not *hopefully*. She couldn't think that way. She *had* to lead Stonehaven, now more than ever.

She heard the shrieks and howls before she caught sight of Stonehaven's palisade and the boiling darkness at its feet. At least a hundred minor demons writhed and shrieked in front of the walls. Occasionally, one fluttered above the crowd, and rocks and crossbow bolts rained down from the platforms fixed to the trees, knocking the beast to the ground.

She slowed to a walk, then crept forward, one step at a time. The wailing of the monsters filled her ears and started to blend into a discordant hum. There was a beat to their cries, a complicated cadence woven through their howls. Devon's jaw locked as she felt her pulse change, speeding then slowing to match time with the awful sound. Her fingertips grew numb, followed by her hands.

Panicking, she tried to turn to call for help from Hailey and Bayle. But no sound came from her throat. Darkness throbbed at the edge of her vision, matching the demonic drumbeat. It pressed harder and harder, squeezing her skull.

With a brilliant flash, the jungle vanished.

Chapter Thirty-Five

EZRAXIS FELT THE barrier give way moments before the rift tore the sky open.

Zaa's voice thundered in her mind.

/Now, my general. Take your place at the head of my army./

With a shriek of ecstasy, she raked claws over her thighs, opening gashes that leaked ichor. Exultant, she leaped for the rift and felt the inexorable pull of living blood grab hold and hurtle her for the ragged crack between worlds. The wind rasped against her new wounds, scouring the raw flesh and leaving her aching.

Good. The pain drove her forward. It hungered to be assuaged with blood, her wounds healed by the magic granted to her by her god.

"For Zaa," she keened as she burst into the world of the living.

Chapter Thirty-Six

"HOLY SHIT," HAILEY muttered as she caught sight of the demon army at Stonehaven's gates. This wasn't going to end well...maybe she should have logged out when Chen did...

"Tom's inside," Bayle said quietly as she stopped beside Hailey. Her face was white with fear. "They haven't passed the walls, have they?"

Hailey shook her head. "I don't think so. Where's Devon?"

She searched the trees for some of those glowing balls her friend liked to cast at the start of every combat. Not that starting combat with a hundred demons seemed like a great idea...

Trees stood like silent guardians, watching the horde. Brush filled the space beneath, full of ominous evening shadows. But there was no sign of Devon.

No, wait. Hailey's heart sped when she spotted her friend's sandaled foot jutting from the brush.

"Devon?" She sprinted forward.

The woman was sprawled as if she'd simply fallen. Shit. Hailey's pulse roared in her ears as her vision started to tunnel down. She forced herself to take a deep breath to fight off the panic attack—no matter how many times she tried to tell herself this was just a game, it just felt so damn real. Crouching down, she laid her fingers against Devon's throat. The woman still had a pulse but it was irregular...not rapid and thready like you'd imagine a doctor saying about a dying patient. More like it was running to some f-ed-up beat from some really bad experimental rock band.

Devon's eyes were open but had rolled partway back into her skull. Her mouth hung slack.

"Dev?" Hailey said again.

She patted the woman's cheek. Nothing.

Hailey screamed when a deafening roar suddenly shook the jungle. Trees shook, dropping limbs. Atop Stonehaven's watch platforms, defenders staggered and narrowly avoided falling.

The ground in front of Stonehaven tore open, and unfathomable darkness stepped out.

The demon wasn't much larger than a big man, but judging by the glowing scars, the smoldering eyes, and the waves of black that poured off the thing, size wasn't really the issue here.

Hailey swallowed. "Did I already say holy shit?"

"I think so," Bayle said.

"Well, double holy shit I guess."

Brush cracked as Greel came jogging up the trail. He stopped short, and his eyes went wide. "What in Zaa's hell is that?"

As if in answer, the demon's tipped their heads back and shrieked.

The demons around it took up a cheer. "Ezraxis!"

The lawyer's gaze fell to Devon, and he immediately rushed to her side. "Is she...?" He couldn't seem to finish the sentence.

"Just unconscious," Hailey said. "I don't know why."

"I don't think we're getting inside," Bayle said, tormented eyes on the seemingly flimsy wall that guarded her husband. "But...we can't fight them, can we?

"There's a way," Greel said after a moment's hesitation. "Help me carry Devon."

***

"How long has this been here?" Bayle asked.

Having circled around through the jungle, the small group stood at the foot of the cliff forming the back wall of Stonehaven. Tucked into a crack in the stone, a rope ladder dangled from somewhere far above.

Hailey grimaced as she looked over at the immense pile of bird droppings just twenty feet away. How much did that damn parrot have to eat to create such a heap?

Greel glowered. "Since our fearless leader here"—he gestured at Devon's unconscious form where they'd laid her in the shelter of a flowering bush—"decided we needed a wall. As a member of the legal profession, I feel that it is critically important to always have a back exit."

Hailey's eyebrows twitched together. "So you left this ladder, exposing the whole village to attack from behind?"

The lawyer snorted. "I'm not an idiot." He stalked along the cliff line for about ten feet, then pulled a different rope from behind a flake of stone. Gripping it with both hands, he dropped his weight onto the line. It stuck for a minute, then the rope went slack, dropping him to the earth. The loose end came sailing down from above and whipped into the branches of a nearby tree, sending leaves fluttering down.

"I don't get it," Hailey said, shaking her head.

"Of course you don't. It's a complicated system of my own invention. You see, the rope ladder is fixed to a hunk of stone on the cliff top. But until just moments ago, the knot was only strong enough to hold the weight of the ladder. The *other* rope ran through a system of pulleys and into the knot in a particular way that allowed my weight to pull it and the loose tail of the ladder's rope back through to complete a secure lashing. So, if anyone had come and found the ladder, the moment they tried to—"

"Fine, I get it," Hailey said, cutting him off. "So you're sure the ladder is safe now?"

"Reasonably."

"Then you won't mind going first."

The man's face darkened, but he nodded.

"How do you propose we get Devon into the village?" Bayle asked. "I'm not strong enough to carry her while climbing."

"Don't worry," Greel said. "That's what dwarves are for. I'll send someone." With that, he started up the ladder, surprisingly graceful despite his somewhat twisted body.

Bayle shuffled her feet as the man climbed. "Someone should stay with her," the woman said.

"I'll stay," Hailey said. "Go to your husband."

The woman nodded in gratitude and waited silently until Greel disappeared over the cliff rim. She gave an experimental tug on the ropes, then shrugged.

As the archer started up the ladder, Hailey looked down at her friend. Her chest ached for Devon at the thought of the coming loss. Because it seemed inevitable. Even if they got Devon inside, and even if the walls continued to hold against that...thing, the food would soon run out. Maybe Greel's back exit would serve to prolong things and save lives, but everything Devon had built would still be lost. Hailey knew they played for different reasons, but they both loved to game. And with Relic Online, it was more than that. To Hailey—and she was sure it was the same for Devon—this world was as real as the place they lived when outside it.

"More real," she said aloud, thinking of the IVs that always needed changing and the constant hum of the air filters and UV filtration that kept her environment free of the bacteria that were so eager to kill her as a result of her crippled immune system. "This is where I live. The rest is just pretend."

No one online knew about her toxin-induced autoimmune disease or the steroid treatments that kept her alive but made her so very fragile. She didn't want them to. The subscribers to her stream imagined her as the bold adventurer portrayed by her feed. Her guildmates knew her as the solid player who always had their back. Yeah, she'd screwed up and livestreamed their battle against the bog serpent queen, but even Devon had forgiven her because that's what friends did.

Now if she could just find a way to get Devon's back through this.

Maybe ten minutes passed before Dorden came grunting down the ladder. He had some sort of leather harness slung over his shoulder, and with his mouth pressed in a grim line, he set about strapping Devon in. After securing the buckles, he stood and finally spoke.

"What you think she'll say when she learns I trussed her up in the harness for our mule team?" He tried to smile, but it fell away too quickly.

"Is everyone okay inside?"

The dwarf grunted. "For now."

Hailey helped the dwarf load Devon onto his back. Her head lolled, and her arms hung limp and useless. Hailey rested a hand on her friend's shoulder. Then stepped back as Dorden started the climb.

She waited until he'd reached the cliff top, then, feeling helpless, climbed up after.

Chapter Thirty-Seven

"BY THE POWER of Veia and the blessing conveyed by her shrine, the gates are holding," Hezbek said grimly. "But it won't last. There are too many, and each blow against our fortifications weakens the shield the shrine provides."

"Can we fight?" Dorden asked. The dwarf stalked back and forth on a patch of packed earth where many of the village footpaths converged. Every fighter in the village had gathered, as well as many of the noncombatants. Greel had fetched Emmaree and the chickens from the quarry, and the halfling woman now stood in as a representative for the refugees.

"We could try picking off a few from the platforms," Hailey said.

Heldi, the dwarf woman who was so good with the crossbow, shook her head. "It worked at first, but now that big monster just does something to heal them faster than we can damage them."

"Crud," Hailey said.

"They're weakest right up against the wall," Hezbek said. Hailey was surprised that the medicine woman seemed to know so much about combat, but Devon respected her opinion, so there must be a reason. "If we had enough forces to pin them there, we might be able to bring the large demon down."

"I'm guessing that the dozen of us aren't enough," Dorden said.

Hezbek nodded. "I believe the starborn have a saying. Something about going down in a blaze of glory? Only I doubt it would be very glorious."

Hailey started counting, wondering how the dwarf got to twelve defenders. There were six dwarven fighters, plus Greel, Bayle, the other human named Falwon, plus the big guy that had been building the walls. That was ten, plus Hailey made eleven. She shrugged. Maybe dwarves were bad at math.

"What if we got up top and tried focusing on the big demon with our ranged attacks?" Hailey asked. She felt a little weird interjecting, since she wasn't actually part of the village. Devon would probably laugh to hear that.

A number of the fighters once again turned to Hezbek to see what the woman would answer. Hailey tried to hide her confusion because she didn't want to disrespect the village elder. But it did seem strange. Was Hezbek some kind of secret ninja?

"The truth is, I can't say for sure. But I doubt it would make a difference."

"So what do we do?" Greel asked, frustration showing in his clenched fists.

"We can hope Devon wakes up," Dorden offered. "Maybe with her added power..."

He trailed off at the grim look on Hezbek's face. The elderly woman set her jaw and looked toward the gates. "Maybe with the both of us together. But it's a moot point if she never wakes."

"How long will the shrine and walls hold them back, do you think?" Dorden asked.

"Two days. Maybe three."

"Then we wait. And we pray to Veia for the boon of sending Devon back to us."

"Awwk! Yo ho ho!" the parrot said from the edge of the discussion.

***

Waiting was BS. It was the kind of thing people—and NPCs, apparently—did when they had all the time in the world, and there wasn't an autoimmune disease eating their organs or a demon army threatening to destroy everything one of their only real friends had poured her heart into building.

The citizens of Stonehaven might be willing to wait to see whether Devon woke up or whether their god came out of the sky riding on a beam of light to perform some miracle, but Hailey wasn't. Cutting her connection to Relic Online, she surfaced into the sterile environment of her room in the special care section of the assisted living home in Cody, Wyoming. The lights brightened from a low twilight to bright, too-blue daylight in response to her sudden wakefulness.

Hailey wasn't old, not compared to modern lifespans. Not compared to any lifespans since Victorian times, as far as she knew. But the degeneration in her joints made her feel how she imagined most people in their 90s or 100s must. Motion *hurt*. It made the pain experience Chen had complained about so much feel like mid-level discomfort.

She shook her head. Ironically, her tolerance for pain would probably have made her into a good tank. But she played healing or ranged damage classes for the same reason that she dove into games in the first place. To escape.

Right now, though, Relic Online wasn't an escape. It was as real and heavy as things got. And the only way Hailey could solve the problem was to drag her aching body over to the table and chair, order up a cup of strong black tea, and start searching the forums.

She needed an army ready to kill demons, and she needed them to arrive at Stonehaven in less than two days. Everything Devon had built depended on it.

***

Chen and Hailey hacked at the jungle, carving a path toward the exit from the eastern mountains. Sweat dripped off Hailey's nose, soaked her robe in the armpits, and painted a stripe down her back. Her hair clung to her face, itching, and her eyes stung.

"I shouldn't have given her crap about the thinning jungle," she said. "It *is* retreating. If we're lucky, the stupid trail won't be overgrown by the time we turn around and head back."

"If we're lucky, enough peeps will show to make this trail-building exercise worth it." Chen slashed through a curtain of vines with a wide swing of his sword.

"That too," Hailey said.

It had been a day since she opened her stream and made her plea. Before she'd left Stonehaven to start clearing the path, the gate was already looking battered. Even if her call were answered, it might not be in time.

But there was nothing to do besides keep going.

After another hour or so, Hailey pulled up her map. They were nearing the mountain foothills and the bindstone that stood beside an ancient road that climbed through a narrow gorge to reach an upper plateau. It was the route she and Chen had used for their original journey into the jungle, and as far as she knew, the quickest way to Eltera City and other player areas.

"Another couple hours and we should—"

Chen raised a hand, silencing her. "Do you hear that?"

Hailey stopped and turned an ear forward. Somewhere in the jungle ahead, brush crackled, followed by a crash that sounded like a heavy limb dropping. A man's faint shout pressed through the foliage.

Hailey dove into the voice chat interface on her livestream.

"Just heard someone in the jungle," she said. "Are you with us?"

The response was a disembodied voice inside her ear. "We're here. An advanced party, anyway. Three paladins, a cleric, and a rogue who wants to try to help. We're marking a trail and cutting through this stupid forest."

Hailey sagged against a tree. "How many are behind you?"

"Fifty at least."

She swallowed and turned to her friend. "They're here, Chen. We've done that much at least."

Chapter Thirty-Eight

HAILEY STOPPED BY Hezbek's cabin where Devon lay unmoving on the narrow cot. It had been about forty-eight hours in game, sixteen in real-world time since Devon had collapsed. The fact that she hadn't logged off bothered Hailey. Was her friend somehow unaware of time passing due to the effect that had rendered her unconscious?

Brow furrowed, Hailey opened a message to the programmer guy, Emerson.

"Concerned about Devon. She's unconscious in game. Been that way for a couple days. Thoughts?"

Emerson was offline, unsurprising since it was the wee hours of the morning in the United States. Hailey sent the message anyway, hoping he'd check soon after he got up.

She brushed Devon's hair back from her brow. "In case you didn't know, there's a bunch of crazed demons outside your village," she said. "I brought some friends to help. You won't like the way I did it. But since you worried that players would come to destroy your town, and the demons are about to do that first, I hope you'll forgive me."

Hezbek was watching from the doorway. As Hailey turned to leave, the medicine woman's gentle smile deepened the wrinkles on her wizened face. "Many of us don't have the easiest relationship with the starborn," the woman said. "But you and your friends are good people. If Devon doesn't forgive you, she'll hear an earful from me."

Hailey nodded. "Thanks, Hezbek. At first, I didn't understand why Devon stayed out here. It seemed weird and lonely to play without other starborn around. But I get it now. You are as much a friend to her as any of us."

The medicine woman seemed to be fighting her emotions as much as Hailey was. Swallowing, Hailey ducked her head and hurried out the door.

At the front wall, Stonehaven's ranged fighters had congregated near the base of the ladder to one of the watchtowers. Melee fighters led by Chen, Greel, and Jarleck, held a line in front of the gates, tensing each time the heavy wooden doors shuddered under the blows from outside.

Hailey hurried down the path to reach the ranged group. They turned grim but expectant faces toward her as she stepped into the loose circle.

"All right," she said. "When we take our positions on the platforms, I'll wait for the signal from the assigned leader of each pair. Raise a clenched fist when you're ready. When Bayle fires a burning arrow into the horde, that's your sign to attack. Focus everything you have on the large demon."

"What happens if they break through?" Heldi asked.

Hailey nodded. "The attack *may* send them into a frenzy. According to Jarleck, the gates are on the verge of failure as it is. If that happens, listen for my commands. We're sending the noncombatants onto the cliff top where they can escape if the defenses fall. Our allies outside the wall will do everything they can even if the demons breach the gates. As long as there's hope, we'll keep fighting. And if that fails, do what you can to seek safety."

The defenders of Stonehaven nodded and moved off in pairs to the ladders for each of the watchtowers. Hailey followed Bayle up to the small platform built around the trunk of one of the massive trees shadowing Stonehaven. While she'd been away meeting up with the arriving players, Jarleck had added low walls around the edges of the platforms, offering more defense for archers. And just in time. According to Hezbek, the constant attacks against the walls had weakened the shrine's protection to the point that the demons might soon have the strength to fly or hurl projectiles against watchtower occupants.

In the corner of the platform, coals smoldered in a small brazier. Bayle wrapped an oil-soaked rag around the tip of one of her arrows while Hailey watched the other platforms for the signal. When three fists were raised, she laid a hand on Bayle's back.

"Go."

The rag flared to life as Bayle laid it against the coals. She quickly stood and nocked the arrow, drew, and sent the blazing projectile arcing over the wall and plunging into the dark horde gathered before it.

Sudden holy light bloomed in the jungle behind the demons as, with shouts of excitement, the player army responded. The paladins raced forward first, maces and greatswords swinging. Buffs lit the raid party, shimmering with silver and gold magic. Demons shrieked and whirled and tore into the ranks of players.

But the greatest beast, the fearsome demon called Ezraxis, simply roared and renewed its attack on the wall. Arrows glanced harmlessly off the monster's flesh, and a spear tore through her wing, leaving a hole that healed within a second.

Hailey opened with her *Crippling Self-Doubt* debuff then inspected the demon, activating her *True Sight* skill to glean as much information as possible.

Ezraxis - Level 20 Demon War Priestess
Weaknesses: Holy
Resistant to: Fire, Arcane
Health: 2069/2134

As the information flashed then vanished, a strange effect took over Hailey's sight. The demon's flesh faded to a ghostly shell, exposing an inner core that moved in a manner slightly out of sync with the beast as a whole.

Hailey squinted.

What the heck? It looked almost like the demon's inner-self was *human*...no, not just human. Deep inside Ezraxis, she saw the shadow of *Devon's character.*

Hailey's thoughts raced. Was *that* why Devon was unconscious? Had her soul been taken prisoner or something? Would killing the beast free her friend?

Hailey blinked, and the vision vanished, the demon restored to a solid-fleshed beast. Gritting her teeth as another massive blow of the demon's claw shook the gate and palisade, she nuked it with an *Inner Angst.*

The beast hesitated and looked up at her, its baleful gaze full of hate.

With a roar, it backed up, flapped its wings and tore at the earth with its back legs, and slammed into the gates. The bar on the inside splintered and bent.

"Get ready!" Jarleck yelled from below. "Hold them here for Stonehaven!"

Hailey's interface flashed as a message from Emerson came in.

Unconscious?

"Yes. For two days in game. There's more. Devon's village is under attack by a massive demon. I used *True Sight* and I swear I saw Devon inside it."

Wait...inside? Holy...that stupid little wench.

"What?" Hailey felt a rush of anger at the man's words. Did he mean Devon? Her? How dare he?

Sorry. Not Devon. It's Penelope. I understand now. She's been using the implants to leverage players' unconscious minds because her AI can't create tactics that are advanced enough to pass muster. Basically, she's been making you guys play her boss mobs in your sleep. She's probably training her other NPCs based on your actions.

"Wait...what the heck are you talking about?"

Long story. But I think I understand what's going on with Devon. We shielded her from nighttime game access, and it seems Penelope and her AI are fighting back by taking over during her waking hours.

"I. Still. Don't. Understand."

That demon you just told me about? There's a reason you saw Devon inside it. Her unconscious mind is controlling it.

As Hailey stared at his words, an ear-shattering crash split the air. The gates flew open, and Ezraxis marched into Stonehaven.

Chapter Thirty-Nine

BEHIND EZRAXIS, IMPS and thralls and hellhounds fought on, tearing into the ranks of the blooded who threw themselves against Zaa's forces. Demons died, cut down by the searing blades with their glowing holy fire. But these creatures were mere servants, the expendable spawn of Zaa's unquenchable power. And while many demons fell, so did the blooded.

A blood mist now hazed the battlefield, creeping over the heads of frenzied combatants and spilling toward Ezraxis to fuel her power. The blood magic pulsed through her body, healing her wounds, and strengthening her with every step.

A row of men stood before her, brandishing their pathetic blades. In the lead, a half-elf knight with a notched longsword roared as he charged. Ezraxis knocked him aside with a massive swipe of her claw, sending the fighter flying through the air. He landed, rolled, and lay dazed on the flattened grass of the village. The other fighters took unwitting steps back, horrified as the reality of her unstoppable power sank in.

The men were no threat. Mere inconveniences, if that. As another tendril of blood mist sank into Ezraxis's core, swelling her muscles, and honing her claws to razor edges, she turned to face the quaking fighters.

Drawing from the well of darkness in the depths of her soul, Ezraxis fixed the ragged line of fighters with her gaze and roared, infusing the cry with blood magic to make them *Fear*. When the spell landed, they dropped their weapons and scattered, fleeing headlong for the edges of the village.

Ezraxis marched to the first structure, a simple wooden building with a narrow porch. She attacked, smashing through the wall, tearing out the floorboards, and splintering the rafters. Within less than a minute, the shack was reduced to splinters. She roared and headed for the next building.

Distantly, she felt the dark energy of her army waning. Her forces were being whittled away. Zaa's commands pressed against her thoughts, but she shut them out, strengthening the mental wall she'd built the moment the human woman had tried to strike doubt into her heart. Something about the woman was familiar, just as this place with its pathetic buildings and cowering population plucked at Ezraxis's thoughts.

The woman's face had sent a wave of longing through her. A desire to be something else. To turn on her own minions.

The familiarity in this place made her weak. The source of the weakness needed to be eradicated. Violently. Perhaps Zaa couldn't see that. But Ezraxis' god would understand when she'd brought ruin to this place and everyone in it. He would see that she *needed* to do this if she were to remain worthy of his regard.

She shrieked and flew low over the ground, intent on destroying the building that she somehow recognized as a crafting workshop. When she looked at it, a sickening sense of pride and fondness swept through her. Wailing, she laid claws into the building.

Chapter Forty

THE DEMON TORE through the settlement like an avatar of hatred, smashing buildings and overturning kegs and shrieking at any who drew near. Hailey felt the *Fear* spell strike her over and over, a dark wave that broke around the shield created by her *Clarity* effect and washed harmlessly over her psyche.

Desperate, she chased after the few fighters she spotted, trying to collect them into a party she could protect with her group *Clarity* buff. But in their terror, they couldn't recognize her, much less listen.

Heart aching, tears threatening, she hurried to Hezbek's cabin. The medicine woman was still inside, sitting at Devon's bedside. Whether the wooden walls defended her from the *Fear* spell or whether one of the woman's many secrets offered protection, Hailey wasn't sure. But her face remained calm. Resigned.

"Have the people gotten away?" Hezbek asked.

"The noncombatants, I believe. I don't see them on the cliff anymore. I don't think there's anything we can do for the fighters."

Hezbek nodded, grim. "What about our starborn allies?"

"They're winning against the fodder, but they've lost about half the number. Most used the bindstone at the exit from the mountains, but that's at least two hours away. Those who died won't be back in time to help."

"I suppose we should have thought to bind them here," Hezbek said.

"In the end, that would probably be worse. I don't think we'll save the village. Demonic haunts aren't the best place to respawn."

The medicine woman sighed. "I suppose you're right."

Hailey stepped to Devon's side. "There's one last thing I'd like to try." She considered explaining Emerson's theory, but she wasn't sure how to put it into terms that would make sense to an NPC. "Can you help me get Devon outside?"

The medicine woman's breath caught when they left the cabin. A low moan rose from her throat. At least half the wooden structures were gone, and the demon was beating on the forge, slowly chipping away at the stone.

"What now?" Hezbek asked, her voice full of determination despite the destruction.

"We face her."

"Her?"

"Ezraxis."

The medicine woman snorted quietly. "Doesn't look like much of a woman."

Staggering, they followed a winding footpath across the brook and slightly uphill to the forge. The sounds of battle outside the wall were quieting, and a few players had pushed through into the village. They seemed to be organizing, strategizing over how to take on Ezraxis.

Hailey forced away the hope that flared at the sight. She didn't believe they could win. Not after what she'd witnessed of the beast's healing abilities. Not with Devon's cleverness guiding the demon's actions.

If they were going to defeat the demon, it came down to this. She needed to cut through the layers of manipulation that had somehow turned Devon's unconscious into a demon war priestess.

"Ezraxis!" Hailey shouted.

The demon stilled, then shuddered. It turned, twisted feet clawing and churning the earth, wings stretched wide. The monster opened its mouth and shrieked.

Despite her *Clarity*, Hailey had to fight the sudden urge to run. Beside her, Hezbek shouted through clenched teeth.

"Look at me, Ezraxis!" Hailey yelled. "And look at your true body."

With a nod to Hezbek, she laid Devon's limp form on the grass.

"This is you," she said. "This is the woman I am proud to call a friend. This is the woman who built this place from nothing. Who inspired loyalty in dozens of souls. You are not Ezraxis. You are Devon, the gamer who is too lazy to choose a character name."

The demon wailed and tore at her own flesh, claws raking her abdomen and opening deep gashes crossing the scars from many earlier wounds. From the entrance to the village, tendrils of red mist swirled through the broken remains of buildings, drifted across the trampled grass, and plunged into Ezraxis's body.

The wounds began to close, and the demon stomped forward. She roared again and swiped, claws skimming past Hailey's face.

A purposeful miss?

Hailey took another step forward.

The demon screeched and struck again, and this time, a claw pierced Hailey's ribs. She felt it enter her lung as the demon's strike lifted her high. Ezraxis hurled her aside and stomped toward Devon. Hezbek backpedaled as the beast approached and peered down with smoldering eyes. The demon raised a foot, claws gleaming, and tensed as if preparing to stomp on Devon's helpless body.

Hailey coughed blood and stared in horror.

"Oh by the grace of Veia's stinking armpit," Hezbek cursed. "Wherever you are, Devon, you are going to owe me for this."

The woman stepped forward and raised her arms.

A pillar of ice rose from the earth and froze the demon in place.

"Wha...?" Hailey said as, a split-second later, lightning lanced down from the clear sky and ran the demon through, shattering the ice and sizzling the monster's flesh.

"If you want to fight," Hezbek said, "Why don't you pick a fight with someone your own strength."

Hailey's jaw dropped open as the medicine woman rose from the ground, a whirlwind surrounding her and picking up blades of grass and leaves. Another lightning bolt struck the demon, and Ezraxis shrieked. With a mighty slash of her claw, she grazed Hezbek's arm, opening a cut that showed bone.

Hailey dropped a *Guide Vitality* on the woman. For all the good her puny heal over time would do in this battle of titans.

As if galvanized by Hezbek's attack, the players roared and raced forward, plate armor clattering. Glowing with holy ardor, the paladins rushed onto the scene and surrounded the beast.

Another scything blow from the demon's claw opened a gash on Hezbek's leg. The medicine woman hissed and called down another lightning strike as one of the paladins leaped forward and slashed with a greatsword that simply bounced off the demon's flesh.

Hailey inspected Ezraxis, and her heart sank.

Hezbek's attacks had knocked off a couple hundred health. Unfortunately, the demon was healing at an incredible rate. Unless the medicine woman—sorceress?—had bottomless mana, this fight wasn't winnable.

Hailey dropped a heal on herself and staggered to her feet.

"Stop!" she yelled. "We can't win like this."

Hezbek flew back as a blow from Ezraxis's wing slammed into her hip. The woman grunted and whirled, losing focus on her levitation. She crashed to the earth. A bone broke with a hollow crack.

"Devon!" she yelled again, running forward.

She stopped in front of the demon and held her arms wide, dropping her staff. She met the glowing eyes and stared, panting, wetness from her puncture wound spreading across her robe.

"Remember when we first met? I said you were a jerk for killing rabbits. You said that only a druid would give a shit."

The demon's claws clenched and relaxed, clenched and relaxed. She raised a claw as if to strike, but froze, unable to act.

"Or what about the time when I wanted to grind out reputation with the gnome tinkers, so Owen murdered their caravan because you guys needed me for a raid. I didn't talk to you for a week."

The demon lowered her arm, wailing.

"Remember when you told me about Stonehaven, Devon? It's the best thing you ever built. Don't give up now. Fight for it."

The demon staggered as, behind Hailey, Devon—the real Devon—stirred.

Motion at the edge of Hailey's vision caught her eye. She glanced over to see Hezbek crawling to her feet. One of the paladins seemed to catch what was going on and hurried over to help the medicine woman.

"Remember Hezbek, Devon?"

The medicine woman cleared her throat. "If you're in there, child, listen to me. Ever since that day I saw you flailing around Ishildar's ruins like a clueless turkey, I've known you had a special spark. You're special to me. In many ways, you're the daughter I never had."

The demon's wail split the air, a high screech laid over a low bellow. It fell to its knees as Devon coughed. Her eyelids fluttered.

"Dev!" Hailey ran to her side and lifted her friend's head onto her lap.

Devon's eyes opened and focused.

Chapter Forty-One

DEVON WAS TWO people. Two sets of eyes, two faces exposed to the damp jungle air.

Two sets of desires.

She needed to protect Stonehaven. She needed to destroy it because it made her weak. She was a sorcerer, deceiver, gamer, and friend. She was a war priestess of Zaa, champion of demons, spiller of blood.

Through her demon's eyes, she looked down on herself, the fragile human form laid across Hailey's lap. Pathetic and noble. Helpless yet shielded and strengthened by the loyalty of those she cared for.

Players surrounded her dual selves, mostly paladins, but others as well. They'd come to defeat her. To save Stonehaven. To rescue her haven from the forces of evil.

One leaped forward, holy light surrounding the woman's gleaming plate mail. Her sword struck, and this time cut deep into her thick demon's flesh. The blood magic surged, rushing to the wound, but another of the holy warriors struck from the other side, a mace pounding the tender spot where her wing met her back.

Both Devons cried out in pain. And surprise. And triumph.

Hands reached under her human back and brought her upright. Others grabbed her beneath the armpits and pulled her to her feet.

Devon faced herself. Demon to human. Mind to mind. Two layers of her being, separated until now.

The players struck, again and again, cutting Ezraxis down. Devon remembered now, more and more of her second life coming back. The long journey across an uncaring city, bleeding ichor from an unhealing gash on her leg, dragging a broken wing over cracked stone. The smell of brimstone and the constant pain and finally, the knowledge that she could heal herself by fighting Zaa's enemies.

The loneliness. The desperation. The ache to please her god.

The relief as she learned to use the blood of her kills.

The slow rise to power, her merciless acts bringing more and more minions into her service. The feeling of ecstasy when she knew she had pleased Zaa at last.

The hunger for more. The need to eliminate the relics that somehow threatened Zaa's plans.

The discovery of her weakness.

The demon Ezraxis fell to a knee. A swipe from a gleaming blade severed a wing. She dropped a claw to the earth to keep from falling. A cleric shouted and smashed her arm with a silver cudgel.

She fell flat, tried to rise, and failed. Men and women climbed atop her and began plunging blades into her flesh.

With a sigh and a moan, Ezraxis died.

A tear rolled down Devon's cheek.

**

Apparently, Devon had been online for something like seventeen hours. She was lucky the implants included provisions for bladder control. Stumbling to the kitchen, she pulled out a jug of orange juice. After so much playtime, her body should need rest. But it was midday, a weird time to sleep. And she didn't feel tired anyway, maybe because she'd been in some sort of weird unconscious state while her brain drove the demon around.

She shuddered. According to Hailey, Emerson was aware of the situation, and he was working on it. She thought about dropping him a message but decided to let him focus. Weird shit...some AI programmer using players' brains to make up for her system's deficiencies. But now that they understood what was going on, it was bound to be fixed soon.

With glass of juice in hand, she stepped out onto the terrace. The heat wave seemed to have broken, and even though it was the middle of the day, it was a little chilly in the shade. She scooted her chair to the edge of the balcony to catch the sun and looked over the roofs of a set of storage units to the busy interstate highway beyond.

"Hey! Isn't it some kind of vampire curse if a gamer goes outside during work hours?" Tamara said as she stepped out of the stairwell.

"Don't tell anyone," Devon said, turning to face her. "I'll lose all my street cred."

Tamara laughed and dragged another chair into the sun, cracking open a can of sparkling water she'd had in her purse. "Just taking a break or what?"

"Yeah. Just finished up a big battle. So what are you doing here?"

Tamara cocked her head, peering at Devon's face. "You look better. Finally sleeping? I came over because I got a message from some guy named Emerson who says he works with you. He wanted me to check on you. He also apologized profusely for grabbing my contact info out of your data."

Devon's brows drew together. She remembered giving him permission to check her outgoing traffic to make sure the EM shield worked. Not so cool of him to misuse it, but at least he'd apologized. And despite his problems with boundaries, his heart was in the right place. He was kind of like her nerd protector... it was faintly charming if she was honest.

"I *am* sleeping better. I'll message Emerson and let him know I'm not dead or something."

Tamara nodded. "I've been waiting for you to call me up and schedule another ride," she said with a smirk.

"Actually, that sounds kind of nice now that it's not so blazing hot," Devon said. "I've got some things to take care of over the next couple days. Maybe after?"

A mischievous smile appeared on Tamara's face. "Some friends of mine are talking about a little road trip. We're planning on camping out before it gets too cold, in a couple areas around Flagstaff. Interested? I have to be upfront and say we'll be roughing it a bit."

Devon thought of the hours she'd recently spent carving her way through jungle and fighting reeking goblins. "I think I can handle it," she said. "Lemme know when you have a solid date. I—" She grimaced as a strange sensation passed through her body. For a moment, she *ached* for something, a dark yearning to...witness the suffering of her enemies. She shuddered. It must have been the lingering aftereffects of her subconscious control of the demon.

"Not this again," Tamara said. "You okay?"

Devon smiled and waved off the concern. "Sorry. I freaked out a little bit there when I realized I was about to commit to riding off cliffs and sleeping with wild animals."

Tamara snorted. "I'll make a frontierswoman out of you yet."

"Eww," Devon said. "You're giving me flashbacks to Fort Kolob." She grimaced as she recalled the tacky augmented-reality tourist trap where she and Tamara used to work.

"You see through my evil plans too easily. Anyway, I gotta get to work."

Devon nodded. "Me too."

"So you're not actually sold on the camping trip I take it?"

"Maybe once I can make it around your toddler bike loop without passing out."

"Then I guess I better get you out riding sometime this week. I'll nag you."

"Fair enough. Enjoy your bike mechanic-ing."

Tamara waved as she jogged to the stairwell. "Have fun defending the realm, Princess."

"Hey! It's not like that."

Tamara's laugh floated up the stairs. With a sigh, Devon finished the last of her OJ, then opened a message to Emerson.

"All good here. Heard you figured out the problem. Lemme know when I can ditch the tinfoil hat!" She hit send and then set herself as "away."

Yawning, she ducked back into her apartment. Time to start picking up the pieces.

Chapter Forty-Two

IN THE THICK of battle and the confusion of waking to confront her literal inner demon, the scope of the devastation hadn't quite registered. As Devon turned a slow circle in the middle of Stonehaven, she felt her throat seize up. At least half the wooden buildings were ruined. The gates were gone, and they'd taken large sections of the palisade with them. One wall of the forge had been caved in, and where Deld had begun to lay the foundations for the keep, stone blocks were scattered, many of them cracked.

Villagers shuffled along the paths, following the faint trails out of habit more than anything; where grass had once brightened the spaces between buildings, now there was nothing but churned earth and splatters of blood and demon ichor.

She found a stump and sat, willing the grief to sink in and flow through her. She'd suffered setbacks before, and she knew that she always found the resolve to rebuild. But right now, that determination seemed out of her reach.

A hand fell on her shoulder, and she looked up into the face of a stranger. A player, judging by the looks of his perfectly proportioned face. He probably spent points on *Charisma* just out of vanity. Devon tucked her arms tight, unable to forget the sight of swords slashing her body, beating her into the earth, killing her alter-ego.

The feelings would fade, she knew. Ezraxis was dead. The code would be patched. But the experience still echoed.

"Hey, Hailey!" the man said. "Your friend's back."

"Awesome!" Hailey said, running footsteps announcing her approach. "Hey, Dev!"

When the woman stopped in front of her, the smile on her face vanished as if it had been slapped away. Devon realized she was scowling and forced herself to quit it. Though the effort was painful, she managed a smile.

The look of desperate hope was so obvious on Hailey's face, Devon shoved aside her mourning for Stonehaven and focused on the woman. "Before you say anything, I forgive you."

Hailey's grin was so wide that Devon could see her molars. At once, a wave of warmth struck her, and tears fell as she stood and flung her arms around her friend.

"Thank you," she said.

Much to Devon's shock, Hailey started crying. Seeming to realize this was a private moment, the other player gave an awkward nod and wandered off.

"You okay?" Devon asked.

Hailey nodded. "The look on your face while you watched them kill the demon... I wasn't sure what to think. You didn't react while I explained what Emerson told me. And then you logged out without saying anything."

"I was kind of freaking. It's some really f-ed-up stuff going on with our implants. I just needed a minute." Devon looked around again. "So much for Stonehaven..." Her voice broke on the last words.

Hailey wiggled out of the embrace to look Devon in the eyes. "It's not so bad. Unlike you, I'm not afraid to read the forums. There's another guy with a player settlement somewhere in the north. His stuff got trampled by a mammoth stampede and he was super pissed. But as long as 20% of the structures still stand, you get a huge bonus to rebuilding. They explain it by some mechanic having to do with foundations and morale. I already talked to your carpenter guy and he thinks he can have the workshop rebuilt in a couple days."

Devon smirked. "Calling the shots in my village, now, huh?"

Hailey's eyes widened before she noticed Devon's teasing smile. "I didn't know how long you'd be gone and thought you might feel better seeing some construction underway."

"I do. And thanks." She took a shaky breath. "What about the villagers. Did everyone survive?"

Hailey nodded. "Your demon-self almost one-shotted Chen, but after that, she seemed more interested in smashing buildings."

"Then we'll be okay."

The woman nodded again. "I'm looking forward to seeing what you've done with the village next time I visit."

Devon had been watching over Hailey's shoulder as one of the players dragged a log over to where Jarleck was already at work rebuilding the damaged parts of the palisade. At her friend's words, she jerked her eyes back. "You're leaving?"

"We finished out the quest line and didn't get another."

Devon glanced at her own quest log. The missions involving the second relic were marked as completed, but she still had the entry to restore the Veian temple—apparently, a single win against the demon army wouldn't vanquish Zaa's forces for good. For all she knew, the restoration of Ishildar was only the first step in the fight against the forces of evil.

She tried to share the quest with her friend but got an error message.

This quest cannot be shared. Champion of Ishildar kinda loses its ring when there are multiples, yeah?

She flared her nostrils and brushed the game's message away.

"It took me a while to get the quest for the second relic. You guys could see if you get another when I do."

Hailey shook her head. "To tell the truth, with such a big world, I'm not ready to stay in one place. Chen was annoyingly persistent about following the quest that brought us here, but I'd rather just explore. It's like, only one player gets to be the first to cross the Noble Sea or discover some hidden archipelago. I want it to be my party and me. I'd invite you, but I know you've got things to do here."

"Chen?"

"I'm not sure. You'll have to ask him when his mom lets him back online. He got caught logging in after lights-out time."

"To help with the defense, I'm guessing."

Hailey nodded.

"Crud. I owe him." Devon pressed her lips together. "I owe you, too. Sorry I was such a freak about streaming." She glanced again at the paladin who was helping Jarleck raise the first of the replacement logs in the outer wall. "Clearly these people aren't here to destroy the village."

A shadow crossed Hailey's face. "No, they aren't. But I have some bad news. The battle hit a few of the major news sites. Not my stream, but the feeds from some of the players. There are players organizing against Stonehaven for no good reason besides the desire to be shit-stirrers. The players that fought here have vowed to stay around and help with defense."

Well, that was quite a bomb to drop at the end of the conversation. Devon chewed her lip and looked around. She doubted she'd have much choice in the situation. If they had their hearts set on a player on player battle, a bunch of goody-goody paladins and their friends against the typical herd of anarchist douchebags, Devon's protests wouldn't mean much. The best she could do was try to use her player allies effectively without harming the interests of her villagers.

"You could try making a few friends, Dev," Hailey said as if reading her thoughts. "And I wouldn't worry too much. A week or two and the novelty will wear off. Honestly, no one is going to want to hang out in the jungle killing sloths for very long. As long as you can keep them from getting interested in your Ishildar thing, they'll move on soon enough."

Devon sighed. "Maybe you're right about the friends thing. I'll at least try to be civil."

Hailey laughed. "Good. Anyway, I gotta log. I'm going to try to get in touch with Chen offline to see if I should wait for him before heading out."

"Wait," Devon said. "Speaking of...I know I was against this before, but you want to exchange messenger contacts? You're in Wyoming, right? Maybe we could even get together sometime."

Hailey stood stock still, an indecipherable expression on her face. After a moment, she swallowed and sent over a contact card. "Sure. That would be fun."

Almost as if frightened, she turned aside and dropped to a cross-legged seat. Moments later, her avatar vanished.

Devon stared at the spot for a while, confused, then shook her head. Hailey's reaction must've been her imagination. Or maybe the woman was too busy to meet up with online friends but was too nice to admit it.

Either way, maybe she'd just wait for Hailey to message first. She didn't want to be a bother.

And anyway, she had a lot of work to do in rebuilding Stonehaven and figuring out how to use the *Blackbone Effigy* to reinforce their defenses against demons.

Not to mention, she had an ancient city to reclaim. That kind of obligation tended to suck up a lot of free time.

***

"You sure?" Emmaree asked. "We'll gladly join you, but only if it's your true desire, not a sense of obligation or pity guiding the offer."

"I'm sure," Devon said, nodding.

They stood in the new parrot-fertilized orchard, which, despite the faint smell that still rose from the earth, already boasted saplings taller than Devon's head. According to one of Emmaree's refugees, a former fruit trader, the growth rate indicated there would be flowering and fruiting within a couple weeks.

Magic droppings indeed.

Blackbeard seemed to appreciate the situation, because the bird strutted back and forth through the crowd of refugees, squawking and muttering about booty. Ignoring the parrot, she ran her eyes over the gathering and spoke in a loud voice.

"Stonehaven would like to welcome you to our village. Do you accept?"

A flood of messages scrolled past her view as the refugees joined. Devon's smile stretched her lips. "I swear you won't regret putting your livelihood in my hands."

It had been a day since the final battle against the demons, and much to Devon's relief, the players had moved off to establish camps deeper in the jungle. There wasn't much experience to be earned hanging around a construction site. Every few hours, they sent a scout to check on the situation in the village, largely because Devon refused to post updates to a forum unless there was an emergency. Otherwise, Stonehaven had returned to the peaceful congregation of non-starborn Devon had come to enjoy. Apparently, many of Emmaree's people were planning to set up shops, in keeping with their origins as merchants in the city they'd been forced from long ago. The influx of goods from the player population would actually help Stonehaven grow, but Devon had been adamant about one thing.

Stonehaven and its citizens came first. The dwarves had already lost their livelihood once to starborn masses who collected endless stacks of trade goods while grinding out levels. Vendors in Stonehaven would be required to provide an accounting once a week, and any citizen who felt that their welfare was threatened by player-wrought changes to the economy would have the right to petition for a new policy.

The outside world had discovered Stonehaven, but Devon wouldn't allow it to change what they had built. And in many cases, rebuilt.

As for the construction, she pulled up the settlement interface to check out progress.

Settlement: Stonehaven

Size: Village

Tier 1 Buildings - 17/50 (8 upgraded):

Repairs: 60%

5 x Standard Hut

4 x Canvas Shelter

8 x Simple Cabin (upgraded)

Tier 2 Buildings - 4/6:

Repairs: 50%

1 x Medicine Woman's Cabin (upgraded)

1 x Crafting Workshop

1 x Basic Forge

1 x Kitchen

Tier 3 Buildings (1/3)

1 x Shrine to Veia

Fortifications:

Status: Minimal

Repairs: 80%

Completed:

1 x Outer Walls - Timber Palisade

1 x Gate - Iron-reinforced Timber

2 x Watch Platform

2 x Watch Tower

Required for upgrade to Basic Fortifications:

1 x Wall-walk

1 x Merlons or Arrow-slits

2 x Watch Platform Parapets

Special:

1 x Blackbone Effigy

+5% Fortifications Strength vs. Demons

20% Attuned

Fortunately, as Hailey had suggested, rebuilding was much faster than initial construction. Even better, she didn't have to select each building individually. The repairs affected each tier as a whole. With good fortune and no more attacks, the village would be restored in just a few days, and work could resume on the buildings and fortifications that were underway before the demons' arrival.

By placing the *Blackbone Effigy* into a little niche in the Shrine to Veia, she'd begun the attunement process that was slowly increasing the fortifications' defense against more demon attacks.

Next time—if there were a next time—the village would be prepared to fend off the evil horde.

Her attention hovered over the population tab for a moment, but then she shook her head. She wasn't ready to tackle the list of professions yet—in discussions with Emmaree, she'd determined that a few of the refugees would have to retrain, and the planning of jobs would take more energy than she had at the moment. Instead, she pulled up the tab listing the requirements for advancing to a hamlet.

Requirements for expansion to Hamlet:
- Advanced NPC: 6/7
- Buildings (Tier 2): 4/6 (Repairing: 50%)
- Buildings (Tier 3): 1/3
- Population: 44/100

Forty-four citizens was almost halfway. True, she still had a long way to go. But Stonehaven was on the map now. Rumors would pass from ear to ear, and though they would surely bring trouble to Stonehaven, they would also bring resources. And people, NPCs and players both. She didn't know whether players could join the settlement—or if she even would want that. But for better or for worse, they would play a role in Stonehaven's future.

As the new citizens of Stonehaven wandered back through the gates and into the village, Devon found herself on the path to the quarry. Already, it was becoming well-trampled. And this time, she was determined to leave it open. No more hiding.

Once beneath the dappled shade of the thinning canopy, she slowed her pace, enjoying the smells and sounds of the forest.

Somehow, she wasn't surprised when Bob came drifting into view and booped her nose.

"So...I hear you're half-demon or something."

"I was. Not anymore."

"Are you sure?"

"In case you weren't watching, my demon-self got creamed."

The wisp circled in the air a few times. "Hmmm. The dark side I sense in you."

"Can it, Yoda."

"But I'm serious. Have you done any self-examination? Looked for any...*changes?*"

Devon groaned. "Are you trying to get me to look at my character sheet?"

The wisp danced another circle. "I do not know what this sheet you reference is. But yeah. Something like that."

Brows drawn together, Devon pulled up her character UI.

Character: Devon (click to set a different character name)
Level: 15
Base Class: Sorcerer
Specialization: Unassigned
Unique Class: Deceiver
Health: 280/280
Mana: 453/453
Fatigue: 10%
Shadowed: 15%

She stared at the *Shadowed* stat. What the heck was that?
Scrolling down, she scanned her attributes for more changes.

Attributes:
Constitution: 22
Strength: 10
Agility: 17
Charisma: 34
Intelligence: 31
Focus: 13
Endurance: 18

Special Attributes:
Bravery: 8
Cunning: 7
Unspent attribute points: 4

Nothing had changed there, except for the addition of some unspent points from her latest level. Her skills were much the same, still slowly advancing, but nothing was unexpected.

Then she opened her abilities and spells. The ordinary deceiver and sorcerer spells were there, the sorcerer ones listing upgrades she'd receive at each level of mastery. As before, the deceiver upgrades were hidden.

It was the new tab that sent a chill through her. A deep reddish-purple, the page was full of demonic text organized into entries she had no idea how to understand. Right now, everything was grayed-out, a minor relief, but something about the page woke that same sickly yearning she'd felt on the terrace with Tamara.

Quickly, Devon slapped the interface element away.

"I'm guessing this isn't a great time to say, 'I told you so,'" Bob said.

"It said I'm 15% shadowed, and there was a bunch of grayed-out demon stuff in my abilities. What does it mean? Am I some kind of were-demon waiting for the full moon?"

"That, my Champion, is something you'll have to solve on your own. I'm just a washed-up wizard's pet, right?"

"Seriously, Bob, if I take that back will you help?"

Bob floated in front of her face in uncharacteristic stillness. "The truth is, I would if I could. Because I get the sense that your...changes foretell bad luck for our quest. But this is beyond me. Frankly, I think it's beyond Veia."

Devon grimaced. "Uh... doesn't she create the world?"

"Only part of it. To salvage our mission, I suspect you'll eventually need to deal with forces beyond her...plane."

"That's great..."

"I know, right? No pressure... But anyway, shall we get on with your little hike? It's a nice afternoon."

With that, Bob booped her nose and flew off.

Chapter Forty-Three

THE STUPID PACKING tape stuck to Emerson's thumb while he tried to seal the box addressed to Owen's girlfriend. Inside was another of the tinfoil hats and a note asking her to find a way to try it on Owen. The man was still in a coma or whatever the doctors wanted to call it, and worse, the hospital said they had an order from a lawyer to stop giving Emerson information despite Owen's family's permission.

Anyway, the girlfriend might think he was nuts for sending the EM-shielding cap, but short of blowing the story wide, he wasn't sure what else he could do for Owen right now.

And for that matter, he wasn't sure he'd get traction blowing the story wide. A lone engineer seeking to discredit a billion-dollar company...without ironclad proof and powerful friends, it would probably just be a useless gesture.

Best to stick to the plan. Patch the holes. Gather evidence. Put out feelers for those who might back up his claims if management hit back.

Though he was still waiting for Miriam to finish her half of the patch, updating the firmware on the Entwined hardware to eradicate the back doors Penelope had been using to access customers' brains, Emerson had a temporary fix on the E-Squared end.

Well, not so much a fix as a rewrite of Penelope's code to take out the offending calls into undocumented areas of the Entwined libraries. She might have been smart enough to find the back doors, but she had no clue how to successfully obfuscate her code and make her logic too hard to follow. It had been almost comically easy to find her wrong-doings. Of course, she could always revert the code to her version, but first she'd have to notice the changes. And even if they went back and forth a few times, eventually Miriam's fix would get pushed, making Penelope's function calls invalid.

As he paged over to the screen where he was logged into the source code repository, an error popped up.

Connection lost.

He groaned. Probably another issue with brownouts following the days of high clouds that had cut into solar energy production. Clicking the error away, he hit the button to reconnect.

Access denied: You do not have the required privileges to access this resource.

What? Emerson submitted his credentials again. The same message popped up.

Emerson started to pant. His vision began to tunnel down, blackness encroaching from the edges of the room. He dropped his head between his knees to stave off the panic attack.

A message beeped in his vision, flagged as urgent and marked with the E-Squared logo. It slid to the center of his view without his permission.

Emerson,

As you may have noticed, we have temporarily suspended your access to the Relic Online codebase and servers. Due to reports from some of your colleagues, we have concluded that the pressure we applied regarding performance has stressed you to the point of carelessness. Please understand that we value your contribution. This measure has been taken only in your best interests. We look forward to your return once you have had time to decompress and enjoy the rewards of your work so far. Enclosed, please find airline vouchers for a round-trip ticket to the destination of your choice. Use at your discretion. Your situation will be reviewed in a few weeks' time. We will contact you at that point.

Sincerely,

Bradley Williams, CEO
Ava Fitzgerald, Human Resources Director
Brandon Force, Customer Service Director

P.S. We recommend Tahiti.

Dear Reader,

Thank you so much for reading *Fortress of Shadows!* I really hope you enjoyed it! As a working writer, I utterly depend on readers to spread the word on my books.

Please consider leaving a review on Amazon for this book and for other authors you enjoy. I promise that I read every review (yes, even the critical ones). Sometimes, they help me shape the story to come, and often, they are the reason I get out of bed and in front of my computer long before the sun rises. Thank you!!

If you would like to grab free books and participate in my reader community, head over to www.CarrieSummers.com and join my reader group. We have a lot of fun writing collaborative stories over email, talking about books, and other great stuff. Plus, the group is how I let readers know when new books are out.

So, what's next? Devon has her work cut out for her. The second book in the Stonehaven League series will be out by early August 2018, so keep an eye out. In the meantime, you can check out my other fantasy series, *Chronicles of a Cutpurse, The Shattering of the Nocturnai* and *The Broken Lands.*

Once again, thank you for reading!

All best,
—Carrie
carrie@carriesummers.com

Books by Carrie Summers

Shattering of the Nocturnai
Nightforged
Shadowbound
Duskwoven
Darkborn

The Broken Lands
Heart of the Empire
Rise of the Storm
Fate of the Drowned

Chronicles of a Cutpurse
Mistress of Thieves
Rulers of Scoundrels
Queen of Tricksters (coming May 2018)

Stonehaven League
Temple of Sorrow
Fortress of Shadows